Honoria and the Family Obligation

The Fentons Book 1

Alicia Cameron

Copyright © 2017 by Alicia Cameron

All rights reserved.

No portion of this book may be reproduced in any form without written permission from the publisher or author, except as permitted by U.S. copyright law.

Contents

Dedication	V
The Main Players	VI
1. Blue Slippers	1
2. The Harrogate Assembly	10
3. Benedict and Mr Wilbert Fenton	36
4. Genevieve's Marriage	47
5. To Bassington Hall	59
6. The Card Shark	69
7. Honoria In Love?	79
8. Mr Scribster's Bargain	90
9. Genevieve to Bassington	98
10. A Card Party	109
11. A Dastardly Attack	122

12.	Arrangements for London	128
13.	Mr Allison's Desire	135
14.	Benedict's Condition	147
15.	Lord Sumner Receives a Letter	159
16.	Mr Scribster Cuts His Hair	168
17.	Mr Wilbert Fenton Makes Plans	178
18.	Genevieve Talks to Benedict	193
19.	Confiding	199
20.	Lady Cynthia Departs	207
21.	Genevieve Saves Herself	218
22.	Sir Ranalph Fails His Wife	225
23.	A Proposal	239
24.	Lady Cynthia Returns	250
25.	Mama Untangles the Knots	259
26.	Epilogue	280
About Author		286
Also By		287
A chapter of Clarissa and the Poor Relations to tempt you…		292

To every reader of Clarissa and the Poor Relations who took the time to let me know how much you enjoyed my first Regency romance. You inspired this second

The Main Players

In Yorkshire

<u>Fenton Manor</u>

Sir Ranalph Fenton, baronet, owner of Fenton Manor

Cynthia, Lady Fenton, his wife

Benedict Fenton, 21, his eldest son

Honoria Fenton, 20, his eldest daughter

Serena Fenton, 18, his next daughter

<u>Ottershaw</u>

Sir Henry Horton

Genevieve Horton, now Lady Sumner

In Kent

<u>Bassington Hall</u>

Mr Rowley Allison, owner

Mr Angus Scribster, his friend

Lieutenant Darnley Prescott, his cousin

In London

HONORIA AND THE FAMILY OBLIGATION

Mr Wilbert Fenton, younger brother of Sir Ranalph and friend of the Prince Regent. A womaniser and a gamester

Pierre, his valet

Lord Carstairs, Fluff, university friend of Benedict Fenton

Lord Sumner, Genevieve's husband

Lady Harrington, his wealthy aunt

Dowager Lady Sumner, his mother

Countess Overton, who runs a gaming house

Mr Rennie, a card shark

Lord Grandiston and the Honourable Charles Booth, who appear briefly - but are major players in *Clarissa and the Poor Relations*

Chapter 1

Blue Slippers

'He has arrived!' said Serena, kneeling on the window seat of their bedchamber. She made a pretty picture there with her sprigged muslin dress foaming around her and one silk-stockinged foot still on the floor, but her sister Honoria was too frozen with fear to notice.

'Oh, no,' said Honoria, moving forward in a dull fashion to join her. Her elder brother Benedict had been sitting with one leg draped negligently over the arm of the only comfortable chair in the room and now rose languidly to join his younger sisters. After the season in London, Dickie had begun to ape the manners of Beau Brummel and his cronies, polite, but slightly bored with the world. At one and twenty, it seemed a trifle contrived, even allowing that his long limbs and handsome face put many a town beau to shame.

Serena's dark eyes danced wickedly, 'Here comes the conquest of your triumphant season, your soon-to-be-fiancé.'

Dickie grinned, rather more like their childhood companion, 'Your knight in shining armour. If *only* you could remember him.'

'It isn't funny.'

Serena laughed and turned back to the window as she heard the door of the carriage open and the steps let down by Timothy, the one and only footman that Fenton Manor could boast.

'Oh, how did it happen?' Honoria said for the fifteenth time that morning.

Someone in the crowd had said, 'Mr Allison is approaching. But he never dances!' In confusion, she had looked around, and saw the throng around her grow still and part as her hostess approached with a tall gentleman. With all eyes turned to her she stiffened in every sinew. She remembered the voice of Lady Carlisle introducing Mr Allison as a desirable partner, she remembered her mother thrusting her forward as she was frozen with timidity. She remembered his hand lead her to her first waltz of the season. She had turned to her mother for protection as his hand snaked around her waist and had seen that matron grip her hands together and glow with pride. This was Lady Fenton's shining moment, if not her daughter's. Word had it that Mr Allison had danced only thrice this season, each time with his married friends. Lost in the whirl of the dance, she had answered his remarks with single syllables, looking no higher than his chin. A dimpled chin, strong, she remembered vaguely. And though she had previously seen Mr. Allison at a distance, the very rich and therefore very interesting Mr Allison, with an estate grander than many a nobleman, she could not remember more than that he was held to be handsome. (As she told Serena this later, her sister remarked that rich men were very often held to be handsome, strangely related to the size of their purse.)

There was the waltz; there had been a visit to her father in the London house; her mother had informed her of Mr Allison's wishes and that she was to receive his addresses the next afternoon. He certainly visited the next afternoon, and Honoria had been suffered to serve him his tea and her hand had shaken so much that she had kept her eyes on the cup for the rest of the time. He had not proposed, which her mother thought of as a pity, but here she had been saved by Papa, who had thought that Mr Allison should visit them in the country where his daughter and he might be more at their leisure to know each other. 'For she is a little shy with new company and I should wish her perfectly comfortable before she receives your addresses,' Sir Ranalph had told him, as Honoria's mama had explained.

Serena, when told, had thought it a wonderful joke. To be practically engaged to someone you could not remember! She laughed because she trusted to good-natured Papa to save Honoria from the match if it should prove unwanted; her sister had only to say "no".

'Why on earth do you make such a tragedian of yourself, Orry,' had said Serena once Honoria had poured her story out, 'After poor Henrietta Madeley's sad marriage, Papa has always said that to marry with such parental compulsion is scandalously cruel.'

And Honoria had mopped up her tears and felt a good deal better, buoyed by Serena's strength of mind. To be sure, there was the embarrassment to be endured of giving disappointment, but she resolved to do it if Mr Allison's aura of grandeur continued to terrify her.

'And then,' her sister had continued merrily, 'the rich Mr Allison may just turn out to be as handsome as his purse and as good natured as Papa — and you will fall head over heels with him after all.'

The morning after, Honoria had gone for a walk before breakfast, in much better spirits. As she came up the steps to re-enter by the breakfast room, she carelessly caught her new French muslin (fifteen and sixpence the yard, Mama had told her) on the roses that grew on a column. If she took her time and did not pull, she may be able to rescue herself without damage to the dress. She could hear Mama and Papa chatting and gave it no mind until Mama's voice became serious.

'My dear Ranalph, will you not tell me?'

'Shall there be muffins this morning, my dear?' said Papa cheerfully.

'You did not finish your mutton last night and you are falsely cheerful this morning. Tell me, my love.'

'You should apply for a position at Bow Street, my dear. Nothing escapes you.' She heard the sound of an embrace.

'Diversionary tactics, sir, are futile.'

Honoria knew she should not be privy to this, but she was still detaching her dress, thorn by thorn. It was incumbent on her to make a noise, so that they might know she was there, but as she decided to do so, she was frozen by Papa's next words.

'Mr Allison's visit will resolve all, I'm sure.'

Honoria closed her mouth, automatically continuing to silently pluck her dress from the rose bush, anxious to be away.

'Resolve what, dearest?' Honoria could picture her mama on Papa's knee.

'Well, there have been extra expenses – from the Brighton property.' Honoria knew that this was where her uncle Wilbert lived, her father's younger brother. (Dickie had explained that he was a friend of the Prince Regent, which sounded so well to the girls, but Dickie had shaken

his head loftily. 'You girls know nothing. Unless you are as rich as a Maharajah, it's ruinous to be part of that set.')

Her father continued, 'Now, now. All is well. If things do not take with Mr Allison, we shall just have to cut our cloth a little, Madame.' He breathed. 'But, Cynthia, I'm afraid another London Season is not to be thought of.'

Honoria felt instant guilt. Her own season had been at a rather later age than that of her more prosperous friends, and she had not been able to understand why Serena and she could not have had it together, for they borrowed each other's clothes all the time. Serena's intrepid spirit would have buoyed hers too and made her laugh, and would have surely helped with her crippling timidity. But when she had seen how many dresses had been required — one day alone she had changed from morning gown to carriage dress to luncheon half dress, then riding habit and finally evening dress. And with so many of the same people at balls, one could not make do - Mama had insisted on twenty evening gowns as the bare minimum. However doughty with a needle the sisters might be, this was beyond their scope, and London dressmakers did not come cheap. Two such wardrobes were not to be paid for by the estate's income in one year. Honoria had accidentally seen the milliner's bill for her season and shuddered to think of it — her bonnets alone had been ruinously expensive. She had looked forward to her second season, where her wardrobe could be adapted at very little cost to give it a new look and Serena would also have her fill of new walking dresses and riding habits, bonnets and stockings. If she were in London with her sister, she might actually enjoy it.

'Poor Serena. What are her chances of a suitable match in this restricted neighbourhood?' Mama continued, 'And indeed, Honoria, if she *does not like this match. Though how she could fail to like a charming, handsome man like Mr Allison is beyond me,' she finished.*

'Do not forget rich,' teased her husband.

'When I think of the girls who tried to catch him all season! And then he came to us – specifically asked to be presented to her as a partner for the waltz, as dear Lady Carlisle informed me later — but she showed no triumph at all. And now, she will not give an opinion. She is strangely reticent about the subject.'

'Well, well, it is no doubt her shyness. She will be more relaxed when she sees Allison among the family.'

'So much rests upon it.' There was a pause. 'Dickie's commission?'

He laughed, but it sounded sour from her always cheerful Papa. 'Wilbert has promised to buy it from his next win at Faro.'

'Hah!' said Mama bitterly.

Honoria was free. She went towards the breakfast room rather noisily. 'Are there muffins?' she asked gaily.

'How on earth do you come to be engaged to *him*?'

Honoria was jolted back to the present by Serena's outcry. She gazed in dread over her sister's dark curls and saw a sober figure in a black coat and dull breaches, with a wide-brimmed, antediluvian hat walking towards the house. She gave an involuntary giggle.

'Oh, that is only Mr Scribster, his friend.'

'*He* you remember!' laughed Serena. 'Is he as dull as his hat?'

Honoria remembered Mr Scribster's long, miserable face, framed with two lank curtains of hair, at several parties. She thought it odd that a gentleman so patently uninterested in the events should bother to attend. And indeed her mother had whispered the same to her. Honoria must be present where her parents willed her — but surely a gentleman should be free not to? But Mr. Scribster attended in company with Lord Salcomb or Mr Allison with a face suitable for a wake.

'Yes,' said Honoria. 'He never looks happy to be anywhere. And generally converses with no one. Though occasionally I saw him speak to Mr Allison in his grave way and Mr. Allison *laughed*.'

'Maybe it's like when Sir Henry Horton comes to dinner.' Sir Henry was nicknamed among the children "The Harbinger of Gloom". 'Papa laughs so much at his doomsday declarations that he is the only man in the county that actually looks forward to him coming.'

Honoria spotted another man exiting the chaise, this one in biscuit coloured breaches above shiny white-topped Hessian boots. His travelling coat almost swept the ground, and Serena said, 'Well, he's more the thing at any rate. Pity we cannot see his face. You should be prepared. However, he *walks* like a handsome man.' She giggled, 'Or at all events, a rich one.'

The door behind them had opened. 'Serena, you will guard your tongue,' said their mama. Lady Fenton, also known as Lady Cynthia (as she was the daughter of a peer) was the pattern card from which her beautiful daughters were formed. A dark-haired, plump, but stylish matron who looked as good as one could, she said of herself, when one had borne seven bouncing babies. Now she smiled, though, and Honoria felt another bar in her cage. How could she dash her mother's hopes? 'Straighten your dresses, girls, and come downstairs.'

Benedict winked and walked off with his parent.

There were no looking glasses in their bedroom, so as not to foster vanity. But as they straightened the ribbons of the new dresses Mama had thought appropriate to the occasion, they acted as each other's glass and pulled at hair ribbons and curls as need be. The Misses Fenton looked as close to twins as sisters separated by two years could, dark curls and dark slanted eyes and lips that curled at the corners to give them the appearance of a smile even in repose. Their brother Benedict said they resembled a couple of cats, but then he would say that. Serena had told him to watch his tongue or they might scratch.

The children, Norman, Edward, Cedric and Angelica, were not to be admitted to the drawing room — but they bowled out of the nursery to watch the sisters descend the stairs in state. As Serena tripped on a cricket ball, she looked back and stuck her tongue out at the grinning eight-year-old Cedric. Edward, ten, cuffed his younger brother and threw him into the nursery by the scruff of his neck. The eldest, Norman, twelve, a beefy chap, lifted little three-year-old Angelica who showed a disposition to follow her sisters. On the matter of unruly behaviour today, Mama had them all warned.

As the stairs turned on the landing, the sisters realised there was no one in the large square hall to see their dignified descent, so Serena tripped down excitedly, whilst her sister made the slow march of a hearse follower. As Serena gestured her down, Honoria knew that her sister's excitement came from a lack of society in their neighbourhood. She herself had enjoyed a London season, whilst Serena had never been further than Harrogate. She was down at last and they walked to the door of the salon, where she shot her hand out to delay Serena. She took a breath and squared her shoulders. Oh well, this time she should at least see what he looked like.

Two gentlemen stood by the fire with their backs to the door, conversing with Papa and Dickie. As the door opened, they turned and Honoria was focused on the square-shouldered gentleman, whose height rivalled Benedict's and quite dwarfed her sturdy papa. His face was nearly in view, Sir Ranalph was saying, 'These are my precious jewels!' The face was visible for only a moment before Serena gave a yelp of surprise and moved forward a pace. Honoria turned to her.

'But it's you!' Serena cried.

Everyone looked confused and a little shocked, not least Serena who grasped her hands in front of her and regarded the carpet. There seemed to be no doubt that she had addressed Mr Allison.

Honoria could see him now, the dimpled chin and strong jaw she remembered, and topped by a classical nose, deep set hazel eyes and the hairstyle of a Roman Emperor. Admirable, she supposed, but with a smile dying on his lips, he had turned from relaxed guest to stuffed animal, with only his eyes moving between one sister and another. His gaze fell, and he said the most peculiar thing.

'Blue slippers.'

Chapter 2
The Harrogate Assembly

Serena's confidence seemed to have ebbed with her break in good manners and Honoria moved a little towards her to grasp her hand in support — an upturn of the usual.

Papa looked his astonishment. 'Can it be that you are acquainted with my younger daughter Serena, Mr Allison?'

'We have not been introduced.'

Honoria, no longer the centre of attention, was able to look at him closely and wonder at the stiffening of his already rigid mouth.

Serena had recovered herself. 'It is just that I recognised Mr. Allison as the gentleman who returned my slipper to me when I – I lost it at the Harrogate Assembly,' she lowered her head and put out one blue toe as demonstration, 'this one, in fact.' Honoria, fascinated by the slightest twitch in Mr. Allison's face, saw that he did not look down like the rest of the company, but rather raised his eyes a fraction as though to keep from doing so.

Mama frowned her down, not pleased that Serena's liveliness had led her to speak before the formalities were performed. 'Be that as it may, might I introduce you now? Mr Allison, Mr Scribster, my younger daughter Serena. Honoria you already know.'

The gentlemen bowed slightly and the ladies curtsied. As she rose, Honoria met the gaze of the phantom Mr Scribster, animated for once by an expression of surprise. She felt her lip curl slightly and he looked away. The pressure off her a little, she amazed herself by saying, 'How was your journey, gentlemen? I trust it was not too fatiguing.'

Mr Allison replied, looking through her, 'Thank you, no. It was without event.' His voice was dry and colourless, very unlike his gentle attempts to get her to talk on the other occasions when they had met.

'And how do you like our Yorkshire countryside, sir?' asked her papa.

'Very well, sir. My cousin, Lord Royston, has a place but ten miles from here. I am well acquainted with it.'

'That accounts for your being at the Harrogate Assembly!' declared Lady Fenton in a tone that disclosed she had been ruminating on the little incident.

Mr Allison merely inclined his head.

After a few more stilted observations, Mama invited the gentlemen to see their bed chambers. Mr Allison expressed his intention to have a rest before he dressed for dinner and the party dispersed.

'Not you, Serena. To the Yellow Salon. Now.'

Honoria and Serena exchanged glances, following their mama.

'I do apologise for my outburst, Mama,' said Serena. 'I just wasn't expecting to know Honoria's Mr Allison.'

Honoria frowned.

Lady Cynthia gave her famously probing regard.

'When Lady Hayes took me to the Assembly, I suppose I danced too much and the strings on my slipper came undone and it came off. Someone kindly retrieved it and that someone was Honoria's Mr Allison.'

'He's not *my* Mr All—'

'Is that the whole tale, young lady?' interrupted their mama with the basilisk eye still on her younger offspring. 'For it does not seem enough to account for Mr Allison's altered manner. He was all charm before you girls arrived and a trifle — reserved afterwards.' Her eye brooked no contradiction of her understatement. 'You did not indulge in some hoydenish behaviour such as to give him a disgust of the connection?'

'Mother,' declared Serena, 'I'm shocked.'

She curtsied and turned out of the room with dignity, Honoria following. Lady Cynthia rolled her eyes.

Walking up the stairs, Honoria whispered. 'Do pray tell.'

'Well, it was all as I told Mama. Only, I left the middle bit out.'

At that moment, Mr Scribster entered his friend's bedchamber. Allison was thrown down on the bed, boots still on, in an almost theatrical attitude of despair. He sat up drawing his hands through his hair.

'Gus, you've got to get me out of here.'

'What on earth?' Never having seen his friend less than in control, Scribster was at a loss.

Allison bent forward with his head in his hands and laughed shortly. 'It is a short and ridiculous story, but right now I just wish to get out of here and I cannot seem to think—' He ran his hands through his usually immaculate hair.

His friend was more concerned than he appeared 'Nothing easier, I'll go to the stables with a letter addressed to you that Belcher can deliver to the house. He'll still be with the horses - the butler won't have seen him. Emergency in London — must depart.'

'Brilliant! I knew I must have kept you around for some reason, it certainly isn't to lighten my mood.' The feeble joke was an attempt at a more usual manner.

Scribster's lips twitched, 'We Scots wear our misery without disguise. It is the honest way.' He saw Allison's face lighten and was relieved. 'Will you not tell me your ridiculous story?'

'On the way. First find Belcher. Wait!' He folded over a piece of paper from the small desk in his chamber and found a wafer to seal it with. He dashed off his name 'Mr. Rowley Lascaux Allison'.

Scribster moved quickly to the servants' stairs at the end of the corridor. He dashed down looking less like a corpse at every step, had anyone been there to see it.

Benedict Fenton could find no good excuse for Rufus' fall — not one he could explain to Genevieve Horton. Well, Lady Sumner, now. He had seen her ride across the hill in the old way, her ancient brown habit and boots, her mouse-coloured hair escaping from the perfectly simple flat hat and letting the wind tie it in knots. His heart had lifted and he rode towards his old playmate, pushing Rufus when his sure feet tried to turn a little to avoid the rabbit hole. He'd ridden over to see her when the servant's gossip had let him know she was here. It had given his morning ride a direction, and a pleasant one. Genevieve was the closest of the Hortons to his family. She had spent more time in their easy going home than at Ottershaw. He'd seen her briefly in London, but it wasn't the same as on familiar ground.

But now, because of his fall, she was berating him as of old. It was the work of an 'absolute cluncher', as Genevieve told him. She sent Ned, her groom, back to fetch some help and he soon found himself on the sofa in the nursery, where she and her sisters had once swapped secrets with Honoria and Serena and allowed him to stay and be mocked or made use of as the young ladies desired.

They were alone now, apart from the old nurse Curtis, who had tended the three sisters, (Veronica, Genevieve and Rosalind) since birth until they had all left the Manor, each to marry after a single season.

His own mama had been surprised at this success, for the Horton girls were not handsome, as everyone held that *his* sisters were. But they had birth and good portions, and Genevieve's sister Veronica was heir to Ottershaw, since there were no male heirs. Genevieve was almost two years his senior, with a 'distinguished' nose, as Rosalind, her youngest and sweetest sister, called it, but that her father referred to as a beak. She looked down it at him now. 'Let's see if there is anything broken at that shoulder,' she said.

He was holding the right arm with his left when suddenly her probing arms made him squeal. Before he had time to protest she had pulled and rotated the arm, and he found only a dull ache instead of burning pain. 'Jenny!' he protested.

She grinned, but something made it go wrong. 'Lady Sumner to you, you miscreant.' She put her hand up to straighten her thatch of hair and put it beneath the pins that were supposed to hold it in place and he thought – is she nervous? Jenny, the fearless rider to hounds, the scourge of all male pretenders to courage in the saddle. Nervous of what? Of him? She had cuffed him more than once in their youth, usually for shying at a fence (he was ten, she was twelve and taller) or for playing pranks on his sisters. He wanted her to cuff him now, not look as strange as she did. The nervous fingers moved from her hair to the jabot and ruff at the top of her habit, and she pulled at it as if it was unbearably tight.

He saw discolouration of her skin there and was amused. 'You, Lady Sumner, have been injured yourself. What was it,' he teased, 'another rabbit hole? Or did you finally meet a fence too big for you?'

Genevieve's hands clutched at her throat in a gesture he had only seen in a booth theatre production at Harrogate Fair. She looked aghast for a moment, then her hands dropped to her sides. 'No fence you could clear that I could not – even though you've grown less spindly since I saw you last.' It was said with an assumption of her old manner. 'Bind the ankle tight, Curtis. Mr Benedict has a nasty sprain.' She strode from the room, no doubt to make for the stables, as his sister Serena did whenever she was put out of temper.

Curtis came with some linen torn into strips and began to bind Benedict's ankle in a business-like, but unusually silent manner. She had bound other such wounds in his childhood, he knew her well, and saw that her silence tried to hide some trouble. Despite himself, Benedict asked, 'What is it, Curtis? What's wrong?'

She looked up from her labours and looked into his serious, honest eyes. 'It's bad, Mr Benedict. As bad as can be.'

He left in the cob as soon as he could, denying himself the dinner that the Squire punctiliously, but unenthusiastically, offered him. Curtis had sworn him to secrecy (about the secret he did not know) by putting her finger across her plump lips. He felt burdened with the weight of it, as he seldom had been in his rather comfortable, hedonistic young life.

The groom was evidently ignorant as to cause when Benedict asked him casually about the length of Lady Sumner's visit.

'I think it be a while, Mr Fenton, sir. For the master do say we should get the horses ready for the next public day which is a month off. "Make it a good job, Ned" he says to me, "or Lady Sumner will have at you." Mayhap Lord Sumner will join her soon.'

Benedict Fenton sat silently for the rest of the journey. He had no notion what to do, but his whole instinct told him he must do something. He had met Sumner once at the wedding and once again at a club in London. He strove to remember him and could not, rather like Honoria with her beau. Sumner was medium height, medium colouring, talked too much. He seemed a bore, and that was all. Now Benedict remembered he played deep that night at the Faro table, and he strove to see it as a sinister sign. But many people played deep and he didn't hold it against the others.

He'd seen Genevieve in a green ball gown and her hair held tight in an unbecoming style wearing a wreath of flowers that seemed to accentuate the red at the tip of her long nose. She looked stiff and uncomfortable and Benedict had thought, amusedly, that she would much rather be in the stables. He'd meant to ask her to dance, and tease her about her new love of finery, but his friends had taken him to the card room and somehow he'd forgotten his childhood friend and her coronet of dead flowers. He remembered now how quite alone she had been, and how uncomfortable.

What he was imagining was not what he could ask her. To her he was a silly boy. And if she confirmed the dark suspicions, what then? Nothing at all to be done.

He and Father were somewhat at outs at the moment. A little matter of London debts. He had gambled away his allowance and failed to pay his tailor and so on. Everyone did it – but his father, usually so good-natured, had cut up strong about it. But he must talk to Papa, he could think of no one else so straightforward and true before whom he could lay this problem.

'The bit I did not wish Mama to bother herself about,' Serena's eyes were very merry with mischief as she said this, 'was that during my dance with Captain Redmond, I agreed to take the air in the gardens for a moment.'

'Serena!'

'I know, but Lady Hayes was in the card room and it seemed harmless. It was very hot inside.' There was a pause. 'Captain Redmond wanted rather more than the air, however – and he's forty if he's a day, I daresay – so I had to run off to the gardens. I lost my slipper on the way and hid behind a hedge. Mr Allison found my slipper and returned it, and escorted me to the doors. He was kind. Thankfully, the set hadn't finished and her ladyship had failed to notice my absence. And so I joined her, said I was fatigued, and we went home.'

That she guessed there was still more to this story, Honoria's intelligent eyebrow let Serena know, but the younger girl was saved by a summons to the stables, issued by a disapproving Macleod, the butler.

'Why Jenkins needs bother you when he has trouble with the horses is beyond me, Miss. Can't he do what he's paid for?' But Serena had haunted the stable since she was a slip of a thing and the former groom, Woodward, had recognised her passion and encouraged it. When his eyes were failing and Mr Fenton had employed Jenkins to help him, the old man had shunned the help of his replacement and confided all his renowned remedies for poultices and balms to his young Miss Serena. And on no account would Serena divulge them. Papa might not let her at the horses so frequently otherwise.

'Whatever has happened?'

'Mr Benedict drove over to Ottershaw, and his horse stumbled on a rabbit hole.'

'Idiotic,' said Serena.

'Is Dickie alright?' asked Honoria.

'I believe so, Miss. The Squire's groom brought over the horse and a message that he has a sprained ankle and will be sent home in the cob after dinner.'

'Serves him right!' declared his unsympathetic sister. 'Fancy falling into a rabbit-hole. Rufus might be injured—' Serena headed for the door.

'Serena, delay a moment,' said Honoria, 'at least change your shoes.'

It was the work of a moment to cast off the satin, beribboned slippers for her sturdier walking boots in half jean, and while Serena laced them, she affected nonchalance at Honoria's probing. 'Did you have much conversation with Mr Allison after he had given back your shoe?'

Serena affected to think about this, then smiled. '*After* he gave back the shoe? Well, hardly any at all.'

Honoria knew enough of that smile to suspect it. 'Serena!' but her sister had danced away. 'Your dress!' said Honoria to the door.

In the end, Serena delayed too long in the stables to assure herself of Rufus' recovery, and had only just become cognisant of the time. Papa had a heavy appetite and liked to be punctual at his meat. Especially since Mama had decreed that with their fashionable visitors they must delay dinner by at least an hour. Still country hours but more genteel than five of the clock, which was their wont.

She hurtled in at the side door and pulled up her skirts to take the stairs two at a time.

'No blue slippers,' said a dull voice.

She perceived Mr Allison on the landing, staring down at her tightly laced boots. Conscious of her harum-scarum appearance, Serena dropped her skirts and said conspiratorially, 'I am shockingly late to change for dinner, sir. I was in the stables checking on a horse that was injured due to the most ridiculous accident. Never mind, but please sir, say nothing to my father, I was expressly forbid to be a hoyden.'

Despite himself, Allison grinned. 'And *are* you?'

Serena considered, 'I'm afraid that I am. I seem to be constantly considering my own opinion before others'. And then I act on it, which is the definition of hoydenish behaviour, my mother says. It leads me into many scrapes.'

'I remember.'

'How ungallant of you. As though I should have known Captain Redmond was so lacking in gentlemanly virtues.'

'But I'm pretty sure your mama would have told you never to leave the ballroom with only a gentleman for company.'

'But it was *so* hot and I thought no harm ... Captain Redmond was so *old*.'

Redmond, Allison knew, was but seven years older than he. He bristled, but adopted a mock-severe tone. 'And your opinion was unfounded. Experience guided hers — which is why young ladies should listen to their mamas.'

'And not be so hoydenish? Thank you Mr Allison, I shall remember this advice from my *elder* and depart chastened.' She swept a deep curtsy and darted past him to continue her ascent of the stairs. She turned to say, over her shoulder, 'At least I would if you were not such a fabulist ... I have a good mind to tell my sister why you remembered the blue slipper so well.'

He had been grinning, but this last comment swept it from his face. 'Can you tell your sister and brother how sorry I am that I will not meet them at dinner? I have been called away on urgent business and am just going to inform your papa.'

Serena stopped. 'Really?' she said, 'I hope it is nothing too distressing?'

'No. But it demands my urgent attention.'

'I should not have asked. I am too impertinent, Mama says. Only, I do not like to see people in distress and not acknowledge them.' She held out a frank hand. 'Goodbye Mr Allison, I do hope you have a pleasant drive back to town.'

He looked up at her, then her hand left his and she ran upstairs, in the most cheerful manner possible. He stood, stunned, and then remembered his mission. He went downstairs to find his host.

The upshot of this was his departure within the half hour.

Sir Ranalph Fenton was put out rather more than usual by the gentlemen's sudden departure from the Manor. He was rattled by his wife's questions on the subject, since he had no answer. If she had said 'Whatever can he mean by it?' once, she had said it a dozen times, and he could see Honoria blush. She should not have been told until Mr Allison declared himself and he rather blamed his wife for that. He had delayed Mr Allison's proposal in town in order to give Honoria a chance to know him better, and to feel herself practically engaged was too much pressure for his eldest daughter's delicate nature. But her mother had assured him that Honoria was well disposed to Mr Allison and would be better off preparing herself to meet his offer calmly.

And now look! He had been prepared to have Honoria decline the offer, but not to suffer this dreadful insult, for whatever Allison had said about an emergency, he was not convinced that he had not 'sheered off' as the cant phrase would have it, from the commitment. Honoria blushed and trembled. He would not have had it so for the world.

Lady Fenton was still hopeful. Mr Allison had hardly had time to 'go off' Honoria, they had barely exchanged words. She believed Serena had something to do with the affair and kept her interrogative eye on her all through dinner. But Serena only looked angelic, which was deeply suspicious on its own. Had Serena behaved in some way that had given Mr Allison a disgust of the family? She was capable of much trouble, but whatever it was, could her mama only ferret it out of her, she was sure she could explain it to the proud Mr Allison. Girlish naivete could surely be pardoned.

The meat was tough, and the usually sunny disposition of the baronet was sorely tried. So when Benedict said, 'Sir, might I talk to you in the library?' he shrugged him off.

'Not tonight, my boy. I can't deal with your excesses just at the moment.'

Benedict was stung, remembering the last time he'd asked to talk to his father privately was to confess his debts. He turned on his heel. His father stopped him. 'What is it Dickie? I'm sorry, my boy.'

'It's nothing sir, I'm sorry to have disturbed you.'

'No need to pucker up, lad – tell me what it was you wished to discuss.'

Benedict's stiff face gave way to another thought. Though he'd prefer to stay silent, on principle, he saw again Genevieve's neck. 'I drove over to Ottershaw today to see if – well, that doesn't matter sir.'

'And you had an accident. This much I know.' Sir Ranalph looked at his son, 'don't worry, Serena believes Rufus will be alright.'

'It isn't that, Papa. Lady Sumner had come back on a visit to her parents.'

'So I believe. And?'

'There was a bruise at her neck sir, I thought she'd taken some tumble like me, and I teased her with it — but it wasn't so. She was horrified and tried to cover it up.'

'And?'

'Well, sir. I fear someone may have done her harm.'

His father gave a large sigh. 'Well, if so, she is in the right place. A few weeks away from her home may do them both good.'

'Papa — how can she go back there?'

Sir Ranalph's face was grave. 'A husband has the right to be free of interference in actions relating to his wife. It is never for others to venture into the realms of a marriage.'

'And if this were two years hence and the bruises were on Honoria's neck sir?'

'I shall take care that Honoria shall marry no such person.'

'Yes sir. But if she did?'

'This is not the case of your sister. Even if you are right, my boy, there is little to be done. A father has no rights after he surrenders his child to a husband.

'Then you, sir have a graver responsibility than I had previously conceived of.' His father sighed. 'What do you know of Lord Sumner, father?"

'Nothing of any note. I understand he's a bit of a gambler. But everyone plays, after all.'

'What about Aunt Millicent?'

'What has you mother's sister got to do with this?'

'She lives in Bath and never visits London. And her husband lives abroad. Sometimes marital separation can be achieved, can it not? Even divorce?'

'Divorce is out of the question, as is separation. Your Aunt Millicent is a daughter of a peer, it was a very different situation.'

'How was it achieved?'

'It doesn't matter, what is permissible for Lady Millicent is not possible for a Genevieve Horton, no matter how rich her father is.' Sir Ranalph was looking uncomfortable.

'But how, father?'

'It is not your business, young man—' Sir Ranalph encountered look from his son's eyes that told him Benedict was no longer a boy. 'I believe your grandfather made her husband an allowance — but only if he lived on the continent.'

Benedict paced the room while his father looked on. 'I think, sir, that I should go once more to town.' He flushed. 'If you could give me *my* allowance a little ahead of time, there should be no cost to you. I have a standing invitation to stay with my friend, Carstairs.'

'Lord Carstairs plays deep, my boy.'

'I have told you before, Papa, that I do not favour gambling as an occupation. I made some mistakes, and I have learnt from them. I do not intend to waste my money on gaming anymore.'

'That's what every young fool, says,' muttered his father, but with so much humour Dickie could not take offence, 'until the next time.'

He did not tell his father how catastrophic that experiment in gaming was. He carried, in his pocket, a reminder of his own stupidity:

It was the night when his friend Carstairs had taken him to a gaming hell in Curzon Street, an almost respectable address. Indeed, it was run by Countess Overton, the widow of a Viscount, who was rumoured to have squandered her husband's fortune in the first year after his death. But she used her playing skills to good effect, and now ran this house.

She was a handsome woman of his mother's age, with a striking, rather than beautiful face with dark eyes, black hair in a Grecian twist and a sparkling evening gown of the very best quality. She greeted Lord Carstairs as an old friend and seemed to be enchanted to be introduced to Benedict. 'Oh, what a delight,' she said airily putting her arm through his and leading him to the gaming salon, alight with the glow of candles at the centre of each of perhaps two dozen tables placed around the room. 'Your Papa was one of my beaus you know.' She trilled a laugh and some gems at her throat sparkled, 'A long time ago, I'm afraid. You look very like, but taller.'

The ladies and gentlemen one met here were sometimes members of the Beau Monde, though never, of course, the unmarried girls. The younger women who frequented the house might, in dress and comportment, look respectable, but they were never seen in the best circles. All this Carstairs told him. 'So watch out for the petticoats, my lad!' before his slender figure disappeared into the crowd at a table under a large curtained window.

Benedict had seen his Uncle Wilbert at a table with another of the Prince Regent's cronies, where he looked up and merely nodded. His nephew was relieved. He had neither the address nor the money to gamble at such a table, he was sure. After looking around him, a little bored, Benedict had been glad when invited to join a table with one Mr. Rennie, a man he had met a week previously when his uncle had taken him to Jackson's Boxing Salon. He was a handsome looking fellow, a trifle high coloured, with a pair of military whiskers that increased Benedict's respect — to serve under Wellington was still his goal. The dice were thrown, and Dickie was soon in the midst of the game, encouraged by the free flowing champagne. Mr Rennie — "Just call me Rennie, old man, everyone does" — was very gay, and Dickie enjoyed the bonhomie of the occasion. His uncle passed by, nodding his leave and Benedict's eye followed him to the door, where Mr Fenton bent so low over the Countess's hand that Benedict feared for his corset-strings. He smiled, sipped at his champagne, and continued to play.

Soon, he became uncomfortably aware that he had lost the modest sum he had brought with him this evening. But Rennie, his very good friend Rennie, had made no stir about this – it was easy to begin to win back some money by the use of IOUs scratched onto paper. And win he did, for a little while. It encouraged him to go on, somewhat ashamed of his own cowardice. He wanted to leave the table, but there seemed to be no way. Carstairs was enthralled at the play at another table. He longed for someone else to leave, so that he would not be the first to break the play, but no one did —there was nothing for it but to play on.

When Benedict looked up, he saw himself being regarded by a new pair of eyes. It was Lord Grandiston. Of course, Benedict had never been introduced, but the most fashionable man in London (apart from Mr Brummel) had been pointed out to him. Even if he hadn't been, Benedict would have known him for someone magnificent. Tall, he was dressed simply in black with a white satin waistcoat and biscuit coloured pantaloons. Yet his muscular form, coupled with his tailor's genius made him elegant than any man present. His eyes met the young man's from his position at the fireplace — Benedict looked away, lest his eyes give away his fear

He had lost another hundred in just a few minutes, but Rennie, friend of his bosom, now adjured him not to worry, the next throw would solve all his problems. As Rennie lifted the dice to pass to him, a sudden hand grasped his wrist. It must have caused pain, for Rennie gasped and dropped the dice, which fell into the other swift hand of the interloper. Benedict looked up. The Earl of Grandiston.

'Do you mind if I take a turn?' he drawled. As he lowered himself, a chair appeared below him as though by magic, and he threw the dice. Benedict sat back bemused, catching sight of the anger on Rennie's face,

then the smooth transition to the assumption of pleasure. Almost at once, Carstairs arrived at his table with the Honourable Charles Booth at his shoulder. Carstairs grasped his arm and told him he had called the carriage. He rose, with apologies to Rennie who waved them away casually, not quite meeting his eye.

In the coach, Carstairs apologised, ruffling his thin blond hair ruefully. 'Grandiston sent Booth to warn me you were in deep water, old man, I should have kept a better eye on you on your first visit to the old smoke. The thing is,' Carstairs leaned forward confidentially, 'Rennie might be not quite the thing.'

Benedict slumped, rolling his eyes.

The next morning, a package arrived —addressed to him. It contained a pair of dice and an unsigned note. "It might have been worse" *was scrawled on it.*

Benedict was playing with the dice when Fluff Carstairs, peer of the realm, with whom he had bunked for the night in his digs at Half Moon Street, emerged for breakfast. His given name was James, but it was rumoured that in his long list of subordinate titles, he bore the insufferable name of Florian, baron of Loughbridge. Fl-lough ... forever Fluff. He was clad that morning in a loud yellow silk robe at odds with his hunched back, watery eyes, and half shut appearance. The robe added to Dickie's already drumming headache.

'What the devil—?' said Carstairs taking the dice up. He held them and tossed them a few times in his hand. 'Loaded.' He said shortly. He cocked an eyebrow towards the note, which Dickie handed to him, 'Grandiston, I'll wager. Dashed decent of him.'

'Rennie's I suppose,' said Benedict with an effort at the same bored tone as Carstairs, but with a new realisation of the disaster he might be facing this morning without the Earl's interjection.

Benedict threw them – a perfect twelve. 'Why didn't I win when I threw?'

*Carstairs looked at him, for a second, with his fork stopping on the way to his mouth. 'Keep forgettin' you're just a babe in the ways of the world. You didn't throw **these** dice — Rennie would have palmed them.'*

'Oh! And how does one do that?'

'Lord, I don't know, Dickie, What do you take me for? A loose screw?'

Benedict had resolved to carry the dice with him, a symbol of all he still had to learn of the 'polite' world.

'Perhaps,' he now said with a frown, 'it might be time to visit my Uncle Wilbert.'

He marched from the room with new energy before he could hear his father expostulate, 'To *Wilbert—?* What the devil, Dickie—?'

Scribster sat with Allison for miles of silence whilst the carriage rumbled its way through the countryside. At mile seven he asked, 'Drat it man...?'

'You remember Lady Carlisle's Ball?'

'Where you broke the hearts of several young debutantes — stay that — several match-making mamas, by dancing for the first time that season? With *lucky* Miss Fenton?'

'The same. Did you wonder why I danced?'

'I did.'

'I danced with the wrong sister.'

'Hmm. The mystery of the blue slippers is solved.'

'One blue slipper ...'

'The sisters are very much alike, shouldn't think there was much to split between them. Quite a natural mix-up. You like dark-haired girls with kittenish mouths, it seems. Why are you treating it as such a tragedy?'

His friend sat up, eyes wide. 'Weren't you listening? I've all but offered for the *wrong sister*.'

'There doesn't seem to be much between them in looks. What's the difference?' intoned Scribster with a shrug. 'One of them can be as likely to make you miserably leg-shackled as the other.'

Allison threw himself back into the padded squabs with a passion. 'What on earth are you doing here, you dark-hearted villain? Why do I keep you for my monkey?'

Scribster stuck his hands deep into his pockets and leaned back, long legs stretched diagonally across the seats. 'If there is something to pull them apart, you'll have to explain it to me. I'm at a loss. Tell me the riveting tale of the blue slipper ...'

Escaping from the deadly dull Assembly where he had been cajoled into escorting his maiden aunts, Miss Arabella and Miss Hildegarde, Allison had sought the fresh air of the terrace. A couple emerged from the French doors and he instinctively sought shelter behind a pillar, so as not to disturb their tête-a-tête. He saw the shock of frizzy hair and the military bearing of Fanshaw Redmond, Captain in the 4th Hussars, with whom he shared membership of a number of London clubs. Allison determined to walk in the gardens as soon as the couple were occupied enough not to hear him leave. Which, knowing Redmond's reputation, would be soon.

The lady was not very tall and the blue stuff of her dress sparkled a little in the moonlight as did some delicate gewgaws in her hair.

He wanted to leave and sure enough, Redmond acted in character by dropping the arm that had supported her little hand and snaking it around the slender waist. Allison turned to make himself scarce, when he heard an 'ooomph!' — the exact sound Redmond had made when he had last sparred with him in Jackson's Boxing Saloon. He turned around. The little figure was several feet away now and backing towards the steps of the terrace.

'Captain Redmond!' *she exclaimed, but in with the shock and outrage, Mr Allison heard amusement – and was intrigued. Redmond had doubled a little – it could have been that the little fist or elbow had caught the Captain rather lower than his solar plexus – but he recovered enough to jump forward as a way of recapturing the young lady. What was he thinking? A squeal would alert the old martinets in the ballroom and his reputation would be tarnished along with the young lady's. That she was young he guessed from her voice. "Not well done, Fanshaw," he thought. "I thought married ladies were your usual flirts." Redmond was almost upon her and she turned quickly and ran down the terrace into the gardens beyond. Leaving, Allison noted, one fairy-tale blue slipper, with long beribboned strings, on the bottom step.*

'Redmond!' said another voice. 'Hello old fellow, insufferably hot in that cauldron of old ninnies, ain't it?'

Redmond turned reluctantly from his prey and met with another military man — Allison made his escape.

He picked up the slipper and walked in the direction she had fled, until he heard a rustling from a bush.

'Oh, sir. Is that my shoe?' came a voice from behind it. 'Could you give it to me, for the set will finish and Lady Hayes will miss me.' The voice

was a little worried when she mentioned her ladyship, but amazingly confiding all the same.

'I might.' An arm emerged from the bush and Allison held the shoe near and then snatched it away.

'Please sir! As you are a gentleman.'

'I rather feel like a storybook hero tonight. Giving Cinderella back her shoe.'

'But you have not. And I can tell you have not the qualifications for Prince Charming. He would have given it to me directly.'

'Perhaps he would demand a ransom.'

'Oh, you are worse by far than Dickie. What ransom do you suggest?'

'Perhaps a kiss. And who is Dickie – your swain of earlier?' he asked, affecting ignorance.

'My brother.' The voice was still soft, but the arm shot out and clasped the slipper, twitching it from his hand before he had time to realise. He heard the sound of her adjusting the errant shoe. 'My swain, as you call him, was one Captain Redmond, and he was even more uncivil than you.' She emerged from behind the bush, perfectly self-possessed. Allison was distressed to see she was indeed *young, but so pretty with her dark curls, laughing eyes and mouth, that he was gripped.*

'May I take you back to the ballroom?' he asked, looking down at her. 'I always meant to return your slipper, I promise you.'

'That is what all highwaymen say, I believe.' But she put her hand on his raised arm and walked back to the ballroom and her duenna's tender care.

'So a pert young thing bests you—' starts Scribster, still bored.

'Both I — and the gallant captain. Who walked with a strange gait for the rest of the evening,' broke in Allison, with a reminiscent laugh.

'—and you immediately fall under some ridiculous spell. But I still cannot see how you came to make the fatal error.'

'I asked the aunts who Lady Hayes had in charge that evening. To my Aunt Arabella's undying shame, they did not know.'

'But eventually they supplied you with the wrong information. I beg you do not inform them — your Aunt Hildegarde is liable to go off in a fit of melancholy.'

'I've thought of it. But it was not wrong, of course. Her ladyship had charge of Miss Fenton – there was no need to distinguish her as Miss *Serena* Fenton since her elder sister was in town.'

'So what did you then do?'

'I escorted my aunts to two more Harrogate assemblies.'

'Good God!' said Mr Scribster, 'The tedium!'

'Indeed. But Miss Fenton did not reappear. I retreated to London, where at Lady Carlisle's Ball, I saw her. She wore the same spangled blue shawl over her gown and had diadems in her dark hair.'

'Sisters share their finery,' intoned Scribster, in sympathetic accents.

'And Lady Carlisle told me her name was…'

'Miss Fenton. But could you not tell she was different when you were alone in the dance?'

'She was so quiet. I tried to allude to our previous meeting, but she said nothing at all. I attributed it to being under her mother's eye.'

'It could have been so, I suppose. But what on earth impelled you to address her father?'

'I don't know. She was being wooed by a number of beaux, I was given to understand by Lady Carlisle. She might have made an engagement at any time. She is of good family, her uncle an intimate of the Regent—'

'Well, if you take that as a recommendation, Rowley, I've mistook my man ...'

'A dissolute bunch, but no inferior blood.'

'No. Probably just a superior blood-sucker of an uncle, if your suit had prospered.'

'But don't you see, Gus, my suit *did* prosper. I applied to her father. And now I will have to apply to the young lady herself. There is nothing else to be done.'

Scribster's face was no longer so humorous. 'You cannot.'

There was a silence.

'You could explain it to her father.'

Allison raised his brows. 'The elder will have been informed of my intentions. It would be a dreadful insult to her and to Sir Ranalph.'

'Well,' said Scribster after a dispirited moment, 'Let's hope she refuses you.'

'The other sister might. Indeed, I was not at all sure of my success with *my* Miss Fenton. But this one is so spiritless that she will follow her parent's recommendation. I know that, and yet I don't know if she liked me or not.'

'Is this where you damn your fortune to the winds once more?' said Scribster, bored. 'I am all sympathy...'

'I have been sought by fortune-hunting mamas since my eighteenth birthday. Fourteen years is enough.'

'So you attend balls and never dance.'

'So do you.'

'But *I* break no hearts. I do not suffer from a handsome face and thirty thousand a year.'

'Why do you go, then?'

Scribster's face took on a twisted expression. 'To keep my friends company. And for the view.'

'I do dance in the country. But dancing at Almack's leads to infernal chatter.'

Scribster had heard tell of a young lady, years ago, who had been said to die of 'a decline' following a dance with his friend — and speculation of a proposal. More the fault of the chattering women, who had given her false hope, than of his friend, he believed. But it had scarred the young Mr Allison.

'And now?'

'In honour, I can see nothing else for it than to invite the young lady and her parents to Bassington Hall for some weeks in the summer. And there make my proposal.'

'Then I shall take up a post in Switzerland with Lord Otley.'

'Oh, no you don't, you ungrateful cur. You cannot live off me for months on end and then depart just when I need you. To Bassington Hall for you, my lad, and don't think you can escape.'

'Of course, you *could* try to give the girl a dislike of you—'

'The way I'm feeling, that will not be difficult,' said Allison with the voice of the doomed, 'but I don't suppose it will work.'

'Well, of all the conceited coxcombs, you are the worst. Irresistible, are you? Even if you try to be disagreeable?'

Allison grinned. 'Not me, Gus, as you well know. But my infernal pockets.' There was a pause. 'Not one word of this-'

'I do *not* tell secrets abroad, laddie,' this occasional Scots appellation being the only trace decipherable of his Scottish heritage, since he was educated at Eton. 'And you should know it.'

'Ah!' said Allison, 'I knew there had to be some reason I let you and your long legs take space in the carriage.'

The gentlemen stretched out their legs, closed their eyes and were silent for the next ten miles. Then Scribster's body started to shake. Allison ignored him until the vibrations travelled to Scribster's leg and his own seat began to quiver.

'What the hell—?'

Scribster seemed to have difficulty speaking. 'The unavailable Mr Allison caves in to beauty after years of—' he choked, 'And then ... th-the *wrong sister*!'

A guffaw escaped him at the same time as an oath from Allison. He quelled himself, only to be overcome again. He opened his eyes to look at his friend, and Allison gave him a dark stare that set him off more fiercely. He stopped, reining himself in with a heroic effort. He closed his eyes and took his position once more but in a moment, the legs beside him began to shake as well. Soon the two gentlemen were laughing, making the carriage shake to double the effect of the country roads.

'It's not funny!' howled Allison, but that just made them worse.

Chapter 3

Benedict and Mr Wilbert Fenton

After the first day, Honoria was spared the raising of the subject of Mr Allison's departure by her mother's sensitivity to her daughter's feelings of rejection. 'We must not bring it up, my love,' she said to her husband, 'for the poor girl is probably crushed.'

'We shouldn't have informed her of Allison's purpose. Then she would not be crushed.'

However fond her ladyship was of her husband (and she was very fond indeed) she was not pleased to be reminded of this slip in judgement. She paused in the pinning of her cap, a very sheer lace concoction (of a style and quality she herself could not afford) which had arrived from her cousin in Paris just the other day. 'Perhaps so.'

The colder tone alerted her husband to his mistake. 'Is that the cap Georgiana sent you? It is my quite favourite! How charming you look, my dear.' His wife's face unfroze a little. 'Though I must say I prefer to see all of your beautiful hair.' He stood behind her at the mirror and touched the still-dark curls, meeting her eyes with a smile.

Her smile beamed anew. 'Well and do you not, sir, in the privacy of your chamber?'

He bent and kissed her cheek. 'Well, we shan't mention Allison to Honoria, at any rate,' he said, returning to the subject at hand. 'You are right as usual my dear. But what if the town emergency was real? And Allison is of the same mind?'

His wife stood and found her way into his arms once more. 'We shall let matters rest until we are a little more informed.'

'I did not think Allison to be a man of fickle decisions.' Lady Fenton nestled closer to him, 'Well, well, we shall leave it be. And on top of all this, what can Dickie be up to in Brighton with my revered brother Wilbert?'

Lady Fenton hugged him closer. 'Not what you fear, my love, I'm sure. He has assured you that gaming is not his particular failing. We must believe him.'

'I do. But I'm afraid I do not trust Wilbert and the Prince's set. Why needs must my son visit him all of a sudden? I'm sure it is to do with that business with Genevieve Horton, Lady Sumner, I must call her now.'

Lady Fenton looked up. 'What business with Jenny?'

Sir Ranalph cursed silently. Lady Sumner's bruises were not a topic to be discussed. 'I believe he might have something to deliver to Lord Sumner for her.'

He met his wife's intelligent eye as blandly as he could. Her preoccupation with her own children made her drop the subject of Genevieve for another time. 'And what, pray, has Wilbert got to do with Jenny?'

'That,' Sir Ranalph was able to reply honestly, 'is what I have not been able to discover.' He looked down at his lovely wife. 'My love — do we have to go to dinner now?'

But she pulled playfully away from him. 'Sir! You know what occurred the last time we delayed dinner.' Sir Ranalph frowned and his wife saw her way to escape to the door, which she opened.

'What occurred?' asked her husband, with drawn brows.

'Angelica!' She flung over her shoulder and whisked herself from the room.

Serena was suspicious of her sister. They sat in their room making preparations to their toilette for dinner; Mama was as strict as though they were in town. Honoria smiled a little once more and it was this smile that Serena suspected.

'Don't tell me you're glad that Mr Allison did not declare himself.'

Honoria looked at Serena a little guiltily. The family's finances might now be saved if Mr Allison had spoken, but she really could not help her joy. The pressure was lifted. She continued to brush her hair silently, avoiding her sister's eye.

'I could understand before you met him again – he might have been a fright, after all! – but instead he was deadly handsome.'

'I suppose—' Honoria said dispassionately, 'but it makes no odds, he wasn't at all friendly.'

'Well,' said Serena judiciously, 'his manner that evening may have been a trifle stiff—'

'A *trifle*?'

'Well, but I can assure you he is most amusing at other times.'

'There is much more to the story of the blue slippers than you have divulged,' said Honoria in a chiding tone.

Serena smiled, 'Not *much* more. But if I told you all, you would lecture me on impertinence and I already have Mama to do that for me.'

'I am sure Mr Allison can be all that is charming, but I fear we would not suit.'

'But think of his money,' teased Serena, 'all the dresses and horses you could ever want. Surely the thought of this match slipping away from you should have you tearing your hair out!'

Honoria regarded her solemnly 'And would you marry for reasons such as those?'

'Not I!' said Serena, who had eventually stopped rearranging Honoria's curls, 'I shall elope with a highwayman, or a sea captain or some such. It's a life of adventure for me. But you, Orry, you were born to be married and have children exactly like Mama.'

As they went downstairs to dinner, Honoria sighed. It was true – so why *not* the handsome, rich, *sometimes* charming Mr Allison if he desired to marry her? It was something about the pressure to save the family. She had always thought to have a spark with her future husband, not be reduced to a snivelling wretch every time she encountered him. With such a large family to provide for, Honoria had always known it to be her duty to marry well. But she had liked none of the men who might have offered for her during the season. She had discouraged more than Mr Allison — if Mama knew perhaps she would be angry. She was a bad sister. Now there would be no more chance of enticing or rejecting suitors, since there would be no more London seasons – for her or her sister. What a terrible person she was to be so pleased to escape marriage to a man who *may* be perfectly kind and good. Only, what had he wanted with *her*? He knew nothing of her except her birth and her looks – Honoria could not help but think him a man with no romance in his soul and was glad that he'd left.

As they entered the dining room, Honoria saw that Papa was once more in spirits.

'Ah, girls,' he said, opening his arms expansively, 'some good news for all of us! We are all to visit Bassington Hall next week at Mr Allison's invitation.'

Honoria's spirits sunk once more but she smiled faintly.

Serena showed enough joy for both of them. 'How wonderful. It is close to town, is it not? Shall I be able to visit Astley's Royal Amphitheatre and see the horses?'

It was fortunate that Benedict, fortified by a night's stay at an inn, had dropped his bags off at Lord Carstairs' London residence. That inestimable peer of the realm, sitting in the loud dressing gown, with his fair head in his hands, his large blue eyes red rimmed and watery, looked like last night's dissipation might have caught up with him. But he was able to inform him that his uncle was in town.

'He was at Countess Overton's last night,' he groaned as his head followed Benedict's quick figure around the room, 'Stay still, blast you! There must have been bad wine,' Benedict grinned. Carstairs often encountered bad wine, the volume that he drank having nothing at all to do with his sore head.

Arriving at his uncle's address, Benedict was informed by his butler that no one could see that gentleman till twelve of the clock at least.

'Perhaps you might wish to await Mr Fenton in the Chinese salon, Mr Benedict?' that august personage suggested in a repressive tone.

'Perhaps not,' said Benedict, moving past Sinclair with rapid strides and taking the stairs two at a time.

'Mr Fenton, sir!' called the butler.

Benedict stopped suddenly, turning back, remembering some of the most colourful of the rumours surrounding his relative. He looked down at Sinclair whose mouth had squeezed into a tight circle as through he had recently eaten prunes. 'Or...is my uncle alone?'

'Certainly not, sir. It is the hour of his toilette, his valet attends him.' The butler gestured once more towards the Chinese salon, but Benedict was again *en route* to his uncle's bedroom.

He almost reeled at the smell that assaulted his nose at the door of that empty chamber and he followed the expensive scent to an open door past the grand silk covered bed and almost choked on the doorstep.

'Oh it's you — thought I heard a kick up. What the devil do you mean disturbing me at my toilette?'

Benedict was momentarily silenced as he took in the magnificence of this small chamber. His uncle was seated in front of a dressing mirror of the rococo style and his valet Pierre, a haughty, but almost miniature personage, hovered over him with a number of stiffened muslin cravats hanging over his arm. The gentleman's coiffure had already been achieved — a riot of brown curls swept forward from his crown in an exaggerated version of the fashionable Brutus. At either end of the small chamber there were other, taller mirrors in gilt carved frames, to better display his rather dissipated person from every angle. His uncle, though the younger son, looked far older than his hearty, handsome brother, though he was taller, like Benedict himself. There were a number of chairs covered in more silk brocade and Benedict threw himself into one to enjoy the spectacle.

The room was given extra glamour by the purple silk robe that his relative had obviously cast off, and several waistcoats in gaudy hues that his uncle had discarded in favour of the dull gold brocade that his valet had set aside. As a follower of Mr Brummel, Benedict disapproved the display, but he could not help but be fascinated. His uncle now stood up wearing only a flowing white shirt with pale green pantaloons. His valet stopped and raised an eyebrow at his master who nodded. With a quick glance over his shoulder at the intruder, Pierre removed a white cotton object from a drawer and brought it over. His uncle lifted his shirt and Pierre attached the small stuffed cushion around his waist, fastening it at the back. Benedict got a glimpse of his uncle's stomach – as slender as his own – before the appendage was added. The shirt dropped, the tiny Pierre mounted a small footstool to help his master shrug into the waistcoat, and his uncle bore the portly shape Benedict knew so well.

'What the Devil?' he asked.

'Clever, ain't it?' his uncle replied. 'Designed it myself.' He smiled at Benedict's obvious astonishment. 'Ever since the Brummel debacle, Prinny's even more delicate about his weight.' The previous year, the Prince had finally fallen out with his friend Brummel and had 'cut him' (looked straight through him) at Almack's. The Beau's response was legendary. "Alvanley – who's your fat friend?" Even without the Prince's patronage, Brummel's star had not fallen. He continued as the witty, elegant darling of the ton — much to the Prince's consternation. 'He cut poor Humphrey last month just because Jessie Mumford —'

Benedict recognised the name of the reigning beauty, Lady Mumford, '— said he was a handsome figure of a fellow. He hasn't been asked to card games or jollifications since.' He tapped his false stomach. 'Makes Prinny more comfortable to have men of girth around him. When I said I'd have to get my tailor to let out my coats, he even commiserated and said to send the bill to him!'

Benedict was amused and shocked at once.

'Well, it's one less bill to fall on your father.' His uncle frowned. 'You here about your coronetcy? Told your father – the very next win!'

Benedict raised one eyebrow in the manner of his idol. Though he hadn't known this particular, it was of a piece with what he did know. Since his season on the town, Benedict had learnt more about the state of his father's finances than ever before — but strictly from the throwaway lines of his uncle who had taken a lazy interest in the young man and squired him to some of the less salubrious corners of the town. Knowing that his father's tidy estate was a profitable one, it had been a mystery to Benedict why such economies were practised in his household. Occasionally he had heard his parents discuss difficulty with 'the Brighton property' and for months now, he had understood that this meant repairing the fortunes of his dreadfully expensive uncle. His father, the eldest, had inherited everything, and had felt for the younger brother who had received even less than he should have after Benedict's grandfather's death. Papa had immediately paid his brother a generous income, but even that had to be supplemented to support his uncle's ruinous career. Now with seven children to support, his generous father had occasionally 'not come through with the readies' which had led to his uncle sailing ever closer to the wind. Benedict disapproved, but still fell for his uncle's scapegrace charm withal.

'Not the coronetcy. Here about something else entirely. I need your help, sir.'

His uncle regarded him with a wary eye. 'Got yourself in some hot water? Heard you played with Rennie, I could have warned you.'

'Well, why on earth didn't you, sir?' Benedict objected reasonably.

'Good God, boy, if you expected me to make you a list of all the fellows with an inventive line in play, shall we say, it would run to several pages. Burned deep were you?'

'Of course not — just a trifle!'

'Carstairs let you know what's what?'

Benedict looked a little sheepish. 'Fluff? No, he was at another table. Grandiston intervened.'

'The Earl of Grandiston — you walk in fashionable circles, my boy.'

'I don't. I'd never met him. But he sent me these next day,' Benedict handed the dice to his uncle.

Mr Fenton threw them in the air twice. 'Loaded.' He threw them and they showed twelve. 'A bit overdone,' he remarked, '— eleven is less obvious.'

The toilette was completed. Benedict saw that his uncle's raddled face had been treated to the veriest touch of rouge and a wisp of powder, but it was subtly done. 'Not sure what you wanted of me, but tell me over breakfast.'

Breakfast at noon was a lavish affair, but Benedict, though he'd already supped with Carstairs, had a young man's appetite. However, watching his uncle eat, it was easy to believe that his girth was real. Benedict looked on in admiration.

Waiting until the servants departed, Benedict raised the reason for his visit. 'Those dice sir—' he began.

'Nothing to be done about that now my boy, if you suspected anything at all, you needed to call for the dice to be broken open at the table. Or Grandiston should. But he wouldn't. Dashed bad form.'

Benedict looked appalled, he had a young man's horror of being at the centre of such a scene. 'No sir, it's not that. It's just that Carstairs told me Rennie must have, what he called, 'palmed' the dice. And, um, I wanted to learn how to do it.'

His uncle let out a crack of laughter. 'And you thought of me as the man to have the gift! Charming!'

His nephew blushed, 'Well, sir. It's just that you've been on the town for a long time, and—'

'And you think I'm a loose screw? A *triche* as the French would have it!' He wiped his mouth with a linen napkin. 'Well, you'd be wrong my boy. I'd never stoop to cheats' tricks. It doesn't answer—' he said in a tone of rectitude. Benedict was about to apologise when he added, '— except in the case of extreme necessity. So you want to win what you lost from Rennie, my boy? A laudable desire, but you'll never know enough. I knew his father. Up to every rig and row in town since he was a babe in arms. He'd spot you.'

'No sir — I want to cheat someone else entirely.' He smiled.

'Is he a knowing 'un?'

'Let's hope not, sir.'

Mr Fenton senior smiled. 'A lad after my own heart.' They toasted with teacups.

Honoria knew her duty, but her ability to carry off a noble demeanour faltered at times — though no one seemed to notice. In any other extremity she had Serena to confide in. But, of course, she could not tell her sister now.

In the next week, preparations were continuing for Bassington Hall and Honoria was aware that she was going around in "tragedy queen" mode. She knew that the prospects of marriage to a handsome and rich man would have been the pinnacle of her desire. But the *necessity* of it appalled her. And Mr Allison frightened her. He was a man devoid of romance. Honoria had a dread of being married to him.

Serena wandered around, talking happily about Astley's Amphitheatre and the chance to visit the Metropolis. That lowered Honoria's spirits further, for she knew that without her marriage Serena would have no prospect of visiting London again — maybe ever. She sighed the deep sigh that had become usual to her — she would smile and simper at Mr Allison and do everything that was required of her. For Serena's sake.

'I seem to have stained your second best walking dress, Orry,' said Serena carelessly, 'Bunter says she doubts she can get it off.'

'Well, why did you wear it?' asked Honoria, stung from her dejection.

'I didn't think you'd mind — I stained my own yesterday.' Serena explained, as though she was reasoning with a child.

If one's annoying little sister could only know how much she was indebted to one, perhaps one could bear this sacrifice a little better. Despite herself, Honoria sighed.

Bassington Hall was being prepared for its incoming guests. The butler, Blake, let Mr Allison know that all was ready. Despite himself, and the presence of Mr Scribster, Mr Allison sighed.

Chapter 4

Genevieve's Marriage

Genevieve felt much more like Miss Horton than her ladyship now that she was home again, and had to smile as old retainers started sentences with "Excuse me, Miss Jenny—, oh, I mean your ladyship—"

But underneath, her dread still remained. No one in her home knew the circumstances of her visit and they must not. How she had come to so expose herself to Dickie Fenton she could not imagine. Benedict may still feature as a silly young boy in her head, but she knew he was not stupid. When he saw the injuries to her neck she could simply have passed it off, but her nerves were closer to the surface now and for a moment she had betrayed herself. She'd seen that look in his eyes, the one that he'd had when he used to bring back birds with broken wings or try to revive a drowned kitten all those years ago. And now he would wish to mend *her* broken wing, but that was quite impossible.

She'd married Frederick Sumner, because he'd talked to her non-stop about horses. On his estate he bred the beasts and of all the men she'd met on her boring season, he was the nearest to someone she could bear. Her sister Veronica was already married to the man who would one day live at Ottershaw with her, one Colonel Edward Forbes, and after listening to his inane conversation (which Veronica thought charming as it was full of compliments to her person) and his braying laugh, Genevieve was sure that she would need to set up her own establishment before that day ever arose. So when Sumner paid his addresses, Genevieve said yes. Everyone was charmed. It was a good match. Her inheritance would help his struggling estate and his birth and position would reflect well on the family. She'd received a rare kiss from her cold Papa on the occasion of her engagement.

Frederick was not handsome, but ordinary. Medium build and height, mouse coloured hair, and the slightest leaning towards corpulence still allowed a man to be held of as handsome when he was also a Lord. She knew herself, moreover, to be a very plain girl. His eyes moved around the room as he spoke, but Genevieve had put this down to insecurity. To share his acclaimed love of horses and of the country, to share his life and home was what Genevieve had desired, for she was a practical girl and had hardly known how to dream of more. But life was so different, so very different than she had believed. And now this.

She was glad that Dickie had not come back - she might be able to pass off the questions of her old nurse when she came to fill her bath, but she did not know how she would have fared against the wounded-animal sympathy in Dickie Fenton's eyes. She had been sure he would have pushed her with questions as the younger Dickie would have done, but the new sophistication of town had possibly stopped him. She was glad. There was little to be done. What little could be done she was doing now. She'd come home. But it could not be forever - her father was already asking when Sumner would arrive.

Meanwhile, she enjoyed the freedom to practically live at the stables, even if at first she had to field questions from Ned about Sumner's stable. The truth was, her husband bought showy nags who had little or any breeding possibilities. He considered himself an expert and would certainly take no advice from her. He had agreed with her (during their short conversations at balls) that country life was far preferable than town. But now that he could afford it, he spent as much time in London as he could and had her accompany him, though he knew she would rather stay in the country.

At a ball given by the Marchioness of Stevely, the reason for her presence became flesh. She was pushed before Lady Harrington, widow of Lord Harrington, and the aunt of Lord Sumner, who had been travelling on the continent at the time of Genevieve's wedding. Genevieve, squeezed into another satin creation of the Dowager Lady Sumner's dress maker, with her hair painfully scraped into a coiffure that it's natural frizz had resisted with the utmost force, beheld a plump vision in an outmoded gown of purple satin, topped by a turban and a perilously high trio of ostrich feathers. At her breast, her wrist and clasping the feathers in place, were large glittering amethysts, each stone surrounded by diamonds. Her husband bowed low and playfully said, 'You take the shine out of every woman here, Aunt. May I present Genevieve, Lady Sumner!'

Lady Harrington did not seem impressed, but she gave a grunt and shook Genevieve's hand. 'I suppose you agree that I take the shine from all the young girls around?'

Genevieve blinked. 'Well, no,' she said, 'but then I am not at all fond of purple.'

Her husband gasped and Genevieve flinched. She had, once more, let her mouth say whatever came into her head. He was not alone in abhorring this; her mother had repeatedly told her to be careful what she said. But her ladyship, after a pregnant moment, merely gave a crack of laughter and begged her to be seated. 'No, go away Frederick,' she said as her nephew tried to bestow her shawl on her shoulders a little better, 'let me talk to your wife in peace.'

Frederick had gone with a hooded glance at his wife.

'I have three nephews, you know, all equally anxious for me to die.'

Genevieve blinked again. She was tense and her tongue was only under control when she was at ease. 'Well, I must suppose by —' she gave a vague wave of her hand towards Lady Harrington's neck, '—that you are very rich.'

Once more the crack of laughter. 'And I suppose you'll tell me that you will be very sorry to see me die, despite the hope of inheritance.'

'Since I have only just met you, I cannot say I would be very sorry, my Lady, but I have not thought at all of an inheritance.'

'Well, we have established you are not fond of amethysts, but I suspect my diamonds will excite a different response.' She looked at Genevieve under her brows, her little eyes as sharp as needles.

Genevieve was silent. She hardly cared, but was it not very vulgar to be talking of diamonds?

'Not fond of diamonds either, eh? Why not?'

'I can't think what use to me they would be in the stables, your ladyship,' she replied, after some consideration.

This set Lady Harrington off in a paroxysm of laughter, which made Lord Sumner approach from the other side of the ballroom. She waved him away, however, 'Let us be frank,' Lady Harrington continued, and Genevieve had raised a brow. She did not think they had been less than candid thus far. *'None of my brothers have sons who can produce an heir. I trust that you and Frederick will be able to continue my father's name.'*

Genevieve, thinking of the awful nights where Frederick paid his quick visits to her bed, said fervently, *'I hope so too.'* Maybe then he would leave her alone.

The old lady sat up straighter. *'Well, I do not hold with this modern practise of married couples living separate lives. If your husband is here, so should you be. I—'* she said, with raised brows, *'—accompanied my husband always.'* As her husband had lived only two years, this, Genevieve later discovered, was not as strong a claim as it might have been. *'How on earth are young women to have children if they live separately from their husbands? I myself lost two children before they could be born. It is my greatest regret, but my husband at least had brothers who could continue the line.'*

Genevieve was silent. She was certain her mother-in-law, the Dowager, must have complained of Genevieve's reluctance to come to town.

'And I suppose, since you are not fond of my ensemble, that you think yourself dressed more fashionably?'

Genevieve looked at her peach satin gown. *'Good God, no!'* she blushed. *'I beg your pardon. I have the tongue of a stable boy sometimes, my mother informs me. I cannot seem to mind it.'*

But her ladyship seemed merely amused. *'I never choose to mind mine.'* She looked at Genevieve closely. *'So you don't like your gown and you'd rather be in the stables. I suppose you are of help to Frederick in this horse breeding enterprise.'*

Genevieve was silent once more. It behoved her to support her husband by some assertion here, but she was not gifted at lying to order. Her husband's 'enterprise' was doomed to failure unless he let her help. Which he would not.

Lady Harrington didn't appear to notice, 'You are obviously a woman who has little time for London parties. But it is my will that my father's name live on, and for the moment you, my dear, are my best hope of this. So let me see you always with your husband — until you find yourself increasing, that is.'

Genevieve stood up swiftly, finally pricked by the old woman's words — so accurate a portrayal of the duty she was harnessed to that she could hardly bear it. If Frederick had been merely boring, it may have been bearable, but instead she was living a sort of nightmare.

'What is it like, Lady Harrington,' Genevieve said, looking down at her, 'to have the power to order other people's lives?'

The old lady's eyebrows raised and a flush of anger raised on her cheeks. Genevieve felt Sumner at her shoulder and flinched. He could not have heard, but he would hear the old lady's reply.

Lady Harrington spoke to Genevieve only. 'It is a privilege of age and riches, my dear,' she said smoothly.

Frederick's hand was on her shoulder, he squeezed so hard that Genevieve had a difficulty not to wince.

'And how are my favourite ladies getting along?'

Genevieve looked away, waiting for the axe to fall.

'Don't let your mother hear you say that, Frederick,' her ladyship said in her usual dismissive tone to her nephew. 'But your wife and I are

dealing extremely well together. In fact, she's agreed to accompany me to a friend's house tomorrow afternoon.'

Genevieve's eyes flew to Lady Harrington's clear ones.

'Tomorrow at three then,' and she held out her hand.

Genevieve took it. 'Thank you, Lady Harrington,' she said, with a direct look in the old, shrewd eyes. 'I look forward to it.'

Her reminiscences were broken into by a message from the stables. Fever, her father's stallion, was down with a strange colic. He may have managed to eat some forbidden plant yesterday when he'd been out for exercise. The normal preparation had not worked.

Genevieve thought of Serena — the Fenton's old groom had a recipe for a stronger remedy, but it was of no use to send Ned. Serena would not hand her secrets to a servant. She made to ride across to Fenton Manor herself, but once she had her horse saddled she almost gave up the expedition. She could not face Benedict's questioning gaze.

Ned was chattering and she heard Benedict's name.

'—gone away to London, unexpected like, so Sam says.'

'Mr Benedict?' She did not know whether to be glad or not. She could avoid him today, but ... she could be no part in his decision to go to London, could she?

'Yes 'm,' continued Ned, checking her cinch and harness as though she were still a green girl. 'To his uncle's, as I unnerstand,' Genevieve breathed — nothing to do with her. 'And the family set to go off somewhere too.'

'At this season?' Genevieve was mounted and now tightened the reins. 'Never mind Ned. Keep Fever cool, keep her drinking. I'll be back betimes.'

Ned touched his forelock and Genevieve swept out of the stable yard.

With little ceremony, Macleod indicated to Lady Sumner that the young ladies could be found in the yellow salon and let her show herself in, only prompting her by a look to remove her plain little veiled hat. The girls jumped up to embrace her, but Genevieve swiftly imparted her business to Serena. She was instantly concerned about Fever, too, but she point-blank refused to give Genevieve the recipe, instead declaring she would go to the stillroom and make the preparation herself.

'You can trust me!' protested Genevieve, before Serena left.

'I know, but I can't trust Ned. He'll tell our groom, Jenkins, and soon there will be no need for me about the stables and Papa will forbid me to spend so much time there. *You* know Genevieve!' Genevieve did. But she wondered at little Serena, so prettily different from her, today dressed in a frothy muslin with blue sash and matching blue ribbons in her hair. She knew Serena was as interested in her appearance as Honoria was, yet you might find her in the stables any day wearing just such an outfit, tending to a sick horse. 'I will not give up the little bit of leverage I have over Papa, or Mama would have me constantly at my work—' she gestured at the white stockings she had been darning, '—or practising the pianoforte!' She laughed and ran out.

Honoria laughed, 'Everyone agrees that Serena's playing *needs* some practise.'

They both sat down. Not that she much cared, but Honoria made Genevieve feel equally dowdy, she was wearing pink and white striped muslin today; it had long tight sleeves, with just a puff at the shoulder. Lady Fenton had excellent taste. After being offered and refusing refreshment, Genevieve asked, 'Ned told me that the family are leaving the Manor for a while.'

Honoria blushed, to Genevieve's surprise, and put her head down to her work, more darning of stockings. 'Indeed. Mr Rowley Allison has been so good as to ask us to spend a month or so at Bassington Hall.'

'Mr Allison!' of course Genevieve knew one of the richest men in London, 'I did not know that your parents were acquainted with Mr Allison.'

'He is a new acquaintance,' faltered Honoria, blushing and unable to look up, 'that I made during my London season.'

'Good gracious, Orry, you don't mean to tell me Allison offered for you?'

The use of her childhood nickname nudged the reticence from Honoria. 'He has not spoken to me. But, oh Jenny, I believe he has approached my father.' Her soft brown eyes went to her friend's green ones.

'And are you happy, Honoria?'

Honoria gulped. 'Of course, I am very flattered,' she felt she could confide just a little in Genevieve, who had been like a big sister to her. 'It is only that I do not know him very well.'

'You are visiting Bassington for that purpose, I suppose,' her head was trying to remember any snippet of London gossip (which her sister Veronica was mistress of) that she had heard of Mr Allison. She remembered nothing negative. But that meant very little. Women of the polite world were largely sheltered from the worst of men's dissipations. She had met him once, he'd taken pity on her at a formal dinner party and he had kept a pondering conversation going until they hit upon the topic of horses and then she had relaxed. She remembered him favourably. Still, the look on Orry's face was not that of a girl in love. Genevieve leant forward and grasped her wrist. 'Do not agree to marry him if you are not *sure*, Orry. Marriage is not a fate to be trifled with.'

Honoria looked up, amazed. Genevieve was never so passionate or so frank. Genevieve could see her wondering what this meant in regard to her own situation and shut down. She could not speak.

'Of course I will not,' Honoria was saying.

The other relaxed somewhat. 'And your Papa is a dear. He would not ask it of you.'

'Certainly,' assented Honoria. And that was why it was even more imperative that she accept Mr Allison. Her dear Papa would never ask it of her, if he felt she would not be happy, even if the family really needed whatever settlements her parents had talked about. But she smiled at her guest and was glad to be interrupted by Serena, bearing a wax-sealed jar of brown sludge.

Genevieve was up on the instant, anxious to get back to Fever.

'Only give him half, more could be poisonous itself,' she instructed. 'He'll have a temperature, and he should be better by this evening. Woodward did this with Strawberry two years ago and it worked. But I remember him saying that if she hadn't recovered by nightfall, it would be safe to take it only once more to make her well again.'

Woodward's wisdom on such matters was legendary in these parts and Genevieve listened carefully. She was on her way and hardly noticed the strange look that Honoria gave her as she bid her goodbye.

Benedict Horton, meanwhile, was reacquainting himself with Frederick Sumner. For three evenings, he crossed Sumner's path. Once at a low tavern that was frequented by the sporting set, young gentlemen attracted by the company of "fellows in the know" — horse trainers and jockeys, the owners of fighting cocks and some of the best pugilists of the day. Carstairs had led him there, misliking the look he saw in his young friend's eye whilst watching Sumner at a neighbouring table, loud and boring, among a crowd of equally rowdy individuals. Benedict, watching and listening, was thoroughly disgusted with every boastful, idiotic word that fell from the Baron's mouth and did not trust himself to speak to his lordship. When Carstairs insisted they leave, he did. The next night, without his friend, Benedict approached his lordship at a table in White's. Sumner saw him coming and adopted his hearty cheerful manner, 'Young Fenton — still in town?'

'Just come back on family business, your lordship.'

'Well, well,' said Sumner, uninterested, 'I hope your family are well. Honoria was quite a sensation last season, I hear. Very pretty girl. Much admired.'

'Yes.' Benedict didn't hold his eyes. 'Well, I should join my table. Good luck to your play.'

Sumner laughed and turned back to his cards and Benedict joined another table. The club was rather thin of company at this season, so Benedict was able to watch as Sumner lost his stack of chips, and as the house, Mr Semple, quietly refused his vowels. Put out, Sumner rose sulkily from the table and left. Benedict's urge to follow him was just held in check. If this were his father's day, he might have called the fellow out, citing his offending coat or some such thing instead of mentioning his wife. But people would still have talked, and Benedict was determined that nothing would touch Genevieve Horton's name.

On the third night, Benedict followed Sumner through darkened streets to a luxuriously appointed house that his uncle had escorted him to a few months ago. It was enough, he now saw Sumner as a perfect pattern-card of villain. He did not need to know more.

As his rage grew on his walk back to Carstairs' rooms, he laughed at himself. What had he really uncovered? His lordship was a booming bore, he lost at cards, and he frequented a house of ladies that his own uncle and even his friend Carstairs frequented. It just made him a London quiz; that was all. But, on the other hand, his friends were not married.

That would not make much difference to many of his London acquaintance, he knew. But so what if he judged Sumner harshly? He knew what he had done to his wife. At the very least, Sumner was a man without honour, and it looked — from his experience at White's — that society was beginning to know. If Benedict could destroy him without harm to his wife, he would. He was beginning to see a hole in his half-formed plan, but he would pursue it in any event.

Chapter 5

To Bassington Hall

Benedict's tuition in the deeper aspects of play took up an hour or so of his uncle's days. Many techniques that his uncle shared — "only so that you can see what these fellows are able to do and counter it, my boy" — required practise. Lord Carstairs, sworn to secrecy, grew tired of watching Benedict's quick hands repeatedly palm dice, cards, deal from the bottom of the deck, for hours on end.

'I begin to fear that my home, my snug little nest, previously my haven from all of life's trials and concerns, is fast turning into a den of vice,' he shook his head disconsolately. 'I will never be able to share a friendly game of piquet with you beside this humble hearth again, without fearing that you've palmed all the aces or dealt from the bottom of the pack. There is nothing else for it. I'll have to turf you out and cut you dead in the street if I were to see you again. Dash it, I can't be friends with fellows who smell like fish.'

Benedict grinned. 'Let Stoddart push the card table nearer the fire and we'll have a friendly game in our old fashion.'

Carstairs looked suspicious. 'And you won't palm anything?' Benedict's large eyes were innocent and he shook his head. 'Or deal from the bottom of the deck?'

Benedict covered his heart with his palm. 'I swear.'

His Lordship cheered up and rang the bell for the necessary arrangements for their comfort. This included the nice setting of the table (which he directed to be adjusted a number of times) in front of the fire, the bringing of more coals and of refreshments consisting of wine and cake and a suspicion of cheese, the platter of which nearly broke the strength of the small maid who carried it.

With a last placement of a screen, they commenced, to Carstairs' satisfaction, to embark on their usual friendly game, for shillings rather than guineas, with great concentration. It was not long until Carstairs' entire wealth of shillings, (kept for the purpose in a dish in a drawer of his escritoire) was piled before Benedict and he threw his cards down in a rage.

'Dammit Fenton — you swore you would not palm or deal from the bottom! On your word of honour!'

Benedict laughed. 'And I kept my promise.' He lifted a stack of shillings and put them before his friend. 'But I do beg your pardon, I did win these without honour.'

'Wh—?'

'I marked the cards. A little trick my uncle taught me last week. Wanted to try it out. It works,' he added, 'amazingly well.'

'The more I hear about your uncle, the more I fear for his immortal soul. Rum character.'

'But he assures me that these are just counter measures to deal with the cheats of the world who think to rob him.'

'Well ...' said his lordship. 'If you say so.'

'Lord, I don't say so. *I* think he's a dashed rum customer as you suspect, but I would not say it before anyone but you. But his losses at the table are massive, I believe, so one has to assume that he does not practice very much.'

'Or not when he is playing against knowing ones,' Carstairs said cynically. Then with his old insouciance he added, 'Well, every family has 'em,' sipping his wine and eating just a little more of the cheese, cut for him by his ever-attentive valet, Stoddart. 'I ask you again Dickie. Why on earth do you want to be learning the dark arts? I don't think I'll ever feel safe introducing you to a gaming club again. Look at what you can do with only two weeks of study.' The wine seemed to give him inspiration. 'I say, Dickie, do you suppose the facility's in the family?'

'I am learning the dark arts, as you call them, for a purpose purely moral and good, I believe. It may be for nothing, but I hope not.' Benedict's face looked quite harsh for a moment, but his easy grin returned once more as he noted his friend's look of concern. 'As for inherited traits,' he added, thinking of a few tricks his sister Serena had pulled in her time, 'I wouldn't be at all surprised.'

'Well however it is,' his old college friend told him, settling himself into an easy chair with more wine and a smidgen more of the excellent cake, 'keep me out of it. I don't want to know what tricks you get up to. I still remember how you stopped my heart by hanging from the window of our chamber to escape the bursar. Never again — *I* don't want to know.'

'That's what my uncle said — just as though he were a pattern card of rectitude!' Benedict's eyes glittered, 'And as I remember it, you were not the most prudent man at college. There was that time you smuggled Rosa into—'

Carstairs wagged his finger admonishingly, while his receding chin receded even further into his cravat, 'That'll do, old boy, that'll do…'

Bassington Hall was a very grand house indeed, much larger than Fenton, certainly, and larger even than Ottershaw, the largest house in their district. The young ladies had to be reprimanded by their mama for leaning from the carriage windows to drink in the splendour of the house, but she rather spoilt the effect by leaning out herself.

'My love — *fourteen* pillars!'

Their good natured papa handed them down from the carriage himself, proud of his beautiful daughters, one in a heavenly blue pelisse and bonnet, the other in cherry red with a bunch of wax cherries under the straw of her bonnet, nestling in her dark curls. With his wife in the dark green that so became her, how could he fail to be proud?

But when the cherry red pelisse began to follow the groom who had ridden behind on her brother's horse, he drew a line. 'Serena. Jenkins does not need your help to settle the horses.'

Serena broke her stride to look over her shoulder a second, 'But I'm not sure Rufus's gait was quite—'

'Serena!'

She returned reluctantly to join the small troop just as the great doors opened and a number of servants were decanted to welcome and attend to the baggage. Two gentlemen walked towards them, Mr

Scribster at his most relaxed and Mr Allison resembling a military martinet.

After the conventional greetings, very jovial on Sir Ranalph's part, and well-mannered on the part of Mr Allison, the party was ushered into the grand hall, where a royal swathe of curving stairway mounted from the marble floor to the upper rooms. Some young maids awaited them there in a military line to take the lady's bonnets and pelisses, and Sir Ranalph's driving coat and hat. They were ushered from thence by a stately butler to a room off, whose tall oak doors would have accommodated their entire carriage, *even* with the ladies' baggage atop, Sir Ranalph teased his wife later, for they had indeed brought every stitch of finery they owned. "As well to be prepared for every eventuality!" had said his wife when Sir Ranalph had protested.

The room was impressive indeed, with walls lined with green silk, and a ceiling covered in rococo paintings, depicting highly decorative scenes of heavenly cherubs flying in an azure sky. However, it was not as large as they had feared, and the tea tables had been drawn up before a huge fire, and around the chairs screens had been caused to be drawn to make the tea party a little cosier.

Honoria stood entranced, 'Oh, how lovely!' she exclaimed.

Mr Allison looked at her and smiled wanly. 'My mother will be glad to hear you say so. She had it refurbished last year at huge and unnecessary expense.'

Honoria looked crushed. But Serena, entering behind, said, 'Oh heavens, I'm famished!' She received a look from her mama which totally missed its mark as Serena was moving forward, her eyes eventually noting the ceiling, which caused her to utter, 'Goodness!' in a tone that could be taken as either admiration or disdain.

There was a little pause. Allison seemed to feel his lapse in manners and led his guests towards the tea tables.

'Blake has ordered tea for us, pray sit down, ladies, Sir Ranalph,' said Mr Allison, still failing to infuse warmth in his tone, 'I trust you had a comfortable journey?'

Only Serena seemed unaffected by his tone, and whilst she did not precisely talk with her mouth full, she did give Mr Allison a full account of their journey, between making a hearty attack on the victuals provided. Mr Allison looked at her only when manners insisted, but she seemed unaware of much but her own telling of the tale of the longest journey of her young life. She frowned a little as she eventually finished.

Allison could not help asking, 'Yet you seem a little disappointed, Miss Serena.'

'Oh, no!' she said with a return of her smile, 'Well — it's just that Mama was once held up by highwaymen on that road — when she was my age, too.'

'I believe they have cleared the roads on these more enlightened days.'

Serena nodded.

'Am I to take it you would have *wished* to be robbed?'

Lady Fenton shook her head with a smile. 'Forgive my silly child, Mr Allison. I have told her it was not at all exciting, but only most frightening.'

Serena smiled directly at her host, lowering her lashes teasingly. 'Well I have known *certain* highwaymen,' she said with a conspiratorial look, 'that are not at all frightening.'

Scribster watched as his friend, Allison, stiffened even further, but Serena turned away to the dog, which was nuzzling her hand in the hopes of more cake.

It was apparent from the teasing note followed by her unaffected air that she had not been holding the candle for Mr Allison since the evening of the blue slippers.

Mr Scribster watched his friend and the Fenton party with his hooded eyes and long face giving him the air of misery that London equated with his Highland antecedents, and from behind which he could see and enjoy much. Honoria, the delicate flower with an uncomfortable amount of sensitivity, was still recovering from Allison's put-down. Today, in a slender blue muslin dress that became her colouring so well, she looked quite beautiful, he thought disinterestedly, but sad. Mr Scribster wondered idly if she'd borrowed the blue satin slippers and if that might make her more acceptable to his friend. As he lowered his eyes to see, he noticed only a neat pair of half jean boots peeking beneath the hem and when his eyes rose he met hers for a moment. He could not read her expression, but it may have been annoyance.

Serena was enjoying herself hugely, largely unaware of her effect on his friend. She was wearing a pink froth of a gown (with fine cherry red stripes) that became her well. The animation on her face outshone her sister's in vivacity, but then who could judge in this atmosphere? The lovely mama sat a trifle on edge, lest her younger daughter's unschooled tongue betray her. The father, the big bluff man, so fond of his wife and children was ready to be pleased with everything. And then there was Allison, veering between trying to be unaffected by Serena, being slightly off-putting to Honoria and still keeping within the bounds of good manners. Mr Scribster sipped his tea and thought that he'd been to duller house-parties.

He was friend enough to wish Allison well in his endeavours — if only he could decide what his endeavours were. In the days before the Fenton's arrival, Rowley had been determined on the honourable path — to woo Honoria like a gentleman and to discover all the (no doubt) sterling character traits that lay beneath her beauty and timidity. Scribster had advised him to first stop terrifying her if he wished to give her a chance; but that had set Allison off on a rant about being tied to a weak woman who would rule by taking to her bed or casting a mood of gloom upon the house. In this, Scribster understood a reference to his dear Mama. It made him resolve, instead, to give Honoria a disgust of him, in the hopes that she would not have him, but without being less than gentlemanly. Scribster's eyebrows had almost reached his hairline.

'Well, whatever happens, I must, in all conscience, offer for her. And I doubt I can stop her accepting. She is the kind of insipid girl who will do as her parents bid her.'

'I think the term you are looking for is obedient, hardly insipid,' Scribster adopted the tone of a vicar from the pulpit, one of declamatory oration, 'Remember, my boy, that the commandments bid us honour—'

'Stop right now Gus, or I shall throw you in that ditch!' had said Allison, for they were walking at that time. 'No — the only thing is, I must give her a chance and try to get to know her.' This last said in a tone of false optimism.

Angus Scribster had never seen his cool, suave, but kind friend in such a vacillating state, and he found it humorous.

Yes, he was friend enough to wish him well, but not friend enough, he thought now, not to enjoy the situation in all its absurd starts.

The conversation had turned to young Fenton.

'Does young Mr Benedict Fenton not join us?' said Allison politely.

'He's in London,' said Sir Ranalph, looking uncomfortable for the first time, 'Visiting ...' and his wife joined in, 'Lord Carstairs—' whilst the baronet was finishing with, 'his uncle.'

His Lordship and his wife exchanged a rueful look but Allison didn't notice. His eye had been caught by the sight of Serena feeding cake to another of the dogs which had slunk into the room behind Blake as he'd re-entered and quietly taken his place beside her chair.

'But he intends to visit, with your permission, sir.'

Allison turned abruptly just as Serena had looked up and smiled. 'Oh, certainly, sir, he will be most welcome.'

The parents shared a glance of relief that no more would be asked.

Why should a visit to his uncle be a mystery, even if that uncle is known to be a bit of a loose screw? Angus Scribster asked himself.

Sir Ranalph addressed him suddenly. 'We saw you in London this season, Mr Scribster. How do you like the great metropolis?'

'Not at all, I'm afraid,' said he, his voice his usual lugubrious monotone.

'Ah, then, you like your country estate more, Mr Scribster?' said her ladyship encouragingly, 'It's in Scotland, I believe.'

'I cannot say that I do ma'am. Stane Castle is a damp and dreary place overlooking a particularly unprepossessing glen. I never go there if it is to be avoided.'

The conversation faltered, as it often did around him. Rowley had repeatedly told him to varnish the truth with a little good manners, but he felt no desire so to do. He caught the elder sister looking at him with a vestige of annoyance on her face. She did not approve of him. It was the first expression that did not fit with Rowley's bland assessment. Another mystery.

This just got better and better.

Chapter 6

The Card Shark

Honoria rose early with a strange feeling of aloneness, for there was no Serena to share her bed. They had been shown to separate rooms and the footmen were rather too grand to make the request that their bags be moved so that they could share — as they had done since they were but little girls. After dressing quickly, she went to Serena's room to start the day with chatter as they did most mornings, generally before they rose from bed. But Serena's chamber was empty, and it was unnecessary to give much thought to where she was — the stables. Nominally checking on Rufus, but really desperate to get acquainted with Mr Allison's horses. Really, it was Genevieve Horton, or Lady Sumner as she now was, that should be Serena's sister — they had a great deal in common. The mysteries of the stables excited them. Honoria was very fond of horses whilst she rode, but when they were taken away to their abode she had no desire at all to cross the threshold.

There they could remain until presented to her once more, brushed and saddled, ready to ride.

It was better, anyway, that she walk alone this morning. The grounds were tempting, and she spied an interesting knot garden to one side and a rose walk to a grand pergola beyond.

The stiffness between Mr Allison and her was painful. He had brought her here to offer for her — his intentions, her father said, were quite clear — but one would not know it. Perhaps he was shy and embarrassed by the situation like she — but no, a grand gentleman like Mr Allison would not be embarrassed. Perhaps, then, he just *was* this stiff and formal. But she seemed to remember a different tone as he danced with her; and at that dreadful tea, he had tried to put her at her ease, had teased her a little. Her nervousness had very likely given him a disgust of her - but why then did he speak to her father? It was very strange. He was very strange. Could he be moody like Mr. Phipps, the apothecary at Fenton village? His wife had told her mother that she never knew from one day to another whether he would smile or glower.

Whatever it was, she knew that it was her duty to marry him to help Mama, Papa, Serena and the children. She had hardly smiled since she arrived and her mother had remarked it, with a little admonishment in her voice. And what was the problem really? She was to invite the declarations of a handsome, rich man. It was true, however, she did not yet know his character. She stopped walking and worried at the white marble gravel with the toe of her boot. She suspected Genevieve Horton had been mistaken in the character of *her* husband. She remembered her warning — but Genevieve did not know how crucial it was to her family that Honoria accept.

Still, she thought hopefully, if Mr Allison was found to be a libertine, say, or a cruel beast, Papa would never consent. The thought cheered her.

The morning air was shattered by a wail, and Honoria looked around. A shabby child had fallen from a cart that was delivering goods to a side door of the house. Mr Allison, another early riser obviously, rounded the corner at a run. He bent down and from a distance she saw him lift the child back on to the cart. The carter, probably the child's father, seemed to be apologising, and she saw Mr Allison check the crying child's limbs for breaks and with a final word to the carter and a smile, gestured them on their way.

Oh no, she thought, with a tragic pout, it seemed that Mr Allison was not a beast at all. He had re-entered the house and she sighed. It was now absolutely necessary to be as winning and inviting as she could possibly be. She was resolved to smile at Mr Allison all through the day and *not* shake in her boots, she thought nobly. She would bring this thing off. How unfulfilling it was to be noble when no-one else knew.

Her resolve firm, she set off back to the house with purpose. All may have proceeded very well indeed if it had not been for the unfortunate occurrence of her falling in love on the way into breakfast.

Benedict enjoyed his new facility for beating Carstairs at games of chance, but it was hardly a challenge. It was time to go a step further, to challenge himself. Enjoying his uncle's company for another morning, he was once more heading to the smaller chamber off the bedroom, to be present at the delicate process of becoming dressed.

'Your uncle has said to you, M'siuer, that it is *interdit* for to veeseet 'im at the *heure de toilette*. Forbeeden, *vous comprenez?*' The tiny valet was talking quickly as he moved ahead of him up the stairs. 'He is creating 'imself each morning. No-one but *I* know — and I tell no one, me — that he is creating 'imself anew each day. It is the work of a true *artiste* and must never be interrupted. I myself 'old my breath when I see him reach for a new colour, a new twist to the cravat. I tell you, I 'old my breath.'

Benedict looked down on the little man and removed his grasping hand from his arm as though he were swatting a fly. 'Tell you what, Pierre,' he said, moving around the small obstruction in the staircase, 'I promise to hold my breath also.' He patted Pierre's head as he passed. Pierre gave a gasp, tossed his head, and hurried in front of him, head held as high as possible, looking back at him not at all.

The creative *artiste* was standing in front of a mirror, dressed in smallclothes only, arranging his high curls more becomingly around his face. Seeing his nephew behind him caused his eyebrows to raise, 'Now Dickie, this is too bad, really. I am a harmonious man, but how would you like it if I interrupted you before the day had fairly begun?'

'It is half past eleven of the clock. I had breakfast four hours ago.'

'Horrible boy. I'll wager Carstairs didn't. I saw him at Countess Overton's last night.'

'True.' Benedict grinned. 'He breakfasted a *little* later.'

'You, I suppose, were tucked into your bed at a decent hour like your father before you. Desperately clean living fellow, Ranalph.'

He had, by this time, adopted a silk robe that rivalled Carstairs in its roaring at one. Benedict picked up the remains of a sweet roll and ate it, averting his eye. 'Actually, I was up till four. Went to a den in Blackwall Place. Was told I'd see Rennie there.' He shrugged. 'I didn't.'

'Four am. Ah, youth!' Mr Fenton senior mocked a reminiscent smile. 'So you do want revenge.'

'Not at all. But I wanted to play him anyway. I wanted to know ...'

'... How good you are. Well, you have a talent, no denying it.' Despite himself, Benedict felt a rush of pride. 'But he'd probably spot you.' The pride popped like a soap bubble.

'It would be good to try.'

'Well, you have bottom, I'll grant you that. But consider the scandal if you *did* get caught. Ranalph would be more than shocked, and it would reflect badly upon the family as a whole.'

'I wouldn't—' Benedict breathed. 'No, you're right. If there was the slightest chance, I can't—'

'Indeed my dear boy. I'm glad you thought of me. My unblemished reputation might be threatened.'

Benedict gave a crack of laughter. 'We could not have that!'

'No indeed!' smiled his uncle. 'So you may as well tell me — who do you want to topple? What have all these tedious mornings been for? Not that I'm not fond of you, my boy, but if it hadn't been for the delicate matter of the delay in the coronetcy, I daresay I wouldn't have encouraged you to think you could barge in on me at unearthly hours—'

'It's almost midday — and I don't remember you encouraging me!'

'Don't interrupt, I am delivering myself of a homily.' Mr Fenton was being helped into his *pantalons* by Pierre. '—At unearthly hours and disturb my peace. Indeed, when this little visit of yours to the capital has finished, I sincerely hope there will be a familial lapse in time till I set eyes on you again. Say six months.'

Benedict threw one leg over the arm of a chair and continued eating the rest of his uncle's morning refreshments. 'Very nice cake. If I tell you who it is, would you help me?'

'Certainly not.' The coat was going on with delicate precision. The method of throwing back his arms to their furthermost point behind him so that both sleeves could be lovingly put on at once (due to the tight fit of the jacket) caused Benedict an evil grin. His uncle frowned. 'Tell me anyway.'

'I can't tell you *why*. But it is Lord Sumner.'

His uncle gave a short laugh. 'You'll come unstuck there. Tale is, he's been bled dry already.'

'But he can't have been already, I mean—'

'Ah, you mean the wife's dowry. Gone, by all accounts. He has the barony, of course, but he's been bleeding it dry and land doesn't pay well with bad management. He's living on the expectations of his aunt. Lady Harrington, you know. Rich as Midas they say.'

Benedict's grin had faded and he looked sunk. His uncle, catching the look on his face in the mirror as he was giving his cravat a last tweak, frowned. 'Now, why so cast down?' Wilbert looked as though the light had dawned. 'The wife. She was a Horton from Ottershaw— Dickie, you cannot be in love with that red beaked, wan-faced bird?'

'Of course not — I mean to say, Lady Sumner is a very great friend of mine and I do not take your description of her well. A man wearing a cushion at his waist should not throw stones.'

Wilbert tapped his stomach contentedly. 'What's the story?'

'That I cannot tell you. Blast it all.' He paced around the room as far as the space allowed. Then he stopped. 'Who won Sumner's money?'

'Your friend Rennie took five thousand guineas at a sitting. I don't know who else.'

'Could you find out sir?'

'Why should I?'

'So as to enjoy your toilette in peace for at least another six months.'

'Done. Meet me at Jackson's tomorrow at four.'

It happened like this, Honoria was entering the house, with the express intention of showing herself to better advantage to her potential suitor, when she saw a man in the great hall in full regimentals. His back was to her, a strong, manly back, in a scarlet coat, with dark hair a little too long clustering along the top edge of his high, frogged collar. She had not yet seen his face, but her heart stood still. He looked up at Scribster, who was descending the stairs. 'Gus! I've just arrived.' Honoria was granted sight of his left ear and had the oddest feeling of falling in love with it. Its form promised great things. 'Where are Rowley's beauties?'

'One is right behind you! Miss Fenton, may I apologise and present Lieutenant Darnley Prescott, cousin to our host.'

He turned, he laughed, and her hand was taken in a friendly fashion. He looked very much like Mr Allison, with his dimpled chin and laughing brown eyes, but his warm manner, like his handsome face, soothed her soul. Surely here was the embodiment of her dreams. She hardly knew what was being said, her dratted timidity kept her from replying at first. He apologised, then she disclaimed and they laughed, and she felt herself blush rosily.

As she looked up she saw Mr Scribster with his glittering intelligent eyes, and frowned. Why was he always so *there?* And so knowing?

They all moved towards the breakfast room, where Serena and her parents were already installed, and she moved forward on Lieutenant Prescott's arm — Lieutenant *Darnley* Prescott, was there ever such a wonderful sounding name? He was shaking hands with her family, making everybody smile. Serena quipped that it was always wonderful to meet one of Wellington's heroes, and he nobly made little of it, saying he had spent most of his war in offices. As they ate their meal, Mr Allison, who had become almost human when he had greeted his cousin, addressed some remarks to her about the weather, but she did not hear and had twice to be called to order by her mama. She was too well raised to stare at Mr Prescott's heavenly countenance, but her awareness of him, though he was two persons distant from her at the table, was complete — even when she was staring at her plate.

Serena, all this while her usual happy self, felt a little strange. It was not the large, beautiful house or the new company that affected her — why should it when there were such stables and such horses? — it was a feeling of loss. Last night she had gone to Honoria's room, sat on the bed and pulled her knees up as Honoria dressed for bed.

'Well, Mr Scribster hasn't improved on acquaintance. He dresses like Papa's lawyer and I believe his face would crack if he gave any of us a polite smile.'

'What?' said Honoria, 'No, no he hasn't.'

'But Mr Allison is as handsome as I remember, but nearly as stiff as when he visited Fenton Manor. Perhaps he's following *your* example! Is this what you were like your *whole* season?'

No reply from Honoria except an mmm. Her normal reaction to her sister's teasing might have been to throw the hairbrush at Serena. She changed tack. 'Orry, why are you still so nervous? Don't you think we can just enjoy the visit? It is so beautiful here and we can walk and ride every day. Benedict will join us soon and there are no children to annoy us.'

'I *like* the children!' protested Honoria.

'Not all the time you don't,' said Serena, with wide eyes. 'What about when Cedric upsets our walks by begging us to play cricket? Or when Angelica knotted all your work threads?'

'Well, but I miss them being around.'

'You cannot — not *yet*.'

'It is just a little strange that's all,' said Honoria, pulling hair from her brush.

There was something in her sister's voice that made Serena leap from the bed in her impetuous way and rush to give her back a hug. She looked at Orry in the mirror and said, 'It's all just a lark, you know. You don't *have* to do anything at all. I wish you could enjoy yourself.'

Orry smiled then and hugged her back. 'I will, I promise. I'm just a little shy — you know how I am in new company.'

Serena was not exactly satisfied, but with a last hug, she said goodnight.

It was strange to feel distant from Honoria. And she suddenly understood that if Mama's plans for this visit prospered, Honoria and she would soon be parted permanently.

The first time Benedict had been taken to Jackson's Boxing Saloon had been exciting. He was aware that many young bucks about town would give their eyeteeth to attend the saloon and shake the hand of

Gentleman Jackson, legendary fighter, who had the good sense to offer young gentlemen a chance to train with the best. His uncle's entree to many doors closed to less fortunate men was something to be grateful for — although his father had warned him of certain places where his uncle might take him that he was on no account to go. Usually Benedict was anxious to strip and fight — once even with the great man himself — but this afternoon his visit was brief. His uncle, in a small group of ageing dandies, overdressed for this atmosphere of sawdust and sweat, was watching a fight between Freddy Poole and Sir Neville Austen. He looked over the shoulder that Benedict tapped, held up a screw of paper and turned back to the fight. Benedict turned on his heel and had almost reached the door when the lazy but clear accents of Wilbert Fenton caught him.

'Six months, my boy.'

Benedict's laugh wafted back with the clang of the closing door.

Chapter 7

Honoria In Love?

After breakfast, the ladies repaired to what passed for a cosy nook (of only twenty-five-foot square) where they sat at their work. Serena was embroidering a pair of slippers for Papa and the velvet was stretched on a small frame. Mama's nimble fingers were repairing the strings of a lace cap that little Angelica had pulled near off. Having found a tall pin cushion of turned wood topped by stuffed velvet, Honoria was distractedly pinning and pleating some stiff grosgrain ribbon into a confection suitable to wear either in her hair or on a plain straw hat.

'You were very quiet at breakfast today,' Mama said.

'I know, Mama, I will try to put myself forward a little more,' Serena cast her innocent eyes towards her parent.

'Very amusing, Serena,' said Mama.

Honoria shared a glance with her sister, smiling gratefully.

'I rather thought that you had gotten over your shyness with Mr Allison,' pursued Mama, 'but perhaps it was the new arrival that sent you back into yourself. I cannot understand it Honoria, you are not so shy at home.'

Glancing at Honoria's flushed face, Serena answered once more. 'It is these London men, Mama — they are so different to our country acquaintance as to make us quake in our shoes.'

Her mother eyed her, 'Your quaking was not evident, Serena. I will not say you push yourself forward, but you must let your sister shine as well.'

Serena flushed. She was used to gentle gibing from her mother, but this seemed to go further.

'That is not fair, Mama,' Honoria had flushed, too. 'You know that Serena was only filling the spaces I could not — on account of my wretched timidity.'

Her mother's eyes widened at this outburst. 'Well, I'm sure that you are both good girls and perhaps I'm just a little nervous that ... that ...well, that we all enjoy ourselves.'

It was all that was said on the subject, but it was enough to let Honoria feel the heavy hand of fate crush her once more. It was not long before they chatted as they normally did, and Honoria was not again made anxious until Lieutenant Prescott's name was raised once more. It thrilled her just to hear it, but she was unable to join in the conversation. Mama speculated on his situation in life and in his exact relation to Mr Allison, drawing on her slight knowledge of the family and its various branches. 'He must be a sister's child as his name is not Allison, of course. But it may be a cousin's — one frequently introduces one's second or even third cousin as cousin... oh, it that Mr.

Scribster's voice I hear in the hall? Ask him to come in, Honoria, and he shall tell us, I'm sure.'

Honoria ran to the door and performed her office. 'Mr Scribster, won't you come in to the morning room? Mama would like to talk to you.'

He shrugged with an appalling lack of manners. 'Very well,' and divested himself of his coat.

Honoria felt a rush of anger, but controlled it. It seemed Mr Scribster caught it, for he raised one eyebrow, as she could just see beneath the lank curtain of his hair. 'How have I offended you, Miss Fenton?'

Well, thought Honoria, you don't even bother to answer politely or to pretend an interest in anybody or anything, you rude, obnoxious man. But she merely said in a honeyed voice, 'Not at all, sir. I'm sure you never offend anyone.' Both his eyebrows went up, but he followed her obediently into the morning room.

'Mr Scribster! Have you left the gentlemen early?'

'As you see, madam.'

Honoria saw that her mama was thrown for a minute by this abrupt retort, but she soldiered on. 'You must come and admire our work, you know.'

Mr Scribster looked at all three ladies' work and was silent.

'Serena is a fine workman, do not you think?' asked Mama.

Mr Scribster sat on an adjacent seat and answered, 'I'm no judge of stitchery.'

A little 'huh' sound escaped Honoria's throat and he met her eyes for a second, but it was Serena who said, 'Very few men are, sir. But we have not brought you here for that. We wish to pick your brains on the subject of Mr Allison's cousin. Have you known him long, sir?'

'I have known him for many years.'

'And what is his exact relation to Mr Allison?'

'I believe he was introduced as his cousin,' said Mr Scribster blandly.

Honoria got up abruptly and moved to the window.

Mama, though, was undaunted, 'An aunt's son then?'

'Mr Allison has no aunt.'

Honoria spun around from the window and shot him a look that curled his hair. He held her hot gaze whilst her mother continued, 'A cousin's son then?'

'Indeed.' His hooded eyes still regarded Honoria's hot gaze.

'Talking to you is like pulling—'

'Serena!' interrupted Mama. She continued sweetly, 'so Mr Allison's female cousin had a son and Lieutenant Prescott is he?'

'You are correct,' Mr Scribster was continuing to observe Honoria, who turned her shoulder on him and looked out of the window. 'Miss Annabelle Allison, cousin to my friend, wed a Mr Prescott and produced our newly arrived companion.' Honoria turned and raised her brows, but it was Serena who voiced her thoughts.

'You offered some information all on your own, sir. We are honoured.'

'You should be, Miss Serena. I fear it is a rare occurrence.'

Honoria shot him a disgusted look and turned back to the window. There was the noise in the hall of the gentlemen arriving, and soon they had entered in a rambunctious lot, Mr Allison at their head.

'Ladies, we must apologise to you for invading you in our dirt—'

Honoria curtsied stiffly as Mr Allison smiled at her and retook her seat at her work, sitting on the edge of her chair.

'Not at all, gentlemen. I trust you've had good sport,' said Lady Fenton.

'We did, ma'am,' said Sir Ranalph, 'only the rain came on rather suddenly so we dispatched Scribster here to order us some wine before we attempt to clean up before luncheon.' Papa was his usual self, jolly and obviously enjoying the company.

'I'm afraid,' said Mr Scribster at his most bland, 'that I was, ah, entertaining the ladies.'

Honoria gave a little gasp as she stabbed herself with a pin. Lieutenant Prescott, noting it, gave her his handkerchief. 'Let me, Miss Fenton.' Suddenly his smiling face was looming over hers, his large strong hand had taken possession of her little pale one and he knelt at her feet wrapping the handkerchief around her digit, and Honoria was behaving in a way she thought only the heroines in novels did — her bosom was heaving. His touch set her trembling and Serena, noticing, came forward.

'Come sister, I fear we must bathe that finger and get ready for luncheon.' The lieutenant had already risen and was ringing for wine.

Mr Allison bowed as the sisters passed him and Honoria rewarded him with a wan smile. Since Lady Fenton was talking to her husband and his cousin, Allison was able to murmur to his friend, 'That girl may be beautiful but she has all the animation of the stuffed deer in the hall. How can I go through with it?'

'As to the latter, I still cannot see why you must. Your form of honour is a mystery to me.'

'Do you have any of your own to judge it by?' asked Allison.

'Enough to tell you that you are quite mistaken in Miss Fenton. I assure you she can be amazingly animated. I myself seem to arouse her to blazing fury.'

'You have that effect on many, but I can hardly believe it in this case. She is her parents' beautiful glove puppet. What have you done to her?'

'No more than be myself.'

'Well, that's irritating enough. But she displays her anger? You almost persuade me to poke at her till she bites.'

'And what do you want to do to her sister?'

'Nothing. That's over. She's a pleasant young woman—' Scribster laughed. '—but was just— do you know, Gus, I quite see why half the world despises you. I think I might take it up myself.'

Serena was whispering to Honoria as they climbed the stairs to the bed chambers, 'Why on earth would you fall for Lieutenant Prescott?'

'I have not!' her sister hissed.

'Yes you have—'

They had reached Honoria's lofty chamber and they both threw themselves down on the bed.

'I have not — it is just that I get anxious around handsome men. And the lieutenant is very handsome.'

'He's nearly Mr Allison's double, but you don't get breathless around *him*.' Honoria looked up for a second and Serena leaned forward and grasped her hands, 'What is it, Honoria — what are you not telling me?'

Honoria struggled with a half-truth. 'If only Mama had not told me why we are here, I suspect that I could relax and enjoy the visit. But knowing that Mr Allison might offer for me at any moment - well, it makes me so nervous. And that means I cannot relax enough to converse sensibly or—'

'I understand. Only Mr Allison is really very nice Orry, and you call his cousin handsome, so you must like his looks.'

'Yes,' said Honoria, glad to be confessing at least some part of her woes to Serena at last, 'and I saw our host be very kind and attentive to an injured carter's boy — whilst he thought no-one was regarding him — so I know he is a compassionate man.' She sighed.

'Well, don't sound so cheerful about it.'

Honoria laughed. 'I suppose I am making a mull of it. I will try to get to know Mr Allison. He seems very — pleasant underneath his reserve.'

The highwayman thief of the blue slipper "pleasant and reserved"? 'He's a bit more than that. And it wouldn't be the worst thing to be mistress of Bassington Hall. And perhaps Lieutenant Prescott is rich too and I can capture him for a husband and spare Papa the cost of another London season.'

The joke about the season smote Honoria's heart once more. But something she'd said gave her a glint of hope. 'Perhaps he is — we should set Mama on to discover his situation.'

'Oh, never fear, I'm sure she has it in hand. Even Mr Scribster's fabled reticence is no match for Mama when she wants to ferret something out.'

Perhaps the cousin was wealthy enough — perhaps if he cared for her — oh, Honoria, she thought, how ridiculous you are. As soon think that Mr Scribster admires you. The lieutenant was nothing more than a dashing, handsome hero with a kind and gentle nature (evident by the handkerchief that she was already wearing at her breast) whom there was no reason to fall for at all.

Rowley Allison couldn't look at his friend Gus Scribster whenever he was in the vicinity of Serena Fenton. He avoided her as often as he could but there were moments… like when his beloved-but-dim cousin Darnley had repeated something he had heard about Lord Sumner's latest ride. 'My friend sold it to him and as he said, it may initially look like it lacks spirit, but once the horse gets to know its rider, it will be sure to show its paces.'

Serena Fenton had met his gaze, her eyes brim-full of laughter. His eyebrow shot up and she gurgled, then said, 'And how long does the vendor suppose this familiarity will take?'

The lieutenant scratched his head. 'Well, he didn't say. But I suppose it must take some time because he had the beast for two months before, and I saw little spirit in him. But he *looks* very well, you know.'

Serena had laughed aloud and looked straight to Mr Allison to share the joke. He grinned and said to his cousin, 'I trust you will never yourself purchase a horse from your friend.'

Prescott looked confused. 'But you know Papa insists I buy all my nags from Tattersall's. Won't stand the nonsense otherwise.' His father was a sensible man, wouldn't pay for his son getting cheated by one of his showy friends.

As they left the breakfast room, Serena had grabbed at his elbow, drawn him aside, and said, 'Well, my highwayman, has your cousin always been such a lobcock or is it only in respect of horses?'

He looked down at her, the confiding expression in her eyes, and could not push her away again. He relaxed, 'My cousin, Miss Serena Fenton, is never a lobcock. A ninny, perhaps, but a lobcock, no. That suggests a person who stumbles around, looking idiotic. My cousin, on the other hand, always looks handsome and confident and moves throughout the world in the most innocent way, unaware of the chaos he leaves in his wake.'

She laughed, but her mother called her and she swept away. Scribster was in the hall with the others, but his height allowed him to look over the heads of the ladies and give his friend an ironic grin. He had to keep away from her, that was all, away from her twinkling eyes, her teasing smile, so as to stop this reflux of desire from coming at him in waves. He'd watched her then, and he clearly saw that she had no idea of his feelings and certainly didn't share them. Some innate knowledge of him made her offer him looks when something was funny and she thought that he would share her view, and her confiding sought to make him her friend. Eventually, married to her sister, he could perhaps fill that role. But not now. As he walked away, with Gus's sardonic grin following him, he saw the horror of the sisterly visits. But surely by then — surely, he would have come to love her beautiful, dutiful, deadly dull sister.

Her parents were not of the 'pushing' variety, but the mama did suggest several entertainments for the 'young people' designed, he was sure, to allow him an opportunity to offer for Honoria. He looked at the elder Miss Fenton over breakfast that day and he feared that his lack of action was causing her pain. Was that sadness he saw in her face? She did not look at him, but looked at her plate, blushing, or into the ether rather distractedly. When he thought she was distressed, he made up his mind to speak to her after the meal — he had kept her in suspense too long — he could not ignore her distress. But suddenly she gave such a smile of radiance as she looked in another direction, that he thought she was quite alright. It would be fine to postpone his addresses to another day.

They were to ride after breakfast, and five of them were to set off to see if they could achieve the windmill and back before lunch. Nowadays, though the sisters' figures and hair colours were so close, Allison had no difficulty telling which one of them was Serena, even though he only had a view from the back. She wore green velvet today, with a shako hat, whilst her sister wore blue wool with a great deal of military frogging. Scribster was mounting up at his side, but just as he was wondering if his identification was correct, Serena turned her horse towards his cousin, who was leading his nag out ready to mount.

'Who saddled that horse?' she demanded, her face flushed. Serena pointed. 'Take that horse back to the stables immediately.' As the group looked at her in amazement, she added, 'He has a strained fetlock. Can you not see by his gait?'

The second groom, Taft, after a nod from his master, bent and felt the leg that Serena pointed to.

'There is a little inflammation, Mr Allison, sir. But not a lot.'

'Well there will be if you mount a fourteen stone man to ride it for two hours. Take him back and I'll…' she moved to dismount.

'Taft knows what to do, Miss Serena, I assure you.' Allison said to her.

She frowned, her transparent look showing that a groom who had saddled an injured horse was not someone to place trust in. 'Very well, sir.'

He stifled a grin, and took point. 'Sorry, Darnley, there is no other horse in the stable bar Mr Fenton's Rufus that is up to your weight.'

He threw this over his shoulder as he rode away, leaving the rest to follow.

'So sorry, Lieutenant Prescott,' shouted Honoria in his general direction, but her horse was cantering and she needs must pay attention.

Mr Allison sped his horse to a gallop to overshoot the party and clear his head of the pull of Serena in yet another guise, the autocratic beauty. His heart was near to bursting with pride, and he had no right to it. As he rode hard he was surprised, but not very much, that she had nearly caught him up, outstripping Scribster and her sister, who were still cantering.

Chapter 8

Mr Scribster's Bargain

Honoria was riding with Mr Scribster, though her heart was with the noble lieutenant, whom she hoped she would have been able to speak to, just a little, on today's ride. She knew that the more likely outcome would have been that she merely listened to Lieutenant Prescott, because the nearer she got to him the less able she was to speak at all. But it didn't matter, she could merely watch and listen to him. She had been doing that over breakfast, when Serena's laugh had interrupted her. What had she been laughing at? Surely not—

'Poor Lieutenant Prescott.'

She was not aware that she spoke aloud, but Mr Scribster answered her, 'What? Because the poor fool was prevented from injuring a horse?'

Mr Scribster looked at the clamping of Honoria's jaw, and the small muscles of her face fighting for control beneath the skin.

'Spit it out!'

'I. beg. Your. Pardon, sir?'

Mr Scribster laughed, a noise that she had not believed possible to be heard from his long, miserable face.

'I said, spit it out or the bile of it will choke you!'

Honoria did give a choking sound as words arose that she strangled in good manners.

'Told you so. You had better tell me that you find me an unfeeling brute or a whatever it is you are dying to say to me.' Her eyes flashed. 'Yes, you have been giving me that look for a long time now. Do you not have the slightest bit of honesty at your disposal that would allow you to say what you want to say to me out loud?'

'You sir, have enough *honesty,*' she said acidly, 'for the entire nation. If you had any manners to temper it—' Honoria stopped herself, appalled.

'I was brought up by a Scottish mother. In her view good manners were grounded in honesty. I suppose dishonesty grounds yours.'

'Dishonesty, *dishonesty*? If honesty means hurting the feelings of everyone around you with abominable rudeness, then—'

Mr Scribster looked interested, which his face could only achieve with the cock of an eyebrow. Honoria bit her lip and looked down. 'Whose feelings have I hurt — yours?'

'*Mine?* As though I could care a fig for the feelings of a creature such as you!'

'Well,' said Mr Scribster evenly, slowing his horse to the pace of Honoria's, 'That's alright then. No apology needed. Rowley usually tells me when I need to apologise and I do of course, but I can seldom see why.'

'Alright? *Alr*—'

'You seem to have developed the habit of taking a word from my reply and repeating it. It's becoming tiresome'

'*Tires*—' Honoria stopped and suddenly choked on a laugh — it was too ridiculous. 'You,' she said, but in a tone with less vitriol, 'are a horrible person—'

'There, you've said it,' approved Mr Scribster, 'I'll bet you feel better now.'

'—with no manners—'

'Very true.'

'And delight in making other people uncomfortable—'

Mr Scribster considered, 'You may be right.'

'Well, you did not succeed with Lieutenant Prescott. Your remarks about his appointment keeping him far from the war, insinuating that he is a coward, did not upset him in the least.'

'No, he doesn't have the wit to notice.'

'OOOOOH! What a thing to say. Because a man has too much self-belief, too much nobility, to be bothered by a *gnat* like you—' Her voice had ridden to its earlier passion.

'A gnat? Really? I'm a little tall for a—'

'Who is so jealous of his handsome face because he is so *ugly* himself.'

There was a stunned silence. Mr Scribster's mobile eyebrows went down. Honoria's hand had flown to her mouth.

'Mr S-Scribster, I am so, so *very* sorry.'

The horses were stopped and Honoria was frozen. Her hand went to her mouth again as though there was a chance to stop the words she had already said, or stuff them back into her mouth.

Mr Scribster's face had not changed from its immobility, but he looked down. And Honoria was aghast to see his shoulders shake.

She pulled her mare closer, so that she was able to grasp Scribster's arm with her blue kid gloved hand. As she leant forward to offer comfort, she saw a muscle in his face move and she brought the hand up as though burned and slapped his arm with considerable ferocity. Miss Fenton had had to defend herself against brothers.

'You are *laughing*.'

He looked up, a grin dispelling his usual expression, 'I'm wounded to the core,' he said, 'Would you really say *ugly* rather than 'a grave but handsome visage'? People have done their best with the euphemisms over the years, but you are the first woman since my mother to call me that.'

Honoria's quick sympathy was aroused, 'Your *mother*? Oh, you poor little boy.'

Mr. Scribster grinned once more, and Honoria suddenly noticed how those dark hooded eyes could look alive with mischief. 'She told me that only a mother could love an ugly laddie like me — young women of today are not able to see beyond the surface. It turned out that she was quite right.'

'Don't try to flummox me into being sorry for you, Mr Scribster, you won't manage it twice. If you took any pains at all to be winning,

I *would* be sorry. But at any social function where I have seen you, you express all the animation of an undertaker's apprentice.'

'Now, it really isn't polite to mention my face again. It's hardly my fault that I was born with it.'

'*And*,' Honoria continued, 'if a lady does venture to speak to you, you treat her to one of your oh-so-honest replies that leaves her unable to address another remark to you.'

'You are remarkably accurate in your account of my social interactions. Could you have been spying on me?'

'*Spying?*'

'You're doing it again.'

Honoria couldn't help but laugh at this. 'I was not spying, but I heard you give Miss Shaw a set down when I sat beside her mama at the Raleighs' supper party.'

'Were you there?'

'It is customary to pretend you remember if you met a lady before.' Scribster merely raised an eyebrow. 'You are right — it was silly of me to expect it of you.'

'What awful thing did I say to Miss Shaw?'

'You really don't remember?' Scribster didn't bother to reply. 'It was not to her but to her mama, in Miss Shaw's hearing. Her mother asked you if you did not think that pink became her daughter. And you replied that you did not.'

'Well, that was because there was a darker girl sitting next to her in a pink gown that displayed it to much better advantage. I rather think that Miss Shaw might have been better in something else — primrose, perhaps. Though it wouldn't have helped with her complexion.'

Honoria gave a sound. 'Oh, wait a minute — I think I do remember something — was that darker girl you?'

Honoria frowned. 'I think I was wearing my pink muslin that night. But that is not the point.'

'Well, but I assure you, if Mrs Shaw had been your mama, I would have answered in the affirmative, because you looked very well indeed in pink.'

'Yet you didn't even remember me till a moment ago.'

'Of course I did not, the Season is full of attractive young ladies. And pretty full of the unattractive ones.'

Honoria's jaw dropped, 'You are completely—'

'Honest?' offered Scribster. 'I cannot understand why you are annoyed with me, I have just given you a handsome compliment which is something that I'm sure you thought I could not do.'

'*And* made a disparaging remark about Miss Shaw's complexion.'

'I did not disparage her. I commented upon it, as people are apt to comment on mine.'

Belatedly, Honoria noticed Mr. Scribster's pitted complexion.

'Smallpox in my youth. But I survived, as you see.'

Honoria and he rode on a pace, hardly able to see their supposed companions ahead. 'The truth can hurt people,' Honoria eventually said, 'Why cannot you simply say nothing?'

'Well, and so I do, normally. The advice of my friends, such as Rowley, is that I speak as little as possible at social gatherings. And this gives me the reputation as superior and unfriendly, does it not?'

Honoria knew it to be true.

'Of course it does. But occasionally, someone asks for my opinion, and I am honour-bound to give it honestly.'

Honoria sighed. 'It must be nice to be you, Mr Scribster — able to open up your mouth and not care what you say. Be able to sit in society without the need to come up with some conversation or to make witticisms. To think only of yourself.'

'Is that what *you* would wish to do, Miss Fenton?'

This time her sigh was longer. 'Of course not. There are duties to perform, and the social niceties are meant to make us all feel more comfortable. But sometimes—'

'Sometimes, Miss Fenton?'

'No. I will not think this way.' She seemed to consider seriously for a moment. 'If you had told a polite lie, if you had said that the pink became Miss Shaw, you would not have hurt her — and you might have brought her some joy.'

'Yes. But I might have given her mother the idea that Miss Shaw was just the mistress for Stane Castle — a fate I would wish upon no young lady. And Miss Shaw and I should have been forced into social situations where our polite lies might have led to discomfort for both of us. Even if I wished for a wife, it would not be she—' Honoria was frowning again. '—and that has nothing to do with her shocking taste in colour or her bad complexion, just that she was one of the silliest girls I've met.'

Honoria reflected that she herself had avoided Miss Shaw. 'You have an answer for everything.' But she was not unaware of Mr Scribster describing the parallel to her own situation.

'So you will stick to your polite lies, Miss Fenton?' Honoria's eyes flashed. 'Your eyes betray them — but only when you look at me.'

'That's because you have absolutely no desire to be appeasing to anyone, and it makes me furious.' She looked at him. 'I'm sorry, Mr Scribster. I have not been polite.'

'And it has been very amusing.' She smiled at him reluctantly, and he saw a little dimple appear on one cheek. 'You cannot wound me, Miss Fenton, whatever you say. If you must return to your politesse, can I ask that you exclude me? Let there be one place at least where you can say exactly what you think and be as insulting as you like.'

'You are a terrible, vile man.'

'Now that is exaggeration. Let's just say that I have no polite manners to speak of. Will you always tell me the truth?'

They had come to a gate and Mr Scribster got down from his horse to open it, showing unforeseen athleticism. Now he looked up at her.

'Since you take no pains to be polite with anyone, I shall not be polite with you. I believe I shall enjoy it.'

'It is a deal then.' He put out his hand to be shaken, 'from this hour you shall always tell me the unvarnished, impolite, truth.'

She hesitated to extend her hand. 'I will not tell you a polite lie,' she tempered. 'It would hardly be worth the effort — you seem to guess what I'm thinking about you anyway.' His mobile brows shot up again. 'But I cannot tell you what is not your business, so you will promise not to press me.'

He extended his hand further towards her, 'I will not. Do we have a bargain?'

She grasped his hand for a brief moment. 'Very well, you revolting individual.'

'That's my girl,' said Mr Scribster, shaking her hand firmly.

Chapter 9

Genevieve to Bassington

Genevieve, Lady Sumner, had received her husband's missive announcing his imminent arrival on the same day as she received one from his aunt, Lady Harrington, bidding her back to town immediately. In this second missive she found her salvation. She would go back to town as bidden. There could be no argument that Lady Harrington must be obeyed. And if the butler will just tell her husband that his letter arrived just after she had left, he would have nothing to say to it. If Sumner were a rational man, which of course he was not. But still it provided her with an excuse.

Why was he coming to the country at all? She suspected her father may have written to him to recall him to his duties and ask him to join his wife for the country show. He would think it would be a treat for Sumner, as if his lordship would care about a provincial show. So why was he coming? Because he was not sure how she would answer a summons from him to return to London? No, he didn't fear that she would obey, he had taken steps to ensure she would. Her hands crept to her neck. The marks had faded now, but she thought she would always feel them inside her.

He must have his own reasons for coming. A "repairing lease". That's what his friends called the retreat to the countryside to avoid London debtors, or the effects of too much London dissipation. He would wait to quarter day, when his lands would yield payment and then it would be safe to return. But why not go to Sumner rather than make the long journey here? Because it was a long way. Sumner was only two hours from town whereas it was unlikely that anyone would come as far as Ottershaw to dun him.

She could leave today, but would surely meet him on the road. But what if she were to go via Bassington? She'd met Mr Allison a number of times and she could pretend a necessity to see Serena about a horse cure and he would be sure to ask her to stay for a few days — it was good form. She could write to Lady Harrington and to her husband (addressed to London, so that he would not get it till he came back) and explain. If she was really very lucky, he might stay at Ottershaw till quarter day. She felt her own stupidity. He was her husband; she would have to see him soon. But she couldn't. Not yet. She needed time to make herself accept, to build her strength. She had accepted him when he'd offered for her. It was her own fault. She must go back to him. But not yet.

The ride had seemed to Rowley Allison like a space in time outside life. They did not speak, the pace of the gallop had not allowed for conversation, but they sped ahead and laughed with the sheer joy of movement, glancing at each other in an exchange of pleasure. They reached the windmill, with Serena a half second before him and she dismounted perilously. 'Miss Fenton!' he'd protested, but she laughed and led the horse to a nearby tree to be tied off. He joined her.

'Where are the others?' said Serena, looking back along the path.

Allison narrowed his eyes. 'Coming at a safe canter. You might emulate your sister's caution.'

'Do you think I need to be tutored in riding, Mr Allison?' asked Serena, amused.

'No, Miss Fenton,' he said, 'you have proved your superiority in the saddle. But going at that pace over countryside you did not know was foolish in the extreme.'

'Ah, but I was following my highwayman, who is *very* familiar with it.' She laughed up at him in a way that made him itch to catch her in his arms. 'I would not have else. I'm not quite a madwoman — I always think of the horse. The others seem to be a trifle slow,' said Serena, her beautiful brown velvet eyes looking back at the road. 'When I looked over my shoulder earlier, they were stopped. And I thought I saw Honoria strike Mr Scribster.'

'I beg your pardon?'

'I may have been wrong.'

'I can assure you that Scribster is not the sort of man to offer unwanted attentions—'

Serena laughed. 'Oh, I don't fear that. He probably said something offensive. Honoria's temper is slow to light up — unlike mine, I confess — but if she's defending the family or something she cares about, she can be quite ferocious.'

'Can she?' he said doubtfully, regarding the stately pace that Honoria was making with his friend.

'Oh, yes! Why once, when a neighbour berated little Cedric and cuffed him very violently for leaving open a gate, Honoria took her crop to him.' Serena looked conscious, 'But I assure you, he thoroughly deserved it. She is quite the sweetest natured girl in general.'

He was trying to reconcile this with his view of her sister.

'You are so lucky to live here Mr Allison. Such beautiful countryside for riding and so close to London.'

'You have visited London, Miss Fenton?'

'Never. I so wish to. I would go to Astley's Amphitheatre to see the horses, and get to visit all the best dress shops and museums and—'

'And go to balls and develop a following from all the young gentlemen.'

She laughed and looked at him teasingly once more, 'Do you think I should?'

He looked down at her, smiling back, falling into her eyes. 'Undoubtedly. There would be a waiting line to secure your hand for a dance.'

'Well, I should disappoint them all and dance with a friend instead.'

'What friends do you have there?'

'Well, *you*... and Mr Scribster,' began Serena.

'He never dances.'

'And Lieutenant Prescott, of course. He knows nothing about horses, but I suppose he knows how to dance.'

'Very elegantly.'

'Mr. Allison,' said Serena in her best wheedling tone, as her father called it, 'Do you think we might make a short expedition to London — as we're so close?'

'You'd find it very thin of company this season.'

'I live in *Yorkshire!*'

'Well, if you like. We could visit Astley's and stay at my house in Grosvenor Square for a night or two.'

'You are such a friend!' she jumped up from the grass. 'Please, when you suggest it to Papa, do not mention that the idea came from me. He gave me strict instructions—' she blushed and laughed.

'I suspect, Miss Fenton, that you are a minx.'

'You knew that the first time you met me, Mr Highwayman.' She turned away, 'We'll be waiting all day for those two,' she said, standing on a log to remount, 'Let's go and join them.'

It was obvious once more that Serena Fenton had no desire, unlike her companion, to extend their time together. It made his overwhelming desire for her seem like some form of madness.

The only way to cauterise the wound was by offering for her sister.

Benedict had his list. In Wilbert's messy scrawl, he read: *Rennie, Sutcliffe, Dawson. Start with Dawson, he's a relative beginner — he might not notice that he has a cheat playing against him.*

A few visits to places about town, Carstairs' club, a racing tavern, and another visit to Jackson's, meant that Benedict went to Countess Overton's again that evening in search of his quarry. Even though the town was thin of company, the grand salon was still near to full. Now, of course, his visit was very different to his first. Then he had known no-one, but now as he wandered around the room, he nodded to a number of acquaintances, very much the man about town. The Countess had pointed out Dawson to him, but with narrowed eyes. 'I want no trouble here,' she'd said. Benedict, abandoning his Brummel manner, gave her the look of a young innocent, trying it out for size before he took it to Dawson's table. 'You don't fool me, young Fenton,' said the Countess. 'Your father gave me just such an innocent look before stealing a kiss behind a neighbour's orangery.' Benedict was riveted by the notion of his father as a budding rake, a fate his mama must have rescued him from. 'Who could blame him, madam?' returned Benedict, kissing her hand like an old fashioned gallant. The Countess laughed, and touched his face playfully. 'Whatever you mean to do, please do it with discretion or far away from here.' He took her hand from his cheek and kissed it again. 'Your wish—' She rolled her eyes at him, 'Naughty boy!' and she wandered off to her tables. But Benedict knew he would be observed.

By the light of flickering candles, the faces of the gamblers were revealed. A table of the prince's cronies, overdressed and pungent with perfume, looking lazily at cards, never for a second betraying the life altering amounts of money changing hands. At a neighbouring table, Dawson sat with a number of people that Benedict knew slightly, including an extremely tense young gentleman, the flickering candle illuminating the face of dawning horror at his predicament. Hubert Dawson esquire, a florid man with a shock of black hair, was wearing a slight smile which he tried to conceal whilst a pile of IOUs sat by his elbow amongst the bank notes. Benedict observed for a while, nodding at Tubby Danford, who was a friend of his and Carstairs' from Cambridge. Dawson was dealing from the bottom of the deck, but so clumsily to Benedict's accustomed eye that it was a wonder no-one saw him. He looked around the faces gathered there. Dawson's slightly smug one in his round face, Danford, new in town and rich enough to be unconcerned with his losses, two drunken half-pay officers and the young country hick. Benedict drew up a chair beside Danford and began to chat in a rather more animated manner than normal.

Danford said, under his breath, 'How many have you had, Dickie?' Even better. Benedict slurred his speech a little and then Dawson, with a large friendly smile, dealt him in.

It didn't take too long. Benedict fuzzed the cards enough to let Potts, the bumpkin, win back the majority of his IOUs. He left the table before he had them all, but was thanking fate for his lucky escape from ruin. Benedict liked to be thought of as fate. Dawson looked confused but not suspicious, Benedict's clumsy fumblings made him an amateur in the man's eyes. But Dawson's incompetence was beginning to bore Fenton. How had he won 3000 guineas from Sumner? His Lordship must be an idiot. The memory of his own near ruin at the hand of Rennie chastened his arrogance. He grasped Dawson's hand that was palming himself an Ace, rather in the manner that Lord Grandiston had grasped Rennie's. But he did so under the table, where no one could see. He leant forward and gave Dawson a piece of paper. 'All of Sumner's winnings to this address or I expose you now!' he hissed into the man's ear. Dawson tried to pull, but was suddenly very still as Benedict clasped his hand tighter. 'Very well!' said Dawson under his breath, 'let me go.' Benedict leant back, apparently in his cups and 'That's a good one!' and laughed, almost toppling from his chair. Tubby Danford stood up. 'I'd better get this man home!'

The next morning, three thousand guineas were sent in large banknotes to him at Carstairs' rooms. Since the man had fulfilled the bargain, Benedict could not in conscience expose Dawson, and he wondered at how many other innocents would fall under his cat's paw. "I cannot save the world," he concluded. But nevertheless, when he remembered the terrified Potts he believed that he was not yet done with Dawson.

But he had to regroup before taking on Rennie or Sutcliffe — they might not be so easy. And might Dawson have talked to them? Was there a federation of cheats who swapped information on threats to their trade? On the whole, Benedict thought not. But he still needed to be cautious — to think things through for a couple of days.

The next evening, he and Carstairs were heading for their club for a simple supper when they met the Honourable Charles Booth in Half Moon Street, looking dishonourably tipsy.

'Fluff! Thank God!' Booth said. 'You at least are not a dashed follower of Oriana Petersham-'

'You're a little past go for this hour, old fellow. What's Miss Petersham got to do with it? She didn't refuse you?'

'No, no.' Booth ran his hands through his hair and frowned. 'At least, not yet.' He leant forward with his finger tapping his nose. 'On a secret mission of Grandiston's — only in town for a few days — been doing the rounds of the watering holes.' Booth had leaned so far forward as to overbalance and Carstairs caught him, laughing.

'Well come eat with us, Booth, and we won't press you for secrets. You need some mutton in you.' Benedict and Carstairs took an arm each and walked companionably to the club. They talked little because apart from the fact that Booth's feet moved forward, with an occasional veer off in a different direction, his head was on his chest and he bore all the signs of a man taking a little nap. It seemed a shame to bother him.

After the porters at the club had had the familiar task of pouring a young gentleman into a dining chair and bringing him some sustenance safe for his condition (soup, for example, would not be his first course), Booth began to chat familiarly once more.

'Oriana Petersham is at Ashcroft,' he announced.

'Who is Oriana Petersham?' enquired Benedict.

'The Goddess Oriana!' Carstairs sighed, 'the unquestioned beauty of the season before last.'

'Oh,' said Benedict, interested, 'I never was on more than a short visit to town before last season. I must have missed her. Was she very beautiful?'

'Still is. Hair the colour of corn, eyes a heavenly blue,' Booth looked speculatively at Carstairs, 'But I don't remember you dancing attendance.'

His Lordship looked uncomfortable, 'Certainly not. I asked her to dance once and she looked straight through me and said in the coldest possible voice that she was otherwise engaged. I still get chills thinking about it. I like my women warm and inviting.'

'Like Rosa,' Benedict reminisced. Carstairs shot him a warning look.

'She's an angel,' said Booth. He leant forward confidentially, the escaped tail of his cravat dipping into the *sauce Bearnaise* 'She's at Ashcroft.'

'You told us that before. Poor old Bosky Ashcroft's pile: departed and best forgotten,' he said, referring to the young Viscount Ashcroft who stood as a warning to young gentlemen that even a young body will succumb to an excess of dissipation. 'What's she doing there?'

'Visiting a friend. That's where she is — at Ashcroft.'

'Ashcroft. Why do you keep telling us that?'

''S my mission.'

'Your secret mission, is to tell us your secret,' Carstairs recapped.

'Yesh—' he tapped his nose again. 'Grandiston sent me.'

'You'll have all the fools in town bowling down to see her—'

Booth tapped his nose again. 'Zactly!' Booth put himself to eating some dressed crab and seemed the better for it. 'Tell everyone. She's at Ashcroft.'

'Don't worry. We'll tell your secret everywhere we can.'

'You're a good fellow, Fluff. *You* don't want to marry her.'

'I do not. But *you* did as I remember. If you have the advantage of knowing her whereabouts, why the devil are you letting your rivals know?'

'Grandiston.'

'Ah.'

'Thank his lordship for me when you see him again, will you?' said Benedict.

Booth focused properly on Benedict for the first time. 'You are young Fenton — got himself in trouble with old Rennie.'

'That's it,' admitted Benedict. 'Though I wouldn't these days.'

'Don't be too sure,' said Booth. 'Heard he's wrecked lives playing cards in the army.' He lowered his voice again, 'Cheat.'

Carstairs was on his second bottle, 'Don't worry about Benedict. He's been practising fuzzing the cards. Jolly good too.'

'Fluff! Dash it all—'

'Have you?' The Honourable asked interestedly, 'That'll come in handy. But if you were to try him out on the tables, he'd probably notice. Dreadful scandal.'

'Yes,' said Benedict gloomily.

'And he probably hasn't got your money anymore — dreadfully expensive they say,' Carstairs added.

'Oh, I don't know. He has just fleeced young Silverton, I heard today.' Booth said. 'His father has had to bail him out. Took him for over two thousand guineas.'

Benedict sat up. 'That's good news.'

'Not for Silverton it isn't'

'No. But—'

'If you think you can take him, best do it at a private card party.' Booth said.

'If I invited him, he'd think it was suspicious.'

'*I'll* invite him — we went to Eton together — we both like a wager. Used to have him over for card parties until my valet tumbled his lay. But it'll have to be tomorrow night. I'm heading back to Ashcroft the next day.'

Carstairs scratched his head. 'If Benedict gets caught —'

'Then he'll be amongst friends. A peer of the realm,' Carstairs bowed his head in acknowledgement, 'my honourable self and Rennie. Who will anyone believe? It'll be entertaining, too. Who's the better card spinner? You'd better be good or we could all end up with our heads in the basket.'

'Oh, he is,' said Carstairs. 'Frighteningly good.'

'But so is Rennie,' Benedict reminded them.

Chapter 10

A Card Party

Mr Allison had planned their visit to town with the Fentons the next day. Sir Ranalph agreed that a trip to town would be a treat for the young ladies and at dinner the party discussed what entertainment might be had on their brief sojourn. The theatre, museum, Astley's, and Vauxhall gardens were all discussed, and Lieutenant Prescott laughed. 'If we add anything to that list, we might as well stay there for the entire summer.'

'Of course you are right sir,' said Lady Fenton. 'London is not healthy in the summer heat. A brief visit will not be injurious, I hope. But an extended stay must not be thought of at this season.'

'If we knew what Benedict's plans were, we could bring him back with us,' said Serena.

'I will write tonight and apprise him of our arrival,' Sir Ranalph said. 'I must say, it is very good of you to open up your house again, just for the entertainment of my girls, Mr Allison. It will cause you a great deal of botheration sending servants ahead and suchlike.'

'Not at all,' shrugged their host. 'Blake shall travel ahead with the needful servants. He is a magician. An unexpected occasion is his forte. He lives to be surprised by a project and then appear as though nothing is untoward in the slightest.'

Serena was looking a little ashamed. It had not occurred to her that her request would put in motion a great deal of work and bother. Papa's visits to the metropolis involved hotels or hired houses and these could be left behind with no thought. But of course, Mr Allison had a town house that was closed for the summer, with only a skeleton staff on the premises, and no doubt there were holland covers over the furniture and no linen in the bedchambers and her simple desire to see the horses at Astley's Amphitheatre would involve no end of work for a great many people. 'Perhaps we should not go!' she said in a small voice.

Honoria guessed from this that her sister was responsible for the proposed visit and though she appreciated how much Serena wished to visit the city, she too was grasping the scale of it all. Mr Allison's position in society made it impossible to merely take simple rooms in town — he had a very grand house indeed. 'Indeed, perhaps we should not.'

'But you do wish to, Miss Fenton?' asked the lieutenant. 'It would be amusing to go as a party.'

Honoria smiled into his kind eyes. 'Oh yes, Lieutenant. If you think so.' As she raised her eyes, they met the sober face of Mr Scribster. But his immobile expression was no mystery to her any more. His eyes declared his amusement and she looked at him crossly. A hint of a smile traversed his face.

'If we leave on Friday, all should be ready for us. I give Blake a whole day. That should be sufficient, should it not Blake?'

'Undoubtedly sir.'

'But just think of the upheaval!' Lady Fenton declared.

'Her ladyship wishes to spare you, Blake. Let us say that we shall arrive on Saturday.'

'As you wish sir.' Blake almost shrugged.

After dinner, the gentlemen remained in the dining room passing the brandy decanter, whilst the ladies withdrew. Sir Ranalph looked as though his good nature was struggling with his desire to ask Allison a direct question: do you intend to offer for my daughter? Allison knew the answer. He did, he was nearly sure he would. But nevertheless, he was glad to be spared the question by means of the twin figures of Scribster and Prescott. Good manners meant Sir Ranalph would not speak in front of them, but Allison was avoiding the discreet tap on the shoulder and a demand for a private chat. He used Darnley shamefully.

'Is the fighting finished now, Darnley?' he said. He saw Sir Ranalph retreat at this, for to be given an opportunity to hear the state of play with the brave young men who were fighting under the Duke was of course a privilege.

'Well, I've mainly been on Duncan's staff, out of the fray, but now that Napoleon's secured in Elba, we have little to fear.'

After more of this, the gentlemen raised a glass to the Duke, and joined the ladies in the drawing room, where tea was being served.

The arrival of a carriage stopped the conversation.

'Oh, Lieutenant,' said Honoria without thinking, 'It cannot be that you are summoned back to Lisbon. Perhaps there is an emergency? I do hope not.'

Mr Scribster leant forward to set his teacup down on a side table, thus bringing himself closer to Honoria's ear. 'An emergency that only Darnley could save us from? I sincerely hope not.' She cast him a look of disgust and closed her mouth. Mr Allison, listening to the arrival in his hall, failed to see that look, which might indeed have given him another view of the parentally obliging Honoria, but her mother did not.

She moved to the tea tray and said, 'Honoria! Pray assist me to replenish my cup.'

Moving forward automatically, Honoria suddenly noted her mama's reproving eyes. 'I know that Mr Scribster can be challenging, Honoria, but you will be pleased to keep your face from expressing its displeasure. It is not like you, my dear.'

There did not seem to be any way to explain her bargain with Mr. Scribster and that he would not be at all offended, so she merely said, just as quietly, 'Yes Mama.'

She saw across the room that the dratted man had a fair idea of their conversation.

'I think it is Genevieve Horton — Lady Sumner, I mean,' said Serena, who had also been listening to the noise in the hall.

So indeed it proved. Lady Sumner, in an old cape and a plain stuff gown, with her bushy hair escaping from her bonnet and her long nose unattractively tipped in red from the cold, arrived in the midst of them.

'Your ladyship!' said Mr Allison, moving forward, 'Did no-one offer to take your cape?'

'Mr Allison,' Lady Sumner said, shaking his hand more in the manner of a man than the lady she was. 'So sorry to break in in this dreadful way, but I have an injured horse, you know, and I wanted a word with Miss Serena Fenton.'

He hid his surprise very well, but begged her to be seated.

Soon, as she had planned, she had agreed to send the remedy for the non-existent injury ahead to London with her groom, whilst she would stay here and go on to London with the party on Saturday. Only two days delay! She was cruelly disappointed, but she had bought herself some distance from her husband, that was the best she could do.

Honoria and Serena sat at each side of her on the elegant settle, and as they talked and she answered automatically, she looked up and surprised a gaze of pity from Sir Ranalph's kind eyes. Her own eyes misted. Surely he could not guess — but Benedict must have told him — she was ashamed. She looked quickly at Lady Fenton, but she was talking gaily to the lieutenant and Genevieve was perfectly sure she had no idea of her shame.

At one side, Serena was prattling about the remedy, and at the other, Honoria's small hand stole into hers. She turned to look at her. Honoria, too, guessed something. Surely Benedict had not discussed her plight with his entire family? No, but she had said too much to Honoria on the subject of marriage. She had given herself away again. She must be very careful. After giving her kind friend's hand a squeeze, she retracted her own.

Now, she regarded Mr Allison. She had known him to be an interesting dinner companion in an amusing way. They had been placed next to each other once last season and he had been much more entertaining and forthcoming to her than to the young lady at his other side, who strove for his attention. She had recognised the actions of a man not wanting to be caught by marriage and yet friendly enough to a companion who was no threat to his unwed state — and had been amused. Now though, she wished to regard him more narrowly, for if he desired to make sweet Honoria his bride, she would know him better. Nothing had been said yet that she could see, there was none of the distinction in his treatment of Honoria that he must have shown if they were newly engaged. And of course, Lady Fenton, now chatting of village matters with her, would have mentioned an engagement by this time.

So he had not spoken, what did that mean? And what kind of man was he really? He certainly had placed a great deal of weight on Honoria's undoubted beauty if he approached her father after only one dance. Genevieve had seen Honoria during her season. She had been crippled with shyness and though her beauty had ensured she had seldom been without a partner at any ball (unlike the fate of Genevieve on her first season) she seemed to have treated many of these dances as punishments to be suffered through. It was only with she and her sisters, or when dancing with her brother, that her real, sparkling personality showed, so why then had Allison broken his long spell of feminine disinterest (with marriageable females, at any rate — she had heard rumours of his affairs with Opera dancers and the like) and picked on Honoria? It could only be for her beauty, and that, in Genevieve's eyes, made him as shallow as most men. To be married for your beauty or your fortune, as in her case, were two sides of the same, worthless coin.

She would watch him closely and if she felt he could not really appreciate her friend, then she would intervene. She was sure that if Lady Fenton or Sir Ranalph knew what a weight of family obligation she was bearing for them, they would not wish to sell their daughter into unhappiness. The same could not be said for her own father. He'd seen her neck one day and guessed the rest. But still he had written to summon Sumner to Ottershaw, in case the gossips should remark on the separation of husband and wife. But if she saw that Allison was sincere, perhaps the kindnesses he had shown her at that dinner party were real and showed some depth to his character.

Scribster was looking at her speculatively. Genevieve stared back at him blankly. She had no opinion on Mr Scribster and had no wish to know his thoughts on her either. Mr Scribster was a blank page in an otherwise interesting book.

Lieutenant Prescott reminded her of her big handsome dog. A happy black Labrador with a wagging tail to please everyone. His nature was very like Sir Ranalph's, though she did not know its depths as yet. Perhaps he might make a husband for Serena, if he had a suitable fortune. She gasped at herself. Why did women everywhere set the world to partners? Because they were aware, at bottom, that a woman without a husband could be a very sorry being in this world. Without a husband, who would provide for her? For a few widows, like Lady Harrington, and the occasional heiress of large fortune, life without a husband was possible. But for the majority of young ladies, whose father's fortune was entailed to the eldest son, a husband was a necessity. Unless it was a husband like Sumner. Genevieve could find nothing necessary at all about Sumner. Without him, she might have lived some quiet life in the country with a paid companion (another unfortunate unmarried lady) and a couple of horses and if there were few luxuries in that, and a fall in consequence from being the young lady of the big house, she could have lived with it, in retrospect. The notion of having a man of the same fortune or consequence as her father, she should have known to be an empty ambition. Her father was an unfeeling block of ice and his replacement was near to a madman.

Booth's card party was a success. He was a genial host to each of his three guests and Rennie seemed perfectly unaware of anything untoward in his being invited. 'Grandiston not in town?' he asked casually, 'You seem to live in his pocket these days.'

Booth's face froze for a moment, but only Benedict saw, since his back was to the others, pouring out wine for his guests. Then he said, lazily, 'Yes, well his pockets are pretty spacious to live in.'

Rennie gave a laugh. This he could understand. 'I suppose they are! You are a fortunate fellow.'

Carstairs aped himself when he was a little tipsy. 'I shay, gentlemen, shall we play?'

Rennie looked at Benedict, who seemed to have no special place in his memory. He had probably fleeced a number of young bucks since then. And the sum he had lost, though it made up Benedict's entire allowance and more, was small change when measured against some, Benedict was sure. He didn't seem to associate the Grandiston incident with Benedict either, calling the Earl "dashed interfering — no offence, Booth, I know he's a friend of yours—" when discussing his whereabouts. He never looked at Benedict when he said this. He did vaguely remember him, 'Young Fenton, ain't you? We've played before?'

'Yes,' said Benedict indifferently. 'During my first trip to London.' Benedict saw Rennie search his memory and come up with very little.

'Ah, yes!' he said vaguely.

They sat down to a night of wine and cards. They had a plan. Benedict would watch and try to learn Rennie's methods. They knew about the dice, of course, but they were not using them initially, and no doubt Rennie had other cheating methods at his disposal. During this period, they all lost a little and won a little (by Rennie's arrangement, Benedict was sure) to put everyone at ease. They had arranged at the outset that Carstairs was their failsafe. He appeared to be drunk already, and he would continue to drink wine copiously (his specialism) and if they all began leaking too much money to Rennie's machinations, Carstairs would collapse on the table and Benedict would have to break up the party by taking him home.

All four of them drank, but the three friends drank rather more than their guest. He seemed to hold to his second glass of wine, whilst pretending to fill it up, adding only drops on each occasion. Booth and Benedict, who were nearest the window, were replenishing their glasses frequently, secretly taking advantage of a large potted aspidistra that sat on the window sill to get rid of the excess. Carstairs was really drinking, and Benedict feared that he'd collapse before the appointed hour.

The cards were not marked by any method Benedict knew, but this of course was the sort of thing where his newness as a cheat had him at a disadvantage. There may be many methods that Benedict did not know. However, he did not see Rennie give the hands of his opponents any particular attention, as he would have had to do if they were dealing from a marked deck. However, Benedict did clearly see Rennie's diversionary tactics, a spilt glass of wine, a raucous joke, and how they covered some clever palming, some hidden cards on his person — his interesting card shuffling, which kept the cards he wanted to the top of the deck. Booth cocked an eyebrow at him once, asking if Benedict had a clue. He gave the faintest nod and Booth relaxed, putting rather too much faith in Benedict's abilities, that young man feared. How to counter the cheat? There were rather too many aces in the pack now and for Benedict to add his own well-dispersed aces from his sleeve or beneath his coat collar would alert suspicion. By dint of falling drunkenly on Rennie's side, he dislodged a few of the hidden cards, making it look like good luck. Then, with Booth or Carstairs being his diversion at different times, which he orchestrated with lifted eyebrows in either direction, he was able to salt their card hands and allow themselves some wins that Rennie thought were simply chance. This happened for some time, until Rennie took note — but the bumbling fingers of the young drunks were certainly not capable of any sleight of hand. He didn't look at Fenton because he was losing steadily too.

Dashed chance, but Rennie set in motion a game to redress the balance. He began to bid higher and higher, and though Carstairs complained that they were exceeding their agreed limits, he did so only petulantly. The others shushed him and continued the play, with the bids reaching perilous levels. 'Dash it all, Rennie, it's a dashed house party, not Boodles or Whites!'

'Afraid, Booth? You weren't so chicken-hearted when we were at Eton.'

Booth became recklessly indignant. 'Afraid? I'll double the stakes right now!' he said in a voice a little slurred.

There was a tense silence. This was their grand play. Would Rennie bite? His piggy eyes narrowed, but not in fear or trepidation, thought Benedict. In satisfaction. He was being given the opportunity of a larger prize than he had anticipated.

Carstairs complained. 'Don't be silly, Booth. I for one have emptied my pockets. Dashed expensive evening. I'm out.'

'Are you sure, my lord,' said Rennie innocently, 'don't you trust your hand?'

Carstairs looked at his hand. It wasn't bad, Benedict knew. There were two Kings that Carstairs had shown him when Booth distracted Rennie. He'd been dealt them to tempt him into this final bet.

'Oh, very well, we'll all offer our little scripts.'

Booth produced some slips of paper and a quill, and they passed it around, inscribing their names and the varying amounts they all needed to put in to double their stakes. On the table now was over three thousand guineas. Rennie was very sure he would win it and Benedict agreed with him. His hand trembled as he added the last scrap of paper with the unthinkable and un—gettable amount of money he had scrawled upon it. If this failed, he would have to run off and join the regulars. Or become a pirate or some such thing, and his family, his dear mother and sisters as well as his good papa, would be disgraced.

Now was not the time for cowardice. He thought of Potts and his terrified face. He thought of Genevieve's neck, for which her awful husband would pay. But for now this man who was in possession of part of Genevieve's fortune *he* would pay. Benedict would make him — and not be caught doing it.

With the aid of two cards from his person, and one from Booth's hand, Benedict waited till Rennie's hand was down to show his own. The winning hand. For a moment, Rennie was confused. He picked up the cards on the table and looked at Booth. This was not the hand he had dealt him.

'I win!' said Benedict. 'How amazing!'

Rennie met his eye, seeing it all now.

'By God, you monster, so you have,' said Booth. 'If I wasn't away tomorrow I'd get you all back here so I could win it back. Bad luck gentlemen,' he said, looking at the other two. 'Time to call it a night, Carstairs, I think.' He turned to the defeated, 'Bloody play tonight, eh, Rennie? Lucky young pup.'

'Yes. Lucky,' said Rennie in a clipped voice.

'Tomorrow for your vowels gentlemen. I'm leaving for the country soon. Just had a letter from my father,' said Benedict airily.

'Oh, we're good for it, young Dickie, fear not!' said Booth and slapped him on the back.

Rennie was fighting his rage. But he said 'Tomorrow!' and left the rooms with a flourish.

Honoria pulled Mr Scribster's sleeve after dinner as they were leaving the drawing room to ascend to their chambers. They were held back a little.

'You must stop giving me looks that guess at my thoughts,' she hissed, 'Now I am in disgrace with Mama for sending *you* a speaking look.'

'Your look did not so much speak as sabre slash me,' he said, gazing down at her from his great height.

'We said, sir, that we would not lie.'

'Well it would have slashed me, but I ducked. What message did you think I sent to you? I find this very entertaining, most people can only read unalleviated gloom in my expression.'

'Well, they must be idiots,' said Honoria acidly, 'you clearly told me that you think I admire Lieutenant Prescott when I was merely being polite to him.'

'I must hope that one day you'll be so polite to me, Miss Fenton. You look quite beautiful when your eyelashes flutter.'

'I hope that the custard that you ate so much of at dinner curdles in your stomach and that the pain keeps you up all night.'

'I think that a full day of being well-behaved has rather curdled your mood. Meet me before breakfast for a refreshing trade of insults to clear your head.'

'Honoria!' called her mother, 'What is delaying you, child?'

Honoria thrust Mr Scribster behind the drawing room door and caught her skirts up to run forward. 'Merely lost a ribbon, Mama! I'm coming!'

'So *untruthful*. The bower at six?' said Scribster in a lowered tone.

'Half past!' said Honoria, running from the room.

Chapter 11

A Dastardly Attack

Benedict had spent a night playing cards with Sir Philip Sutcliffe, a man on the edge of society (despite his title) since he had married a harridan of a woman whose father was in trade. Her money was one thing, but her vulgarity was quite another, and added to that, it was said, her father kept a much tighter rein on his finances than Sutcliffe had understood would be the case. He was no longer invited to private houses or to Almack's, or to any but the most public spectacles, but he kept in with the gaming set. He was always smiling (a trait that all cheats seemed to have in common) but his smiles could not disguise the bitter lines around his mouth and elsewhere on his ferrety face. A confident Benedict, bored, beat him flamboyantly. He exchanged a look with the man as he left the table, and his eyes were murderous. Of course he knew what had been done. Cheats seldom met their match at their dreadful game, and never one so young and upright as Mr Benedict Fenton.

It wasn't so difficult as Benedict had feared to return the money and vowels to the innocent players. Stoddart, Carstairs' valet, took care of it for him, employing an out of work servant, but an excellent man, to convey the packages to the various abodes and to disappear before questions could be asked. Most were confused but silent, as the accompanying note pleaded. 'For reasons of my own, which I beg you will not ask me to divulge, I must return your losses of last night to you.' It seemed that the gentleman were happy not to press him, excepting another Cambridge friend of his, a Mr Barnabas Smythe, who turned up at Carstairs' place on his dignity.

'Hallo Barney! What you doing here at this hour?' asked Carstairs sleepily, sipping his coffee at a small table.

But Mr Smythe, very upright, instead fixed his eye on Benedict, who was fully dressed and reading a newspaper, which he put down as the visitor was announced.

'Sir!' he said, as though he had not previously thrown up on Benedict's waistcoat and slept sprawled at the foot of his bed on many a carousing occasion, 'I must ask you to tell me what you mean by *this*.' And he threw the packet containing the note, the vowels (amounting to one hundred and twenty pounds, plus a large banknote for £100 and a couple of guineas, onto the table.

'Watch that!' protested Carstairs, chasing an errant guinea under the table, 'What do you want to do that for?'

'It's just your losses back, Barney. What's got your dander up?' asked Benedict interestedly.

'If you have been informed, sir, that I do not pay my debts of honour, then I must tell you—'

'Oh, is that all it is?' said Carstairs, relieved. 'He was late paying off Rennie last year because his old man didn't come through with the readies. He's a bit ticklish on the subject.'

Mr Smythe turned on his lordship, 'I'll have you know, my lord, that I paid him within the week. It would have been sooner, but—'

'I know, I know, Gilchrist backed out of buying your Greys. But I bought them, so it was all right and tight.'

'If you mean to throw that piece of charity in my face—' said Mr Smythe, still furious, 'then you are—'

Benedict stood up and clapped him on the back. 'No, no, Barney. No charity in that. Fluff won a cool thousand on the toll race with those Greys, you know he did.'

'Yes, well, I was dashed sorry to part with them,' said Mr Smythe, somewhat mollified, 'But if you're to be going round thinking I can't pay my debts—'

'Don't think anything of the kind, old fellow.' He grabbed at the letter from the table. 'You see I said it, *for reasons of my own, that I beg you will not ask me to divulge—*'

'What reasons?'

'I begged you *not* to ask me to divulge—'said Benedict, grinning.

'So you *do* think I won't pay my debts!' exploded Smythe. He took out his purse and threw it on the table. 'There. And if that damned Rennie hadn't set it about that I'm a shirker, you would never have offered me this insult.'

'It's not that, Barney, I swear!'

'Well, what is it then?' said Mr Smythe.

Benedict looked at his lordship, who shrugged and then seemed to get an intelligent gleam in his eye. 'Religious conversion!' he said brilliantly. 'Dickie has always gone to church, like the rest of us, but he had an — an experience that made him erm, deepen his religious convictions.'

The two young gentlemen looked at him, mouths agape.

'Since last night?' said Mr Smythe.

'No, it isn't that.' Benedict sat down. 'What a chump you are, Fluff. Is that the best you could do?' Carstairs made an inarticulate noise of embarrassment. 'Look, Barney, I'm going to tell you a story. But however scandalous it is, you can't tell anybody.'

'Did I ever tell about that barmaid that Carstairs brought—'

'Alright, alright!' jumped in his lordship. 'Stow that for later. Let Dickie speak.'

'First I have to say that I am doing this for a very serious reason. And I can't tell you what that is. I can only tell you why I sent back your money. But it's a long tale, and you may not believe me.'

'Have you got something stronger than coffee? I need the hair of the dog,' said Smythe, less stiffly.

'If you'll get all this damned money off my breakfast table, I'll see what can be arranged.

Later that night, after all three young gentlemen had cemented their friendship with ale and some gin, they left the tavern they had adjourned to rather the worse for wear. Barnabas Smythe, who had just had the relief of escaping being heavily in debt, was not very steady and Carstairs volunteered to put him in hackney, if Dickie would just get along home and order some hot bricks in their bed, and maybe some rum punch too.

Thus it was that Benedict, taking a shortcut through a cobbled alleyway next to the tavern, met head on a rough fellow in long woollen coat and scarf, pulled up over the mouth, with his hat shading his eyes, who blocked his way. There was something in his hand and he was raising it — a cudgel. Benedict, trained in the art of fencing, was sorry that these days gentlemen no longer wore a sword at their sides. He cast about the alley for a weapon and saw a broken crate with empty bottles tumbling from it, no doubt for the gin-makers to collect on the morrow. The wood would be useless against the cudgel, so he picked up a bottle. It happened in seconds. The man swung the cudgel at Benedict's head and he ducked and parried with the bottle connecting with the ruffian's arm. The man yelped at the force of the blow, but it only deflected his own, which connected with Benedict's shoulder. The young man jumped back, but his pursuer came at him again, landing blow after blow with the cudgel on Benedict's half-turned body, unable to connect to his head, which Benedict had lowered beneath his arm defensively. As his opponent raised the cudgel once more, Benedict thrust the defensive arm out and smashed the bottle on the wall, moving towards his assailant, instead of away as he expected, and brought it up and under, cutting through woollen fabric and meeting soft flesh. The man dropped to his knees, looking up at Benedict, his dark eyes amazed, holding his stomach. Benedict, breathing hard, kicked the dropped cudgel away and knelt on one knee to check on his fallen assailant. At the last second he felt the air move as the thwack of another cudgel hit the back of his head. The last thing he saw, as he fell, was the toe of a boot - with a mirror-shine.

They began rifling the pockets and cursing, when the cry of 'Who goes there?' alerted them to the appearance of the Watch at the entrance of the alley, two burly watchmen, carrying flaming torches, rushed forward. With a last kick at the prostrate Fenton, both men ran, one holding his stomach.

Chapter 12
Arrangements for London

It was unusual, but Blake, the stately butler of Bassington Hall, was also Mr Allison's butler in London, having an excellent surrogate in Coates, the under butler at the Hall, whom he had personally trained and who now stayed to run things whilst Blake went ahead to prepare Mr Allison's London abode. Even in the off-season there were still eight servants kicking their heels in London, so it only required that Blake took two extra grooms, three chambermaids, two footmen and the French chef with him when he set off to make arrangements. Since he had sent word ahead, he was confident he would arrive to the Holland covers off and a small army of recruits scrubbing and polishing the floors of the main public rooms and the bed chambers, all to host six people for perhaps two nights in town.

London, fortunately, was not sunny, only bright and a trifle chilly for summer. In the heat, the poorer parts of town grew fetid and all manners of smells and disease took hold, which is why the *haut ton* decamped to the country at this season.

When he arrived, Mrs Hunter, the housekeeper at the London address, had the army of servants organised, and put the new recruits to work in quick order. Mrs Hunter, whose body was small and round, but whose energy was indefatigable, had once confided in him that unlike most of her inferiors she loathed the lazy summer months, or indeed any time that her master was absent. No doubt she would wish for a larger party and a longer stay, and she was one of the very few servants (with only Mr Allison's valet, Camden, and Blake himself) who had deduced that one of the party might be their new mistress. This had led her to set the bedchamber windows to be washed once more, an extra task and hardly necessary, but Miss Fenton would find nothing to complain of and everything to admire in any house run by Mrs Hunter.

She would see to the extra flowers, and the house was in a fair way to being creditable, with Antoine taking charge of the kitchen and making a list of his requirements that some minions must source for him in the city, or have the copper pans thrown at them on their return. The stables were already in good order, holding as they did a small string of beasts that Mr Allison used in town, but being made ready to receive and care for the other ten horses and two carriages that were about to arrive. The two carriages that had brought himself, the other servants and some provisions that Antoine had thought it necessary to include were hired, but it was not to be considered that Mr Allison would convey his guests in anything less than his own travel carriage, with himself Scribster and no doubt Lieutenant Prescott taking up another. All for a visit to Astley's Amphitheatre, Blake believed.

He must send to find out if there were any outbreaks of typhus in the area. Large public spectacles, such as the daring equestriennes at Astley's performing amazing tricks whilst standing on horseback, were favourite places for disease to spread.

He had been informed about the proposed trip to Astley's not by his master, but by an overheard conversation that Molly, his favourite squeeze of a chambermaid, who may one day aspire to be Mrs Blake, told him of. After reprimanding her for eavesdropping, he had listened carefully to the conversation she reported as happening in Lady Fenton's chamber. Molly was occupied in a small antechamber, putting away some newly laundered small clothes of her ladyship's, and found herself trapped when Sir Ranalph had arrived and kissed his lady. She was about to show herself when Lady Fenton said, 'For shame! We shall be late for dinner, sir!' and so Molly had stayed put, thinking to avoid the slight embarrassment of interrupting an intimate moment between the baronet and his wife. They would be gone soon. In Blake's experience, this was not always the case and he lectured Molly on the correct behaviour in this situation, which was obviously to make some noise in the antechamber before emerging and asking if there would be anything else, and making your escape in as an unhurried and unconscious way as possible, but he forgave her youthful inexperience and let her continue.

'What do you think of this projected trip to London?' asked the baronet.

'I fear that Serena has something to do with it. She has badgered him with her desire to go to Astley's.'

'I fear so — when our younger daughter wants something, she uses unscrupulous methods to achieve it. Like her mama.' There seemed to be a noise of a playful slap and perhaps another embrace, and Molly was beginning to wonder how to get out of this situation. ("I told you," Blake had told her, but let her continue with her account.) 'Do you think we should nip this visit in the bud? It seems a great deal of upheaval for Allison.'

'I shouldn't think Mr Allison will have more to do than give the order,' laughed her ladyship. (Mr Blake approved — her ladyship recognised a well-ordered household when she saw one.) 'My only fear is that it interrupts the new ease with which we are all getting along here. The Lieutenant's comfortable manners have been a godsend. Even Honoria seems a little more relaxed.'

'Oh, I thought it was all going splendidly,' said her husband, 'they've all been riding together, and so on.'

There was a pause. 'It never fails to surprise me what you miss, my dear. I was used to think Mr Allison a man of address, but he has hardly been relaxed around Honoria, nor she with him.'

'Well, they are nothing but very courteous with each other,' objected Sir Ranalph.

'And do you think such courtesy should have won me, sir?' There was the sound of a laugh and another embrace.

'So all is not going well, in fact?' inquired her husband.

'Perhaps we should not have informed Honoria of his intentions, it does make her so anxious. She does not show her sweet nature to advantage and she certainly does not do much to encourage him.' Her husband made a protesting noise. 'I do not blame her. Honoria does everything I ask of her and she declares herself ready to receive his addresses. But her timidity is such that she is a little stiff, and Allison, rather than quelling her fears, seems rather to have adopted a little of her stiffness himself.'

'And I have been thinking we are having a lovely party.'

'Yes dear, and so we are. But the object of our party is a little in doubt.'

'I will not have Honoria do what she does not want.'

'I know that, my dear, and I have spoken to her on the subject, but she keeps assuring me that she *does* want it.'

'Well, her season was the same. She was not really able to enjoy it as she should have. Being the season's beauty would have delighted most young ladies, but my dear child did not have her head turned by the attention. She is not at all vain, we can say that for her. I'm sure Serena will relish it when it's her turn.'

'But the point it, if this match fails somehow, Serena will never have her turn.'

'We could—' protested Sir Ranalph.

'Yes, perhaps we could visit Wilbert for a few weeks, but only a very few. And you know that being near him brings on your headache.'

'Only when he loses at the tables.'

'Well we cannot bail him out again if he does. It is bad enough that our girls cannot have another season. And what about Angelica?'

'It must be thirteen years at least until we cross that bridge my dear. If I undertake not to frank Wilbert's excesses, I trust our fortunes will have been restored by then. But I would say this: if there is any chance at all that this match doesn't prosper, and I trust your instincts in this, then Serena should have her visit to Astley's at least. For us, it seems hardly worth it — but for her it may be her one chance for that treat. Damn Wilbert and his abominable debts to the devil.'

'Yes, my dear. To London we shall go. Perhaps there our principal players will be a little more relaxed.'

There was a rustle of silk and the couple went down to dinner.

Blake had understood a great deal from Molly's report. That Miss Honoria Fenton might be his new mistress and that her nature was generally sweet and simple. Also that when it came to the day of her becoming a bride, she might need a little guidance and support on the household front, even supposing she was a daughter of the Manor. Blake would undertake that support and education in the most discreet way possible. He had regarded her closely, as was his wont with every guest at Bassington, and when his employer was not around he had found her a lively girl with sound sense of humour and an interest in everything around her. But when in the company of the gentlemen she faded slightly, he felt. Still beautiful, but so much more careful in her speech and deportment as to seem a little, well, stand-offish. The servants reported that every member of the family displayed exquisite manners with their inferiors, no lack of good *ton* there.

No, Blake was content to see his master marry at last and had no fault to find with his choice. There were worse things than a little timidity in a lady, and he would do all he could when she arrived to make her (and the rest of the party, obviously) see how a well-oiled house could run, so that she need not fear to be mistress of it all. Perhaps there would be some occasion to introduce her to Mrs Hunter and when she saw that kindly, efficient personage she would be reassured that the task of being Mrs Allison would not be overwhelming at all.

He would talk this through with Mrs Hunter tonight, over dinner in her small sitting room below stairs, and plan the best way to reassure the young lady whom she was excited to meet in two days' time.

But as it happened, the party arrived that night, in considerable disarray and alarm and no one noticed that the third bedchamber's windows were still a little dull or that the kitchen was thrown into a panic at the dearth of provisions. For a dreadful thing had occurred.

Chapter 13

Mr Allison's Desire

It behoved him to get on with it, thought Allison. He who had lead a troop into battle with decision had delayed enough in asking one of the most beautiful, and kind natured young women of his acquaintance to marry him. Today was the day, he would ask her to walk with him after breakfast. He would enlist her mama in that (he was perfectly sure he could do this with little more than the nod — she had been awaiting it since the party arrived two weeks ago) and she would ensure that the world and his mother did not accompany them. The rest would go riding and he would declare his love, no, rather his *regard* to Honoria and then await her answer. It was beneath him to lie to her. A foregone conclusion, he believed. Not that he flattered himself that her heart beat for him. His moving closer than a chair's width of her seemed to suffuse her face not with passion, but with an expression more akin to constipation of the bowels. He sincerely hoped that he would not have to look at that expression every morning over breakfast for the rest of his life.

But it was simply that she was timid. Scribster assured him that she was in truth a vivacious young lady with a wicked sense of humour, and he trusted in this. Gus had played many a prank on him since their days in Wellington's army, but even he would not prank him all the way into marriage. Her vivacity rivalled her sister's, Gus had said, but when questioned how he knew this or to relate an example of her wit, he only said he could not break an oath. But he smiled, in a very un-Gus-like way when remembering their exchanges, and it encouraged Allison to hope that he was not about to offer for a beautiful idiot or a permanently stiff, pattern-card of beauty. He would not have breakfast, he would not be thrown off his purpose by a teasing look from Serena's dancing eyes — so like her sister's in shape and colour and so different of expression. He would catch the mama first, and casually ask if his invitation could be relayed, whilst he excused himself to the library on invented estate business.

He resolved not to discuss this even with Scribster - he knew himself to be close to bolting, like one of his hunters under any but his own hand. He could not wait until Sir Ranalph sought clarification from him, this was the height of bad manners and would embarrass both of them. However good natured the Baronet was, he might also tarnish his lifetime family relationship with him at the outset. No, today was the day.

At the very moment that Allison was deciding this, his intended was walking with Mr Scribster in an avenue of high hedges some way from the house.

'Why do you wear that dreadful hat, Mr Scribster? It must be a hundred years old.'

'It is my grandfather's hat.'

'Well you ought to give it back to him speedily and get yourself another. One with a very flat crown so as not to elongate an already very long profile.'

'What is wrong with my hat? I do not care to be fashionable.'

'Perhaps you could aim for presentable.' She held out her hand. He took it off and presented it to her.

'Firstly, black felt does not recover its colour once it has turned this rusty shade,' she pointed to the edges, seeing him look at it with the expression the world might take to be grave. She knew better and frowned him down. '—the brim width rivals a hat of my mother's. And silver buckles are no longer worn on the hat-band, sir. Mr. Brummel must groan when he sees you coming.'

'George? Yes, he does. He tells me that being an eccentric is the last resort of the ugly.' He took his hat back and put it on his head. 'So I embrace my eccentricity and I cannot give it back as my grandfather is now deceased.'

'Well, the hat should have been buried with him.'

Her hand went once more to her mouth to stop the words, and he grasped it lightly and took it down. 'Very well, I only wear it because my sister told me when it was bequeathed to me (probably for the silver buckle — my grandfather was a canny man) that I should not under any circumstances do so.'

'Contrary! But your sister is not here to see you.'

'Indeed, but it became rather a habit.'

'Well do not wear it again! And cut your hair.'

'You sound like my sister.'

'I'm sure that she has only your good at heart.'

'Are you?' he said. 'It is clear you have not met her. I do, however, believe that you *do* mean my good, and so I will get another hat and cut my hair at the soonest opportunity — but do not think that an army of hairdressers and a gallon of pomade can make my straight locks adopt the fashionable curl.'

'A Brutus? No, you would have been better off being born a generation ago. You could have worn your hair pulled back into a queue. I expect it would have looked very respectable. Why should you think I have your good at heart?' She sighed, 'I am nothing but rude to you.'

'But I acquit you of being hurtful to no purpose.'

She walked a little, thoughtful. 'That is very kind of you, but I do not acquit myself. I seem to take a deal more pleasure than I had ever thought possible in being perfectly beastly.'

'It is merely the effects of being in a rather oppressive situation.'

Honoria's eyes jumped nervously to his face. 'What do you mean?'

He turned her to face him, grasping at her shoulders, 'You know what I mean, Miss Fenton.'

'You know why we are here then?'

Mr Scribster dropped his hands suddenly. 'I probably do.'

'Now *you* are being evasive!' Honoria said.

'No. Merely careful. You have told me not to press you for the truth of certain things and I feel we are about to approach those things.' He pulled away a little and continued their quiet walk.

Honoria stepped some way before she looked at him. His gait was stiffer than his usual, loose-limbed amble. She laughed. 'Look at you!

You are in grave danger, Mr Scribster, of holding back out of good manners.'

He too laughed and said, 'That will never do! So how serious is your crush on the handsome Lieutenant? Haven't you noticed yet that he is an idiot?'

'Just when I'm beginning to like you, you say something like that!' She picked up her skirts and whirled around, running towards the house.

She calmed down a little as she was within sight of the house and slowed her pace to a walk. Coming from the stables was Prescott, sadly out of his regimentals, but still looking passably handsome in a well cut riding coat of green cloth, buckskin breeches and top boots.

'Miss Fenton — well met!' he said, coming towards her. 'Have you been walking? Do you think you should take a walk with me before breakfast? It is such a lovely day!' Seeing her hesitate, he added, 'Within sight of the house, of course.'

His exquisite sense of decorum was one of the reasons, since the attraction of that left ear, that had drawn her to him. Mr Scribster, for example, walked with her far from the house. But to be fair, this was to allow her to vent her spleen without being overheard. Nevertheless, someone with exquisite manners was just the salve she needed right now, so she took the lieutenant's arm with trembling fingers as her answer, and began to walk towards the little rose garden.

He was so tall. Rather less so than Mr Scribster, but certainly tall enough for her to feel very like a wood nymph being guarded by a handsome Greek god. He had been talking in pleasantries about her visit to Bassington, the weather and the grounds, and she answered calmly, too irate still with Scribster to be terrified of her escort.

'Is your family friendship with my cousin of long standing?' he asked at last.

Honoria was rather caught by this enquiry. 'Not very long, sir. My parents have known him for six months only, I believe.' She said this vaguely, in the hopes of leading the conversation elsewhere.

'Ah, during the season then?' he said speculatively.

'Well, yes.'

'My mother was right! Rowley has met his match at last!' he declared. 'Why are we not to mention it — are there some family circumstances? You can trust me, Miss Fenton — I assure you. When does my cousin hope to marry your sister?'

Honoria stopped, stunned. 'My sister!'

'I beg your pardon, Miss Fenton. Too long in Lisbon to remember my manners. I'll ask Rowley if I choose to be a poke-nose. I have made you uncomfortable.'

'Oh no, Lieutenant. Only, could you take me back for breakfast now? Mama hates if we are late.'

'Of course, Miss Fenton, at once.'

She took his arm again and was so engrossed in her thoughts that she quite forgot to tremble at his touch. Why did he suppose his cousin to be about to propose to Serena? But like little pieces of coloured glass that come together to make a picture in a stained glass window, she knew why this remark had surprised but not shocked her. It was evident that whilst the lieutenant's intelligence might be in dispute, his sensitivity was not. He noticed things. It was why he magically appeared behind your chair when you wanted to rise from the table, why he rescued Mama's wool from tying itself around a chair leg, or redirected the conversation away from Papa's enquiry to Serena as to whether she had visited the stable that morning. He noticed how things were. So did Mr Scribster, but he wouldn't exert himself to do anything to help. Could it be possible that he had noticed something about Serena and Mr Allison? And if it was, what could that mean to her? She must speak with Serena immediately. Not to ask her straight out, obviously, for if she was wrong she could never hide her feelings about the reason for their visit here again.

Surely Mama, who had a seer's insight on her children, would have noticed too. But then Honoria remembered a strange thing. Mr Allison always seemed to be at the furthest corner from Serena. Nearly always... There was no purpose to speculating. She needed to talk to her sister. Mr Scribster would recommend honesty. However, Mr Scribster was a rhinoceros who trampled upon people's feelings, so she would accept no advice from him. What would Mama counsel? Perhaps the same. Suddenly Honoria, glancing over at the assembled breakfast company, realised that the tension she had felt recently was all due to a lack of forthrightness. Not just her own secret, but another that had troubled Mama and Papa, her attraction for the lieutenant, some mystery around Genevieve who was chatting animatedly about stable matters to her sister, the strange case of Dickie going to London when Honoria knew that he had already spent his quarter's allowance and more at a gambling table. She couldn't recall a time when such a web of secrecy clung around the family. Usually, they could all hold a secret for the brief period before Mama guessed and all was aired and discussed around the house. She ate, trying to catch her sister's eye.

Her mama bent over her to whisper in her ear. 'Mr Allison wishes to talk to you, my love.'

Honoria raised her eyes to search for her host around the table.

'He isn't here, Honoria. Have you not noticed that he is absent?' Honoria met her mother's eyes with a faraway look. 'After breakfast you may meet him at the pergola of roses.' Honoria's gaze seemed to follow something else. 'My dear, did you hear me?'

'Yes, yes Mama.' Her eyes encountered Mr Scribster's. They were not as full of amusement as they might be normally. She frowned at him. Serena stood up and Honoria jumped up to catch her. 'Serena! Wait for me.' Her sister did so and as she left the room, she heard her mother's call.

'Five minutes, Honoria!'

In Serena's bedchamber at last, Honoria sat on her bed and curled up her legs, watching as her sister used a soft brush that she kept for the purpose, to brush the debris of the stables from her dress and shoes.

'How would you feel if I did agree to marry Mr Allison?'

'Oh, Orry!' said Serena, throwing herself onto the bed and grasping at her hands, 'Has he indeed asked you?'

'No, not yet,' said Honoria, searching her bright face for a chink. 'What is wrong, Serena, I can tell that you are not quite as happy as … what is it?'

Serena bent her dark curls. 'Oh, it is too selfish. I have just understood that we will be parted when you marry. And it has made me sad.'

Honoria flung off her hands and rose, beginning to pace the room, 'Is *that* all?'

'Well, whatever did you think it might be?' said Serena, at a loss.

'I don't know,' said Honoria testily. 'Perhaps some objection to Mr Allison?'

Serena laughed, 'Don't be silly Orry. What objection could there be to you marrying a handsome, kind, rich gentleman? We could hardly guess how wonderful he would be. I did Mama's trick of getting the servants into conversation, without questions, you know. And you can tell how they respect and like him.' She looked at Honoria's pacing. 'But if you do not wish for the match, you have only to tell Papa.' Honoria was now wringing her handkerchief as well as pacing. 'Are you afraid it has all gone too far? I know how you feel about doing everything that is proper. But I know that even Mama would understand. She is ambitious, yes, but she wishes only our happiness.'

'Yes, yes,' said Honoria, cornered. She bent, and this time she clasped Serena's hands. 'But what do you *think* of him, Serena? Tell me, I beg you. Not as a match for me, just as a man.'

Serena looked confused, but settled back to consider. 'Well both he and his cousin are really handsome! And he is very strong. He threw me onto a saddle as though I weighed no more than a baby. And he is soooo funny.' She saw Honoria frown. 'Really, he is. And he can ride like the wind and is daring in the saddle, but never reckless with the horse, which I really appreciate. His cousin has told me that he was a hero under Wellington, with Mr Scribster, too — if you believe that *that* gentleman can do more than look sour. He is a bit of a highwayman at times....' Honoria looked stupefied. 'He really is.' Serena was looking into the distance, remembering.

'He sounds,' ventured Honoria, rather desperately, 'quite wonderful in your description. Perhaps,' she added with an attempt at levity, 'he would make a better match for you rather than me.'

It was as though she had slapped her sister in the face. 'Oh, Orry, you cannot think that I am after him — just because we rode ahead the other day? Please don't think that,' she said distressed.

Honoria could scarcely say she hoped that she was. 'No, no. It was just a joke.' But there had been something in Serena's face for her to ponder on later. But there would be no later. She had just realised that the person she was meeting at the rose pergola was Allison, and all alone. It could only mean one thing. Nothing could save her now.

She apologised to Serena and left the room. On the upper stair she encountered Mr Scribster, who appeared to have been waiting for her. She moved forward swiftly and grasped his hand. He looked down at it in a confused way, as though no one had ever taken his hand before. 'Can you help me?'

'Yes,' he said. It was like him not to make a pretty speech about it.

'I am to meet Mr Allison and, and I know you know...'

'Yes,' he said again.

'Will you interrupt us? He will perhaps ask a question that I am not — not yet ready for. I will try to keep him talking, but do not delay.'

She drew away from him and ran down the stairs to the marbled hall.

He seemed to wake up and called softly after her, 'If you said no, all this could be over.'

She turned to him, dress still held by both hands and looked sad. 'I can't. I just — it really is not that simple. Only, I'm not *ready*.' She turned and ran lightly to the door, opened in anticipation by a footman.

Mr Allison was awaiting Honoria by the pergola, looking tall, handsome — and eligible. He took her hand and kissed it with great ceremony. 'Miss Fenton — how well primrose becomes you.' The mention of primrose made her think of Mr Scribster and Miss Shaw.

A ghost of a smile lit up her features and Mr Allison thought he had never seen her look better, more natural. This was beginning well.

'I think that you must know, Miss Fenton, how much I admire you,' he continued.

'Do I? And how would I know that precisely?' said Honoria in a tone he had never heard her use.

'Well, um. I do,' he said lamely, but he was beginning to be amused.

She appeared to be looking back at the house for something, but she replied, 'What qualities of mine do you admire the most?'

What on earth was this? The girl who could hardly speak to him on a good day asking such pert questions that might cause her mama to faint if she could hear them. He was confused and ill-prepared. The interview, much rehearsed in the last few hours, had taken an unexpected, but interesting, turn.

'Your beauty—' he began, but stopped when he saw her attention go elsewhere once more.

'Mmm. My beauty,' she repeated, bored. 'And—'

'Your intelligence.'

'You must have sent for references. I don't remember displaying any intelligence in your orbit...' she was still talking distantly, as if the words sprang from her mouth without her will whilst she was occupied by other things.

'Anyway, I have been led to desire to ask you, to request of you—'

'Oh, is that Mr Scribster running towards us?' she asked with what he felt might be relief.

His back was to the house and he said irritably, 'Nonsense — Gus never runs,' but he turned nevertheless to find his old friend almost upon them.

'Gus — what?'

'Sorry, Rowley, Miss Fenton. I'm afraid there is news from town. Mr Benedict Fenton has been attacked.'

'Oh!' cried Honoria, in the tone of the great Siddons from the West End stage, 'I must go to Mama!'

She walked quickly away with Scribster whilst Allison took a moment to collect himself.

'What kept you?' she whispered. 'And the interruption was a little Gothic, wasn't it? Shall Benedict have to wear an interesting sling on his arm to keep up the ruse?'

'I was delayed by the word from London. Your Mama bade me find you. I'm afraid that it is all quite real, Miss Fenton.'

She gave him a tortured look, picked up her primrose skirts, and ran full pelt to the house.

Chapter 14

Benedict's Condition

When the news had arrived of Benedict's attack, Genevieve's heart contracted with guilt. If it had not been that her husband was at Ottershaw, she would have suspected that Benedict, having seen her injuries, had confronted Sumner — and then her husband had bludgeoned him like the coward he was. But Sumner was not there. It could not have been he. Suddenly Genevieve was sure that Benedict's surprise visit to town was to do with her. It shocked her like the shattering of crockery. His nature was such that he could never leave her plight alone once he had guessed it. The silly, wonderful young man would wish to rescue her at all costs — and though Sumner was not in town, she feared he had been responsible for the dreadful costs. None of this made any sense, she knew. What could Benedict have done? And what could Sumner have caused to have done to Benedict?

Thus it was that Genevieve had accompanied them to town, and deposited her bags at Grosvenor Square with the others, since Sumner House in Curzon Street was closed up at this season. She hardly waited for Mr Allison's invitation, just went in the carriage to Lord Carstairs' rooms. As a young gentleman about town, Carstairs had separate rooms from his family's rather large, old-fashioned town house, which had not been in his family for more than two generations, but still terrified him with the pressure of family expectation whenever he visited his mother there. He preferred his rooms, which were not spacious, but cosy, and consisted of only his Lordship's own bedchamber and the sitting room, where Benedict had laid his head this visit on a truckle bed. His valet and maid lived in the attics, like the valets and maids of the other young gentlemen who had rooms here.

So when Benedict's mama and papa, two sisters and a friend arrived, the rooms looked very small indeed. Carstairs took Sir Ranalph away from the ladies and told him the doctor's opinion. Benedict had been hit repeatedly — by cudgels had said a witness. It was very possible that two ribs were broken, his legs and back were severely bruised, but more important were the two blows to the head. The witness, a street-hawker who had been imbibing at a public inn, said that these were the last blows delivered. Benedict having wielded a bottle at one attacker and using it upon him, and the other coming up behind and delivering the blows. The hawker cried 'Watch!' and the two men ran off, leaving Benedict bleeding on the cobbles. If Benedict awoke in the next few hours, there was hope, but otherwise — his lordship put his hand before his eyes. 'Sorry, sir.'

Sir Ranalph put a large hand on his shoulder. 'Thank you my boy, for all you've done.'

His lordship looked at him with his hair flopping over his watery eyes. 'But it's Dickie, sir.' He tried to get a grip of himself, 'I don't think the ladies should see him, sir,' he said, leading the way back into his rooms.

'I don't think that we can stop them,' said Sir Ranalph.

The ladies were in a clump in the middle of the room with Lady Fenton at its head. 'Is my son in there?' She pointed to a door.

Sir Ranalph moved forward. 'Perhaps I will see him first, my dear.'

'You will not keep me from him—'

But it was Genevieve who opened the door, stopped at the threshold in shock at seeing the young man, pale as a corpse, lying unconscious on his lordship's bed. Then she flung herself forward and onto the floor next to the bed, grasping his unresponsive hand.

'Oh, Dickie, what did you *do*?' she cried passionately and burst into tears.

Lady Fenton looked in alarm at her husband, but he shook his head.

The rest of the party nudged around, Serena and Honoria clutching each other for support. Honoria touched Lady Sumner's shoulder. 'Genevieve!'

Her ladyship got up and threw herself into Honoria's arms. 'It is all my fault!' she breathed in his sister's ear. Honoria clasped her close. Serena's eyes met her sister's. They knew Genevieve to be fond of Benedict, but she was not normally an emotional girl. What did this mean?

The news was brought to Mr Wilbert Fenton as he was about to set off for the theatre, less to see the ballet as to mingle with the dancers afterwards — he stood in need of female companionship this evening.

He was about to get plenty. He got a brief note from Richardson, a magistrate in Bow Street.

'Your nevvy Benedict was attacked by ruffians this evening. He was taken to young Fluff Carstairs' rooms in Piccadilly. I hear it's bad. Thought you would like to know.'

Pierre was mounted on a stool adjusting his cravat pin when an oath escaped his master's tight lips and the tiny valet was witness to the gravest expression he had yet seen on his face. 'Stop your trivialities,' Mr Fenton said, brushing him away and cutting into his heart with the words, 'I have to leave.'

Carstairs was not able to stop Mr Wilbert Fenton, dressed inappropriately for a sick room (in knee breeches and an opera cloak), coming in. There seemed to be a great many people in the room, but in fact it had thinned considerably, Serena and Lady Sumner having been sent back in a hackney — Serena profoundly shocked, and Genevieve still crying intermittently.

Carstairs and his brother were standing awkwardly at the foot of the bed, with Cynthia and her eldest at each side of his nephew, who looked completely burnt in the socket.

'Wilbert!' said Sir Ranalph, but his brother paid no heed, only pushed past to get to his nephew.

'Benedict!' he commanded, 'Wake up!' There was a protesting sound from Lady Fenton, on the other side of the bed holding lavender water to her son's bruised temple, but Benedict frowned slightly and opened his eyes. 'Uncle!' he said faintly after a moment where everyone had held their breath, 'is it six months?' His uncle's laugh cracked in the middle.

Lady Fenton looked confused, but Mr Fenton said lazily, 'Not yet. I had an inexplicable desire to see you.'

Benedict winced in pain as he laughed, 'They tried to get it. But I took a leaf from your book. I had a cushion.' He twinkled up at his uncle, then fell back into the abyss once more.

'He's just asleep, now,' said his mama, with her hand on his chest. 'Whatever did he mean, Wilbert?'

'Carstairs,' called Fenton over his shoulders. 'Did Dickie have anything at his waist?'

'Oh, you mean that—' he pointed to a length of linen lying on the dresser with a tumbling of golden guineas and some large bank notes escaping from the folds. 'It was under his shirt, fastened about his waist.'

Sir Ranalph looked at the guineas, then at his brother, his good nature departed from his expression. 'Was this visit to you about *gambling* Wilbert? I swear I'll kill you if it was.'

'Yes.' His brother moved towards him and he held his hands up in a conciliatory gesture. 'But not in the way you think. I'll explain what I can, but not here and not tonight.' The two brothers left the room, Mr Wilbert Fenton's face inscrutable.

'If only we'd known,' said Honoria to her mama in wonder, 'That all we had to do was order him to wake up, we might have done so earlier.'

Their eyes met, and at this stressful period, even such a weak joke was met with hilarity.

Her mother grasped her hand. 'Now will you go home, my dear girl? Leave Benedict with me and I will take care of him. You need rest.'

Honoria looked into her mother's strained face and knew she did not need to worry for her as well as her son. 'Well, I will, Mama, but only after you sit in the chair and sleep for an hour yourself. I can see to Dickie and keep him comfortable till then. You know the corner is turned.'

'What he said was so strange that I almost feared that his brain was affected. But his uncle understood him, didn't he?'

Honoria led her to the chair by the window and put her shawl over her legs, 'Assuredly, he did.'

'And I can get your father to take you back to Grosvenor Square. He is very much in my way—' But her words were slurred and her eyes closed as the break in the tension of the last day washed through her. 'Only an hour!' she said, and fell asleep.

Honoria smiled and turned back to deal with her now restless brother.

Genevieve had control of herself by the end of the hackney ride to Grosvenor Square and was able to meet the gentlemen in better form. Mr Allison did not ask for news, he had received a quick note from Sir Ranalph, but simply met the ladies in the hall and offered them some dinner.

'I need to retire to my chamber,' said Lady Sumner, 'Might you cause some cake and wine to be sent there? That will suffice me, I think.' She gave a wan smile, but turned at the foot of the stairs when Serena followed her. 'No, no. Please, sir. See that Serena eats. She would not have anything at Lord Carstairs' lodgings.'

Mr Allison bowed. He turned to Serena. 'Will you come into the drawing room?'

She looked at him frankly. 'Might I not, Mr Allison? I have not the strength for conversation tonight. I know I must eat, but can I do that somewhere else? Just something simple.'

'Can I bear you company in the blue room? I'll have a tray brought up.'

He nodded to Blake, who dispatched a footman by the wave of a hand, then held open the door of the blue salon.

'Is there any change?' he asked, after the door was closed.

Serena shook her head, beyond words.

He led her to a chair by her elbow and gently pushed her into it. 'He is a strong young man. I saw him try his paces in Jackson's. He'll pull through.'

Serena nodded with a faint smile.

'Lady Sumner seems very upset.'

'Yes. That's the only reason that I left. Mama required me to take care of her or I should never have come home.'

Allison smiled down at her. 'Lord Carstairs' rooms must have been a sad crush.'

This expression, indicative of a very well attended social occasion, made her laugh.

'Yes, he had to send off for chairs to another set of rooms owned by someone he called Rumpy.'

'Viscount Fitzpatrick. He gained the nickname in school when a horse he backed had missed winning, not by a head but by a rump.'

'He came in 'to see how it was all going' quite as though I should entertain him on the pianoforte. He was the most absurd young man!'

'Good gracious! Does Fluff Carstairs have a pianoforte? I would never have expected it.'

'Of course not! You know what I mean. Why is his lordship called Fluff?'

'I believe he has the unfortunate middle name of Florian. Oh, and one of his minor titles is Baron of Loughborough.'

'Oh!' she had lost interest as her exhaustion took over.

He smiled at her. Booth arrived with the tray and a maid ran ahead to place a small side table by Serena's chair.

'I'll leave you to dine,' Mr Allison said, as the servants departed.

'Please don't. Bear me company, if you think your other guests will not object.'

'Gus and Darnley? They are playing a game of billiards so intense that I doubt if they have noticed I have gone.' He took a chair opposite her.

'You see? It is for that that I wish you to stay. You stop me thinking of Benedict every second. I know that to dwell on him will not make me useful to Mama, but I just seem to be unable to stop. He looked so—' she shook her head as though to dislodge the image and Allison would have given his arm to dislodge the pain in her eyes. 'But tell me why the billiard game between Mr Scribster and Lieutenant Prescott is so intense.'

'Well, it began in Lisbon.' He smiled at her again. 'I cannot tell you the tale if you do not eat.'

'You are treating me like I would treat my sister Angelica, bribing her to eat her peas with stories.' Mr Allison's lips closed firmly and she laughed. 'Very well. What happened in Lisbon?' She picked up her fork and Allison smiled.

'You realise I am breaking my code as a gentleman relating this story?' he began. 'Because it concerns a wager. When Gus and I arrived in Lisbon, fresh from the fray, we discovered that Darnley, who had been billeted there for two months as secretary to Lord Duncan, had a reputation as a first class billiard player.' Serena raised her eyebrows and continued her meal. 'Of course, Gus's reputation for billiards is legendary, and if it had not been for the injury to his arm that he laid on a trifle thickly, even Darnley would not have been stupid enough to play him for a wager.'

'I cannot be sorry for the lieutenant when he wished to take advantage of a hero wounded in battle whilst he was far from the fighting.'

'Well, to be honest, Gus had recovered from the last of the three balls that had felled him in battle two months earlier. This last particular injury had occurred when he fell off his horse after a night in a Lisbon tavern!'

Serena almost choked on her sliver of onion tartlet.

'I told you this was no tale for a lady—'

By the time she had heard the scurrilous tale out, and had eaten her meal, Serena was almost exhausted, but lighter in spirit. A note from Honoria had arrived, telling her of Benedict's awakening, and she felt herself able to go and try to rest. Mr Allison, far from the conventionalities this evening, accompanied her upstairs and she stopped at the chamber allotted to Lady Sumner.

'I shall put this on Genevieve's nightstand for her to read when she wakes up,' she said of Honoria's note, 'It will ease her mind.'

'Her ladyship seems extremely upset at Benedict's fate.'

'Yes, well, we were all brought up together. She said something in the carriage about it all being her fault—' Serena frowned.

'Don't trouble yourself about it tonight my dear girl,' he said, his blue eyes looking down at her kindly, brushing his thumb against her chin 'Just rest.'

She looked up at him and took one hand, tiptoeing to give him a chaste kiss on the cheek. 'You are such a good man, Mr Allison. I cannot imagine why Honoria—' she stopped herself abruptly and opened the door behind her with her other hand. 'Goodnight, sir,' she whispered. And then she was gone.

It was nearly midnight when Honoria and her father arrived at the house. Mr Allison had stayed up, but they both refused refreshments and took off their hats and coats and ascended the stairs. They parted with a hug at the top, her father whispering in her ear, 'He will be alright now, never fear, my dear.'

She let her father go to his room and headed for hers, nodding away the footman who had lighted their path. There was a room across the hall with a door ajar and a candle glimmering — she walked towards it fearlessly.

'Mr Scribster?' she whispered before she got there.

'How did you guess it was mine?' said he, coming into sight with a candle in his hand.

She moved past him into the room, closing the door behind her.

She heard him swallow audibly. 'I don't think it is seemly to close the door, Miss Fenton.' He grasped at the handle and she put her small hand on his to prevent him.

'Please — don't *you* speak to me of seemliness too, Mr Scribster. I count on you to be vile and abominable at the end of this horrible day.' She threw her arms around his waist and cried quite as passionately as ever Genevieve had in her arms earlier. He stood stiffly for a moment with his arms extended as though frozen. But in a second he had put down the candle on a handy side table and pulled her close to him, bending his head to rest his chin on her curls.

'You poor girl. Tell me.'

They stood thus for a moment, Scribster holding her up as her knees buckled. He lifted her gently and put her on the armchair before the hearth, where some coals still glowed.

'I know what it is — you have been good and strong for your mama and papa, for Benedict, for Serena, for Uncle Tom Cobbley and all. Have you even allowed yourself to cry before now?'

'Not a lot. Other people were crying so much already. Like Genevieve Horton. I mean Lady Sumner. Why must she have hysterics and become chief mourner — before even my mama?'

'He's not dead — yet.'

'*Oh!*' burst out Honoria, laughing despite herself, 'that is low, even for you.'

'It is low. But do you suspect Lady Sumner of display? She has never struck me as that type.'

'Oh, never. It was so unkind of me to say that. It is just that I was working so hard not to have hysterics when I saw him and she just — oh, how unkind I am.'

'Dreadfully! And fast, too. I noticed it when you closed that door to be alone with a gentleman.'

'It's only *you*!'

'If your mama were to find out—'

'—And you are only barely a gentleman, but you are not a blabber.'

'That shall be inscribed on my tomb.'

She laughed. Then she trembled a little.

'You must get to bed,' he said.

'Yes. But I have to say it aloud first and I cannot say it to anyone else without chafing them sorely.' He nodded sombrely, matching her mood. 'I thought he was near to death. He lay there and I thought he would die and I realised how much I would miss his annoying presence. I thought if he died, I would die too. But first I would like to *kill* whoever had done this to him. Oh, I am so very *wicked*.' He moved to his knees beside the chair and pulled her to him to let the scalding tears fall on his shoulder. She clung to him, saying into his neck, 'This is not at all the thing.'

'Damn the thing!'

She stayed thus for a minute and then pulled away. 'I knew I could count on you to let me behave abominably. I must go.'

She left him before he had time to rise.

She was trembling a little as she entered her room, where a small maid awaited to undress her, but it was not from the cold.

He stayed on one knee for enough time for the truth to hit him like the cudgel to Benedict's head. He had held Honoria Fenton in his arms, and he would strain every nerve in his body to make sure no other man would ever hold her so. He was in love and no longer on the sidelines of this little comedy that had so amused him. It was not a comfortable place to be, but as in the thick of battle, he would find a way through or die trying.

All he had to do, after all, was to convince Honoria (and her family) to refuse a fortune and every advantage in marrying a diabolically handsome, fashionable, intelligent and first class human being and his own best friend — for him.

Chapter 15

Lord Sumner Receives a Letter

Scribster and Allison met on the way to an early breakfast. 'I don't think you should offer for Miss Fenton,' he said, getting to the point.

'Well, I'll hardly do it in these circumstances. I never told you how the proposal fared.'

'You proposed already?'

'I would have if she hadn't kept interrupting me.'

'Did she? And you thought she would wait meekly until her parents' greatest hope came to pass.'

'You wound my pride — perhaps she could like me for more than her parents' sake. Actually, she was delightfully pert and I became interested for the first time. Thanks for that.'

'You're thanking me?' said Scribster at the last step.

Allison put his hand on his shoulder. 'It was you who kept saying she had hidden depths.'

'I did.'

'And it tipped me over into talking to her. The delay was about to get embarrassing for all the family. But she ripped me up — when I told her she must know how I admired her, she said she could never have guessed from my behaviour.' He laughed. 'I had to admire her honesty. I was becoming inured to my fate.'

'How did she reply to your offer?'

'I never got the chance to finish it. You interrupted — I thought you must know.'

'I thought so. Anyway, you must not do so now.'

'Of course not. What kind of self-interested dolt do you think me? And what's it to do with you anyway?'

'You'd be surprised.'

They entered the breakfast room to find only Lieutenant Prescott and Honoria. The Lieutenant's large handkerchief was in Honoria's hand and she looked up.

'Good morning Mr Allison, Mr Scribster,' she said, with a smile, but still a little watery-eyed. 'I am sorry that you see me thus. I assure you that I'm much better now. Lieutenant Prescott was most kind.'

'Are your sister and Lady Sumner still abed?'

'Serena has gone to your kitchens to make a rub for Benedict's bruises. She seems to think if it's efficacious for horses, it will be good for him.' She gave a little laugh. 'Then she is going to let Mama come back here to rest. Lady Sumner and I will stay here and I must wait for the afternoon, when Papa says I may relieve my sister. He wishes me to rest again, as I had such a late night. Papa is already gone, I think. Could you get a footman to find a hackney for Serena?'

'I will take her myself,' said Allison determinedly. 'And you should rest.'

'I cannot. I shall just wait here until I am needed.'

Mr Scribster said, 'You will very likely chafe yourself into low spirits if you do that. Don't be a little f—'

Allison looked askance at his friend. Almost calling a guest a fool was more rudeness than even he could display normally.

Honoria frowned at him, her sadness dispelled for a moment.

'That is why I have invited Miss Fenton to a ride around the park with me in your tilbury, Rowley. I've ordered it to be put to. Clear away the cobwebs before she has to tend to the sick. I trust you have no objection.'

'None whatsoever,' said Allison, hearing the soft step of Serena in the hallway. 'Miss Serena!' he called from the door, 'I'll drive you today.'

'I can go by hackney coach,' she said, appearing in the doorway fastening the ribbons of a pretty straw bonnet.

'I would not hear of it. Anyway, I want to see how your brother goes on.'

'Well, thank you. But you cannot stay, mind, Mama does not want a crowd — like yesterday — around his bed. Honoria told me so this morning.'

'Serena! You are impolite. Not but what it is true. Ever since Benedict regained consciousness, his sleep has been so restless. The least thing awakens him and he is in such pain! The doctor will bring him another sleeping draught this morning, I hope.'

'I promise,' said Mr Allison with a bow in Honoria's direction, 'that I shall only step in for a minute or two to see what help, if any, I can offer.' He smiled. 'And ladies, can we be done with politeness for the present? In this circumstance, I speak for all the gentlemen present in saying that we are at your command, at your family's command, for the foreseeable future.' Prescott and Scribster bowed briefly.

'Well, thank you, but Benedict is swamped with help already,' said Serena frankly, 'And I do not suppose that there is anything else to be done.'

But she was wrong.

By that afternoon, at Mr Allison's instigation, another surgeon — very much more experienced — had examined Benedict and had given exact instructions for having him moved to Grosvenor Square. Serena's liniment was applied, a light sleeping draught was prescribed, his ribs were strapped and a regime for his intake of food and wine established. Benedict was conscious for some of this and bore it with gritted teeth and an attempt at a smile.

At Mr Allison's house, a bed was lumbered down from the attic whilst a great deal of delicate modern furniture was banished from the blue salon. A nurse, a clean and sober middle-aged person who had been Mr Allison's own nurse before her marriage, arrived and tended to the more humdrum and earthy tasks of caring for an invalid, including ejecting visitors who might add to his excitability and very likely give him a fever.

Carstairs rather resented his friend's abduction, but Mr Allison soothed his soul by assuring him that he was always welcome, and that even a bedchamber could be speedily made for him at Grosvenor Square if he was desirous to stay.

In Mr Allison's phaeton, on the way back, Serena said, 'You are a take-charge kind of highwayman, are you not, sir?'

'Too much?' he asked her, taking an eye off the busy road for a second to study her face.

'No, just right.' She smiled at him and then exclaimed. 'Watch your leaders, sir! That cart!'

After a nifty move of the reins and his whip, they passed the cart with only a light scrape of the wheels.

'I was perfectly aware of the cart.'

'Hm-mm,' she paused. 'I know my mother has thanked you, but I must too. You have been ejected from a house party into this nightmare and you have been so good about it. All your amusements have been spoiled.

'How absolutely dreadful. So have yours,' he said, '—or do you wish me to get tickets for Astley's for you this evening?'

'Do not be absurd. As though I could care to go anywhere at this moment.'

'Well, it is the same for me.'

'But he is not your brother.'

There was a pause, as it occurred to both of them that he may soon be — a brother-in-law at any rate.

'But your family are my guests and I am famous for accommodating my guests. It would tarnish my reputation to behave differently.'

She put her hand on his arm. 'Yes, that is what it is. Your pride in your reputation — no kindness involved at all.'

'I'm glad you realise it.' He took a gloved hand from the reins and squeezed hers.

'Your leaders, sir!' Serena laughed.

As he skirted another carriage bowling along the middle of the road, he remarked. 'I cannot imagine how I manage to drive the streets of London without you beside me to avert disaster.'

'Nor I,' she laughed. 'When might you let me take the ribbons, sir?'

'With these young horses? Never.'

'You are too unkind.'

'Dreadfully.'

She sat back on the squabs, smiling a little — her tension eased somewhat, as he had planned.

It was not to be expected, even if the town was thin of the polite world, that an attack on a young gentleman in the street would go unnoticed, and the chatterers were becoming much more interested when the invalid moved from Carstairs' rooms (a peer of the realm, certainly, but of much less social import than the magnificently rich Mr Allison) to Grosvenor Square. That there were a couple of beautiful young sisters involved put speculation in the air, and as Scribster was a sphinx, the last gossips in town targeted Prescott. A tall tree to shake, but assuredly something would fall out.

Thus it was that only two days later, Lord Sumner — now kicking his heels at Ottershaw, and ready to do the same to his dearly beloved once he found her direction — received a missive.

Dear Foxy,

Hope the country air agrees with you, though I doubt it, somehow. No good shooting at this season, surely?

The town is sadly dull in summer, of course, but an event occurred that you might be interested in last week. You know young Fenton? Well, I know you do — some sort of neighbour of your wife's family ain't he? He was done near to death, they say, bludgeoned by a set of rough fellows from quite another part of town. Only saved from death by the Watch, apparently, and if that ain't the luck of the devil, I don't know what is — for a more incompetent shower of blaggards it would be hard to find. My wife is partial to the boy, he danced with her twice at the Fenwicks' ball and complimented her gown at Almack's, apparently, so she's been going on about it interminably to me and I thought I'd try to get to sniff out the juice to quieten her tongue. Well, it transpires that the town is talking about money that the young fellow picked up at the tables. Quite substantial amounts, by all accounts. He won from Sutcliffe and Dawson some considerable sums — took twelve hundred guineas from Sutcliffe at Brooks and also had a regular prayer book full of IOUs — but here's the thing, there's talk that at least two others at that table, the more minor losers, had their money and vowels returned to them. What do you make of that? They were sworn to secrecy, of course, but Southeby's mouth is as leaky as a sieve, as you have cause to know, old man.

There is word of a private party where Rennie dropped a couple of thousand too — he had to leave town on a repairing lease, rather like yourself. I suppose if word leaked about Fenton's recent wealth in one of the rougher taverns that might have been enough to tempt someone to attack — all have reason for a little ungentlemanly try at recovering their losses. I would acquit Sutcliffe, well I went to school with him and I don't think he's as rum as all that, but I've since heard there are other creditors there and who knows what might happen when one's back is to the wall. As you can imagine, talk at the club has gone mad.

What an amazing run of luck the young cub had, but not so lucky when you think of it now. Still, it happens. Just think of Harris, even though he beat old Skipton and won his fortune, it led to him marrying that shrew Gussie Fawkes, so no win at all, really. Anyway, Fenton's lying near to death in Rowley Allison's house in Grosvenor Square, of all places. The great one has billeted the whole family apparently. No mystery there: do you remember Miss Fenton, last year's silent beauty? Well apparently there's a sister just as pretty with a bit more spirit to boot, if Darnley Prescott is to be believed.

Here's the reason I'm writing to you, Foxy: Dummy Prescott has also said something of interest to you — Lady Sumner is staying at Grosvenor Square, too. I thought you'd gone to join her at Ottershaw? Well, I know that's not the only reason, know you'd rather escape the dashed leeches here in London, but the town's asking why she isn't at Sumner House. Allison's put it about that she's bearing her friend Lady Fenton company, and that's holding for now. But your Aunt Harrington's in town and she pinned me down in the Mall the other day asking me about it — told me you'd said you were off to join your wife while she has heard that her ladyship is staying with the most eligible bachelor in town. I denied all knowledge of course. But she was put out, and as she is the honey-hive, I thought you'd like to know. Get back here before the tongues wag too much, Sumner. You can stay with me. It'll be a while before the dunners find you here.

Best get your wife in order, old man.

Yours etc,

Fordyce

Sumner was glad to know where his wife was, and Fordyce's plan appealed. To be in town, albeit not at home, must be more amusing than the County bloody Show – and he had some plans for his erring wife. She would find that leaving without permission had consequences. If she was indeed in Allison's house, he needed to tread warily. But it was no man's place to stop the joyous reunion of man and wife.

Young idiot Fenton he barely thought of. But there was a niggle about the names of those he had won from. All three *he* had played with. But then they were fellows who were seldom from the tables. The giving back of money to some players needed thinking about. What kind of a fellow did that? A soft hearted sap. His head deserved to be split.

The Fentons' falling in with Allison had provided his wife with a hiding place. She would find that nothing in London failed to reach the ear of Frederick Sumner.

Chapter 16

Mr Scribster Cuts His Hair

Benedict's progress was uncertain, it seemed. For the first few days of his removal to Grosvenor Square, he was restless but seldom fully awake. Just when he had been awake for a few moments and spoke some sense to his attendants, then he faltered again and tossed and turned, obviously in great pain from his ribs and head.

Genevieve wished to be in his room for the most part, looking for the moments where he was lucid.

Mr Scribster arrived in the breakfast room the next morning in his usual circumspect manner, but Prescott, looking up, exclaimed 'Good God!' so that every head turned towards him. 'Your hair has been cut—' he continued.

'Sharp as ever, Lieutenant,' Scribster said, sitting beside Mr Allison and accepting a teacup from the supremely uninterested Blake.

'But why—?' continued Prescott whilst the other breakfasters continued to look.

The difference between the two rather lank curtains of hair that had framed his face yesterday, to the short style which revealed his hair as a thick, gleaming thatch which was brushed back from his forehead (disclosing a rather attractive cow's lick peak) was nothing short of sensational. His hooded eyes were no longer hidden behind the hair and their expression was more readable, their hazel colouration more noticeable. He had, himself, been stunned when his valet had finished the task (that he had so long wished to do) and he'd regarded himself in the mirror — a different man. But now the attention was irritating.

'I expect it was too heavy for the summer days,' supposed Honoria helpfully, when the silence had gone on for too long.

'Hmm,' Scribster muttered, and glanced around the table — everyone, including his friend, with their eyes still riveted on his hair. He was glad that Honoria was at his side of the table and he could not meet her eye. 'Oh, for goodness sake!' he said testily, and the ladies' eyes all turned back the matter of breakfast. In his more normal drawl, he asked, 'How's the invalid this morning?'

'He had a restless night,' said Lady Fenton, but the doctor assures us that this is a good sign. He talked a little when he awoke and seemed to know us all.'

'That indeed is a good sign,' said Mr Allison, still hardly able to take his eyes off Scribster. 'His brain is not affected.'

'I never doubted it,' said Sir Ranalph, not quite truthfully, 'He has a head as hard as a cannon ball that boy. Fell out of countless trees when he was young. Never came to any harm at all!'

As usual, the company discussed their plans for the day. As Lady Fenton wished to sit with Benedict this morning, she was very strict that the young ladies should go out in the fresh air for their own health. They decided to go to the park as a group, with Genevieve, Serena, Honoria and Lieutenant Prescott to be driven by Mr. Allison in his phaeton and Mr. Scribster to ride.

'I'll meet you at the park, I have an errand to attend to,' Scribster said, briefly.

'I too, have business with my bank, I shall look in on Benedict and see you all back here,' said Sir Ranalph, unexpectedly. Her ladyship raised an eye to him, but was too concerned about her son to pursue it.

The second of the Fenton men to get past the butler and the attentive valet now entered the sanctity of Mr Wilbert Fenton's dressing room.

'Good God Wilbert, it's a concubine's boudoir!'

His brother, looking at him in the glass said, 'Brother! Always glad to receive your hints on the modes of today. Pierre,' he said to his solicitously hovering valet, 'take notes. The baronet is going to give his thoughts on design.' The little man looked Sir Ranalph up and down, from his slightly dusty topboots to his comfortable but ill-fitting coat and shuddered. 'Is this a familial visit?' continued Wilbert, 'Am I to believe that Cynthia and the girls await me downstairs?'

'Cynthia is with Dickie and the girls have gone to the park with Allison to take some air,' he said as an aside, for he knew this was a diversionary tactic by his brother, 'Came here to talk about Benedict.'

His brother turned in his chair, discarding the comb he'd been using to coax individual curls to cluster around his noble brow. 'He is not worse?'

Sir Ranalph was abnormally angry, but he heard the concerned tone in his brother's voice and warmed to him despite himself, 'No, no! You seemed to have roused him and he's in and out of consciousness now, which the doctor feels is the body's normal response to a head injury.'

His brother returned to his mirror.

'What he said to you about six months — you say it wasn't ravings? We shouldn't be concerned?'

'No. It was perfectly comprehensible.' He met his brother's eyes in the glass once more. 'A joke in fact.'

'About what?'

The comb hesitated on its way to a curl with a mind of its own. 'He was referring to a deal we made. I would find out something for him if he would stop hounding me in my dressing room for six months at least.'

'And you did?'

'I did.'

'And what did you find out?'

'I am not at liberty to tell you.'

'I beg your pardon?' Sir Ranalph held himself at least two inches taller in his indignation.

'I promised Benedict, you see.'

'Are you saying it has nothing to do with the attack on my boy?'

Wilbert put the brush down again and turned around to face his brother. 'On the contrary, I'm nearly sure it does. Just as I am sure that Dickie would not want you to know.'

'You will tell me, Wilbert,' said Sir Ranalph, beside himself with rage now, 'is it anything to do with the infernal gaming tables? Did the boy—?'

'Not in the way you fear, brother. Your son,' he said, a little bitterly, 'is not like me.'

'You will tell me, Wilbert, or I swear I will never frank your debts again. Never!'

There was a silence. Each brother looked into the eyes of the other, Wilbert Fenton's tense, sad, and sympathetic and Sir Ranalph's furious, determined and quite void of his usual good humour.

Wilbert's eyes dropped first. 'I understand,' he said.

Sir Ranalph gasped. 'Then you will not?' he blurted, hardly able to believe it of his self-centred brother.

Mr Fenton turned around to face his mirror again, taking up his comb. His answering voice fell just short of suave. 'I find,' he said, 'that I cannot.'

His brother turned on his heel in regimental fashion and left the chamber.

The little valet busily began to brush his master's shoulders free of imaginary specs of dust. Finally, he met his master's eye in the glass, eyes wide with sympathy and fear.

Mr Wilbert met them. 'I've always been addicted to games of chance, my friend. But now it looks like I've overplayed my hand.'

'Sir Ranalph eez — a kind man, no? If you were to change your mind—?' said Pierre, aware of the large wad of debts and wages due to be paid from Sir Ranalph's generous allowance to his brother.

'And what would my brother do then but make himself a target for the black-hearted scoundrels who attacked his son? No, it is all my fault. I must pay the piper. And my promise to that poor boy was implicit. It may be time to find myself another occupation.'

The valet gave a Gallic shrug, indicative, perhaps of resignation. He reached for a high-necked jacket in pale green.

'Not that!' said Mr Fenton. 'Bring me my riding habit!'

'But m'sieur, you never ride at zees hour—'

'Quick, I say!'

Mr Scribster cantered towards Mr Allison's phaeton, now halted to admit conversation with a gentleman on a horse, who seemed to be addressing the young ladies rather more than Allison himself. As he got closer, he recognised Peter Fairchild, a gentleman of about forty years who had begun to visit town again after the death, two years ago, of his young wife. He was a serious, not to say dull man, but eligible. As he joined the carriage at the other side, Fairchild acknowledged him with, 'Scribster — is that you?'

Mr Scribster frowned a little and just touched his new, low-crowned beaver hat, 'Fairchild.'

'What a very handsome hat, Mr Scribster!' said Serena, looking relieved. 'How well it suits you.'

'Thank you,' he said colourlessly, then caught Honoria's eye. She looked amused and he cocked an eyebrow at her, his expression still bland.

'Are you in town long, Miss Fenton?' said Mr Fairchild, and Honoria turned to answer.

'I am not all sure, Mr Fairchild. A week or two at least, I believe.' She blushed and looked to Allison at this, realising that it was at his invitation.

He nodded, 'The family are residing with me for the moment.'

'Oh,' said Mr Fairchild suspiciously, 'and may I call on you there?' he was looking at Allison as he said this, eager to see how he took this.

But it was Lady Sumner, who had been looking, in a lack-lustre fashion, in the opposite direction to Fairchild's person, who answered. 'You may not sir. You may have heard that Mr Benedict Fenton was wounded, and the young ladies attend him. We are just taking the air at present and will not detain your ride further.'

Mr Fairchild, dismissed, bowed stiffly and rode on.

There was silence, then Serena giggled, 'Well done, Genevieve. What a tedious conservation.'

'You mean, Miss Serena, what a consummate bore. We are grateful for Lady Sumner's dispatch of him,' laughed Mr. Allison.

'Was I rude?' asked Genevieve with little guilt noticeable, 'I'm sorry. Only, we can't have a pack of fools come to call and fawn over our beauties whilst Dickie is so ill. They would expect tea and polite conversation.'

Allison laughed. 'I expect Blake could have dealt with them before it got to that stage.'

'Oh, yes! I'm so sorry. My wretched tongue says what it will. It's only that if Honoria's admirers find out there is another equally pretty sister we shall have the dregs of London visiting us.' She was still sharp and quick, and Mr Scribster wondered anew at her devotion to Benedict, which was rather more than neighbourly in tone.

Allison had begun to move the phaeton ahead on the broad path and Prescott adjusted the rug that covered the young ladies legs, with particular attention to Honoria, who smiled shyly at him. She rated her charms less than her vivacious and equally beautiful sister, he knew. But Serena's sardonic eye could ward off the boring (like Fairchild) or less brilliant, who would feel her judgement, since she did not seek to hide it. Honoria's quiet kindness, on the other hand, would attract the world since she would be slow to judge and even slower to give offence. Prescott, he saw already, was feeling Honoria's warmth and charm and drawn to it, even though Scribster knew he was disposed to marry money. But weighing money against the dark velvet of Honoria's shyly admiring eyes was a battle that money might lose. A limited income and a warm armful of Honoria might be just the bargain the Lieutenant might make. If Prescott knew for sure of Allison's intentions, he might back away, but he did not.

Another rider, never usually seen in the park at this hour, was bowling towards them on a handsome bay, 'Uncle Wilbert!' said Serena. 'The last time he visited, he described that bay to me, with the blaze over his nose.'

And so indeed it proved.

With a sigh, Allison slowed down again to greet the new arrival.

With a deft series of bows to the gentlemen and ladies, Mr Wilbert Fenton, whose blue riding habit was of the first stare, made his object known. He wondered if Lady Sumner would walk in the grounds with him, as he had a particular matter to discuss with her.

Genevieve was rather more than surprised. Mr Wilbert Fenton was a very slight acquaintance of hers and even slighter of her husband. He could not be bearing a message from Frederick, she believed, because although both gamesters, they did not mix in the same set. This must be about Benedict's trouble. With unwomanly haste, Genevieve jumped from the phaeton and went to the head of the handsome bay whilst Sir Wilbert got down from the horse with more facility than one would expect of his portly figure.

'Let us *all* take a walk,' said Mr Allison, conscious that a stroll with a married lady and an old *roué* like Fenton could excite unfavourable opinion, despite the age gap. 'Belcher,' he said to his groom, 'tie up Mr Fenton's bay and Mr Scribster's grey and then take the reins.' Belcher jumped down from the back bar and hastened to do so.

It had been a very informative walk. Mr Scribster would have been mightily amused had he been looking from the outside, rather than as now, fully involved. Instead he felt as though his innards had been ripped out and ground beneath the feet of careless, unaware friends. He watched as Rowley attempted to walk with Honoria and avoid her sister, in which he was fouled by the Lieutenant, who somehow managed to insert himself between his cousin and Honoria.

Honoria looked at him sometimes, when she could do so without turning her head so much that it was noticeable and she exchanged one of the blank stares that echoed his own, but which seemed to convey so much. Her gaze flickered to his hat and he saw approval, he opened his eyes a little as the Lieutenant claimed her attention on the feeble excuse of showing her a perfect bloom. She blushed, and her stare now chastised him not to tease, but so much in the manner of a friend than a rival suitor, that the knife entered again. His expression must have changed somewhat, for she looked concerned for a moment.

He looked at Prescott and wondered if the gallant was in any way good enough for her. He would be a kind and attentive husband. But such a fool that she must surely come to notice it, maybe only when he failed to provide for their third child and they are walking the streets in penury. Until then, his wonderfully good manners and handsome visage would save him.

When Rowley got her on his own at last, Scribster had a ridiculous inability to foresee anything but roses and champagne in Honoria's future. He was a truly good man, his friend. And once Honoria gave up being terrified of him, he could not but enjoy the kindness, the warmth and the humour that characterised her. He would be an honourable and eventually, a loving husband. If only her star of a sister did not visit too often. But even that would fade in time, especially once Serena herself married.

Oh, for goodness sake, why could Rowley not just offer for the sister he wanted? Honoria would recover from the humiliation, he could see to that. He would be her friend and such a friend that when he could spring his other hopes on her (in perhaps two or three years) she might just be brought to think of him in that way.

None of the party showed any disposition to wonder at the two who walked ahead, in sight, but out of earshot. They were too busy caught in their own drama.

Chapter 17

Mr Wilbert Fenton Makes Plans

Wilbert laid Lady Sumner's hand on his supporting arm in the manner of her grandfather. She barely noticed, so concentrated on his words was she.

He was doing the polite, asking pardon for disturbing her outing, inquiring after her father and her husband.

'My husband is out of town, I believe. But never mind that! You wish to talk to me of Benedict.'

'In a sense, yes. But first of all, of your husband.'

'What of him? What has he to do with this?'

'We do not know each other, my lady.'

'Not well, no.'

'My nephew is, I believe, a childhood friend of yours.'

'Say what you wish to say to me. Ask what you wish to ask of me.'

'Benedict wanted some information from me. Information concerning your husband.' She had stopped now and grasped his arm, her eyes wild on his. He looked back at her, open. 'And like a fool, I gave it to him.'

He drew her forward, conscious that the party behind were gaining on him. 'What information?'

'I did not ask myself the question, you see. Why did he want such information? I did guess what he wished to do with it, but I—'

'What information?' she asked again, stopping. Sir Wilbert bowed slightly at an acquaintance who was passing in the opposite direction and he muttered at her, 'Keep walking, madam, unless you want to excite comment.'

Genevieve, almost beside herself since Benedict's attack, said passionately, under her breath. 'I do not care,' but she moved nevertheless.

'I must ask you first. Do you have need of money? Did you confess as much to Benedict?'

'I didn't.' But then she searched her memory and was confused. 'Perhaps, but that was not the subject of— is this about *money*? Please tell me what Benedict wanted from you.'

He looked at her, her figure that of a whippet rather than a lady, her hair caught up roughly beneath her bonnet, a veritable nest for the nearest starlings, her long nose and cheeks flushed unbecomingly, her eyes mad with a passionate desire to know more. The eyes and the passion made Wilbert Fenton understand a little of what it was that Benedict saw in her. A woman with more life in her than many fashionable matrons.

'If I tell you what Benedict wished to know, will you give me the other piece of the puzzle? Will you tell me what occurred between you?'

She flushed anew. 'You may be assured that it was not any of your first thoughts. My appearance might assure you of that.'

Many complimentary words flew to Mr Wilbert Fenton's practised mouth, but under Lady Sumner's raw gaze he could not voice them.

'He knew of a misfortune that I had, that had just occurred, and I think he wished to aid me, I told them there was nothing he could do. But he is the most redoubtable boy. He always wished to aid wounded creatures.'

'I imagine that marriage to such as your husband has made a wounded creature out of you.' He said this lightly, referring to the best known of Sumner's vices, his gambling and whoring, but she froze, holding one hand to her throat. And another thought occurred. 'Ah, I see. Literally, not only figuratively, wounded.' She dropped the hand to her stomach and he saw even more. 'Does Sumner know?' he said, gesturing to the protective hand.

She tilted her chin. 'No! No-one.'

Wilbert Fenton sighed. 'I wish that I had never gotten involved. But it is useless to repine. I was careless with Dickie, I little thought what it would lead to, nor cared, I suppose. But the attack has made a difference.'

'What information did you give to Dickie?' she asked simply.

'I found out which card sharks had won the most part of your husband's fortune.'

'To what end?'

'To win it back, the way they won it from your fool of a husband.'

Genevieve did not even try to protest. She was too weary. 'Cheating? It would be beneath Benedict.'

'But yet—'

'What are the names? Is it one of them who sought to rob and kill Benedict? All my fault!'

He grasped the slender hand on his arm with his other hand. 'Mine too. I cannot give you the names. But rest assured, if one of them is culpable, they will pay.'

Genevieve saw the energy and power in this rather overdressed, stout gentleman.

'I do not know what to do. Give me something to do.'

'Help tend to Benedict. I will let you know if there is any more to do than that.'

Her Ladyship stopped still. In the distance, she saw a familiar figure, walking with another gentleman and unaware of the group approaching.

'It's Sumner! Please Mr Fenton, get me out of here.'

With admirable alacrity, Benedict's uncle turned down a small path at a right angle to them and disappeared with Lady Sumner on his arm. He emerged back onto the original path in a trice and approached the walking party quickly, but alone, taking Mr Allison aside.

'Pray don't ask me why, my boy, but take the party back to the carriage and I will meet you at the gate to the right with Lady Sumner.'

Something in the older man's eyes brought Allison to heel and he bowed, then turned and herded his passengers back to the carriage, lifting Honoria in. He was not surprised when Serena seated herself, though the perch was high.

Before his lordship, all unawares, was upon them, he had bowled around to the gate and picked up her ladyship and was on the way to Grosvenor Square, only half a mile away.

Genevieve thought and thought, wringing her hands. Cheating at cards. Benedict? And Sumner so sure that he was a man about town, up to every fig and fancy. But just as with the stud farm he had been duped by those seeking to profit from him, The fool! And he is my husband before God, so what does that make *me?*

Unconsciously she touched her stomach again.

She had left her husband when he had tried to choke the life out of her on account of her wretched tongue. It was capable of staying shut, but incapable of falsehood if she was asked a question. As Sumner had fallen into her bedchamber and onto her bed, still dressed in the evening clothes that reeked of gin and cheap perfume, he had said, after forcing a kiss upon her, 'Here to do the husband's duty my dear,' he was wrestling her and she was about to tell him that she was with child, that there was no need, when he said, 'You despise me, don't you Madame Prude?'

'Yes,' her stupid tongue answered and then he had tried to choke the life from her. It was not the first attack. He had thrown her across the room once and she had split an eye on a grate — which thankfully required her to keep to her room for a week. Most other times were bruises that could not be seen, some hidden by gloves or long sleeves, most by her gowns themselves. His predilection was a fist in the stomach or a kick on her back when she was down. This time though, her knee had come up of its own volition and he had rolled over, groaning, and cursing in words she had never before heard, then fallen into a drunken sleep. Genevieve had risen, and summoned her maid to pack and a drowsy footman to hire a postchaise for the earliest hour of the morning, well before Sumner could have the ability to rise. When she was packed and dressed and about to await daybreak in the green drawing room downstairs she had looked back at him. His clothes half-off, his slack jaw drooling, fouling the snowy pillow, his face grey and dissipated, and she tried to see any trace of the unremarkable but affable young man that she had wed. She could not. His every line repulsed her now and she was his for life. She must bear it, but for the moment she could not risk that he choke her once more, for he would choke the life from his baby as he did so.

She had gone home to Ottershaw, though she'd had no notion what to do next.

Now was the next. Why had Benedict won back money? What did he plan to do with it? Was he turning into another gamester like Sumner? Or worse than that — a cheat? But Genevieve knew better than that. Benedict had a plan to help her, she was sure. She was furious with him and herself. How could she have let him guess? She knew who he was — he would never let it go. So she must save herself. It was risky, and especially with Sumner in town. Why had he come?

Allison felt fate against him. He had tried to do the decent thing, to propose, and he had been thwarted once more. He ignored the relief that flooded his system and concentrated on his disappointment. Honoria's pertness this morning (which she had not seemed to be conscious of — as if she had her attention elsewhere) had intrigued him, and brought him to believe that if he married her he would not be reduced to staring at a beautiful statue every day of his life. On the other hand, he was no longer so sure that she would consent. That this idea also brought relief he ignored. He had noticed Prescott's interest on her — could have intervened at any time to let him know of his intentions — Darnley was honourable and would have punctiliously withdrawn — but he had not. Perhaps he hoped his cousin might be brought to the point. But the parents would naturally wish their daughter to take her place in the world, not trail around it in the wake of an impecunious husband.

But Honoria's underwhelmed reaction to his attempt at paying his addresses meant something. It would not give her pain if he asked for her sister's hand, and surely, after some explanation on his part, the parents would be brought to understand. But this all depended on Serena's feelings for him. If they were any more than brotherly, he had yet to discover it. And she had met so few men. Was it kind in him to attempt to secure her before even her first season? Her sister had been last season's beauty. Serena would be next season's sensation. A beautiful, vivacious girl, full of intelligence and charm would have every eligible man in London at her blue slippered feet, however limited her portion. Part of him would like to see her conquer all in her first season, but that wasn't a big part. Rowley Allison, he thought to himself, since when have you feared a rival for any woman? Strangely enough, it was Serena's teasing smiles and comfortable intimacy with him that sounded a death knell to his hopes. She had no consciousness of him as a suitor. She did not think of him in that light.

The only rational place for him now was in Bedlam.

The sickbed of Benedict Fenton was a welcome diversion, he thought. The parents were focused on their son and no longer wondering why he had not spoken to Honoria. The sisters, too, were at their most lovely and selfless in tending for him.

Meanwhile, his friend Gus had changed his appearance, if not his demeanour, his cousin was to all intents and purposes wooing his prospective bride and Genevieve Sumner knew something about the attack on Benedict that the rest of them didn't. And why had she ducked her husband in the park? Was he assisting at an adulterous liaison between that beautiful young man and a married woman for whom the description 'plain' might have been invented. Surely not.

But he had no time to worry about his guests' affairs when his own were in such a sorry tangle.

It was all like a bad play at Vauxhall, with even the stock character of aging rogue played by Mr Wilbert Fenton. Allison laughed to himself. There seemed little else to do.

Honoria had seen the touch that Genevieve had given her stomach. It was the same as the touch she had seen her mother give countless times, a mother's protective touch for the child inside her. She castigated herself now, she had been so wrapped up in her own troubles that Genevieve's obvious stress had been pushed to the back of her head, accompanied by the rather unbecoming resentment that had judged Genevieve's upset at Benedict's attack. A horrible thought sped through her brain, only to be dismissed. She knew, from her mother's many months with child, that it was only really possible to know that one expected a baby after two or even three months. Benedict had been in London with her parents and herself, and for some of that time so had Lord and Lady Sumner, but she was sure she could not have seen Benedict alone. No, it was not a thought a young lady should think. But could Genevieve nevertheless be in love with Benedict? She seemed too much affected by his attack. But he had seen her but twice at Ottershaw. No, it did not add up. And then Honoria bethought herself of the lieutenant's left ear. Perhaps the heart could be affected very quickly indeed.

Did her uncle know something of all this? Why had he, who had spent so much time with Benedict lately, wished to speak to Lady Sumner? It was all too mysterious. But she bethought herself that while she would never discuss this with her parents (for telling tales on each other was something the elder Fenton siblings never would do) at least it *was* something that she could discuss with Serena. She so longed for their old relations, but the large secret she carried had put a wedge between them. But now, she thought, to share these thoughts with Serena would be a relief.

In letting down the steps of the carriage, Lieutenant Prescott took her hand and helped her alight at the house. He pressed her hand and said urgently, when she was detaching her short train from the carriage step, 'You are concerned about something Miss Fenton. Please be assured of my discretion if you should stand in need of a confidant.'

She blushed and stared at him, looking into his handsome face. How like him to notice her worry and seek to comfort her. He was so big and strong and handsome and she could see every advantage in laying her problems on his manly breast. But to be talking of her friend or her brother to him was quite impossible. She could only whisper, 'Thank you!'

Serena, waiting for her at the steps to the front door raised her eyebrows. 'What does the gallant lieutenant want with you, Honoria?'

They entered the house and after they had ensured that Benedict was as well as they could expect, she asked Serena to come to her room.

She poured her every fear and concern about Benedict and Genevieve into Serena's ears and Serena listened intently. She pooh-poohed Honoria's first thoughts about a liaison, and then she swiftly got up and found a footman to fetch Genevieve from Benedict's room immediately.

Honoria cried out, but Serena said bracingly, 'You know that there are too many secrets around at the moment. It is time to have it all out. I'm guessing at what can be stopping you from marrying quite the most magnificent man we are likely to encounter—'

'The lieutenant?'

'No— our host! How can you not see him, Honoria? He is just the man for you. He makes me laugh so much, he is quite the handsomest—' she stopped herself. 'Well, it is of no use if you have fallen for his cousin, but be warned. I think you might grow tired of him.'

'I have not at all. What on earth would make you think that anyone would grow tired of—' but she stopped herself, unable to continue, conscious of all she could not say.

'Have you heard him talk about horses?' asked Serena, 'The fellow's a fool.'

'Being a bad judge of horseflesh is hardly a—' she caught herself once more. 'Oh, stop it, Serena.'

But at this point, Serena, who had no intention of stopping the frankest conversation she had had with her sister in a month, was interrupted by the entrance of Lady Sumner.

'Genevieve!' said Serena swiftly, 'May we congratulate you? Orry says that she has seen the signs that you are increasing.' There was a ghastly pause as all colour drained from their friend's face, then she burst into tears.

Honoria shot Serena a hard look and bustled to lead her friend to a small settle and sat beside her, holding her hands. 'Pray do not say anything about this, I beg of you. My husband does not, as yet, know.'

Serena was not finished with plain speaking which had always been the way between them before Miss Horton's marriage. 'Why are you so upset about Benedict? You behave as though there is more between you than we know.'

Honoria was shocked. 'Serena!'

Genevieve blinked. 'You think—?' she gave a peal of laughter that made the sisters' shoulders fall a little. 'I love Benedict as I love you all, but it is not *that*. It is that I feel so responsible for his injuries.' She looked from one to the other of the sisters, 'I believe it happened because Benedict felt he was on some — some business of mine.'

'What business?' continued Serena, now seated beside Honoria. But her voice was softer, moved by Genevieve's evident distress.

'I cannot tell you.

'Genevieve, enough of these secrets!'

'Your uncle has the matter in hand. That is all I can say.'

Honoria, reassured on her worst fear, was sympathetic to Genevieve's discretion. 'We shall not press you, Genevieve, but remember that we are here to help you.'

Genevieve frowned. 'No one can help me. Look at what has happened to Benedict when he tried.'

Mr Wilbert Fenton had topped the morning off by a visit to Lady Overton.

She was charmingly déshabillé in the fashion of the last century, when grand married ladies, dressed in only their commodious slips and a robe, allowed their beaux to visit their boudoir in order to watch them dress. Mr Fenton thought it a tempting reminder of his youth, as was Countess Overton herself. She moved to lounge on a silken daybed accepting her chocolate cup from her maid. She held out one hand and Mr Fenton bent low and kissed it reverently. During this process she had allowed a pale shoulder to escape her slip and Mr Fenton said with more genuine feeling than he had anticipated, 'Countess, what a truly enticing woman you are.'

'Wilbert Fenton, what on earth are you doing loose upon the world at this hour?' He raised his eyes significantly to her maid. The countess waved her away and she left with a repressing look at Mr Fenton.

'What a dragon!' Mr Fenton remarked.

'She protects the proprieties. She does not often leave me alone with a man in my boudoir.' Her ladyship smiled, 'Or at all.' She smiled, sipping her chocolate. 'Despite my reputation as a shocking spendthrift and keeper of a gaming house, I believe my honour is still intact. What brings you to my boudoir at this unearthly hour, Wilbert?'

'I came here to make you a proposition, my lady, but now that I am in your presence, it becomes more of a heartfelt plea. You look quite beautiful today, my dear Aurora.'

'And you are looking at me as you did twenty years ago.' He got up and she held up a palm. 'Do not approach me, I believe you are no more to be trusted than you used to be.'

'In Vauxhall Gardens, along that quiet path — and you so lovely in that silver gown, who could blame me?'

'I gave you a sharp shock!'

'But only after you let me steal that kiss. What happy memories.'

The countess looked at him fondly. 'What is it, Wilbert?'

'I have come to ask for your hand in marriage.'

She laughed so hard that she almost spilled her chocolate. 'You ridiculous creature! And you without a feather to fly with, I'll be bound.'

'You'd be right,' said Mr Fenton, crossing his legs negligently, 'but I could be of genuine help in running your little establishment.' He sipped his own chocolate, 'Indeed, I suppose it is the only thing I am qualified to do.'

'I have no urgent need of any help,' she said, regarding Mr Fenton speculatively, 'that I know of.'

'Your establishment is getting a bit of a reputation, you know. For card sharks who prey on the innocent.'

'Whenever I learn of such persons, I refuse to admit them again.'

'But that is only after the damage is done. I could spot them long before that.'

Her ladyship sat up with energy. 'If you did this, you would be like me, Wilbert. Admitted to only half of the polite world's homes. Shunned by others. Even the regent will fail you.'

'I believe I can make do.'

'You would have no objection to being a kept man?' He raised his brows. 'I have a different proposition for you, if you mean it.'

Mr Fenton frowned.

'I would accept your offer of marriage, but close the gaming club.'

He was stunned.

'And you would have to give up gaming, as would I. It is what destroyed me in the first place and after two years of this place, I have had my fill. But it is in your blood, Wilbert, and I cannot marry another gamester.'

Mr Fenton surprised her by saying, 'I have had my fill for some time, but it has rather become a habit. But what could we live on?'

'In the past two years the Faro Bank has made one hundred thousand pounds.'

There was a stunned silence. 'Then why, my dear, would you consent to marry this old reprobate?'

'We are old friends, are we not? And however much of a devil you are, Wilbert Fenton, you are admitted everywhere. You are my ticket back to respectability. To my old life. Almacks! Balls!'

He thought about it. He believed she was right. His connections and her money would admit them to every but the most stuffy of the haunts of the polite world. He thought with relish of how they would cause talk, but it would die away. There had been no scandal of the risqué kind about Lady Overton. His fellows would rake him over the coals about becoming leg-shackled at his age, but he would not be blackballed. Of course his nights of dissipation with Prinny would lessen, but to tell the truth they had palled in any case. Marriage would supply the perfect excuse to lessen his duties there. He walked over to her and pulled her to her feet and into his arms, kissing her neck and shoulder as he had twenty years ago.

She giggled and then made quite another sound. 'My dear, remember this is only a marriage of convenience!'

'So I thought, my dear Aurora,' said Mr Fenton, suavely, 'but it seems to me that it might become quite another kind of marriage.'

Sometime later, with her head on Mr Fenton's chest, both sitting on her daybed, Lady Overton murmured, 'There have been many men who attempted to flirt with me, you know.'

'I have seen, but you always carried it off with magnificent detachment my dear.'

'Thank you. But it was not always pleasant.' He squeezed her lovely shoulders with his comforting arm, feeling suddenly protective. She sighed and then said playfully, 'But Wilbert, I should let you know that I intend to put you on a reducing diet. It is not healthy for you to be so portly my dear, no matter how well you carry it off.'

'Losing my girth might be much easier than you imagine, my love,' said Mr Fenton.

Her ladyship raised her face, and he kissed her once more. He found that he was much more satisfied with his bargain than he could have guessed.

Chapter 18

Genevieve Talks to Benedict

Genevieve, Lady Sumner's, excess of emotion relating to Benedict's injuries had of course been noted and cogitated upon by Lady Fenton. She was nearly sure that there was nothing scandalous at its root, but nevertheless, she took pains to ensure that Genevieve never nursed Benedict alone. In his moments of consciousness, he'd looked pleased to see Genevieve, and had muttered a word that she could not quite catch, and once, when she and Serena were in attendance, he had asked for her by name. But this morning she left Honoria with Benedict whilst she took the air in a carriage and did a little shopping for things that could make the invalid a little more comfortable. Some lavender pastilles to burn, some of *Doctor Elcott's Elixir*, which had worked so well as a tonic when Benedict was a boy, and some softer flannel to bathe his head (which she would strive to keep Mrs Hunter from seeing, since the housekeeper would no doubt be affronted).

That morning, though, Benedict awoke much better than before. He wanted to sit up and it was no use Honoria adjuring him to stay still, he struggled until a footman took his other arm and lifted him to seated position. Genevieve, seldom far, came in and arranged the pillows at his back to add to his comfort.

'Thank you.' After his struggle, he closed his eyes, woozier than he would admit to. He opened them to two pairs of anxious eyes looking down at him, whilst the footman left. 'I am quite well. Don't send for the vicar just yet.' The two girls looked at each other and laughed. 'I take it I'm in Mr. Allison's house — I think I've seen him once or twice when I woke up.'

'Yes. Oh Dickie, you have no notion how good it is to see you awake. Your head was broken by those dreadful ruffians. I am sure Mama feared you may awake an imbecile, but I see you are no more imbecilic than before.' Benedict laughed and winced simultaneously. Honoria sat on his bed and grasped his hand. He groaned. 'Do you remember any of it?'

'Lord yes! There was a man with a cudgel. I think he meant to finish me, but they only hurt my head. It's a hard thing to break. One of them I cut in the stomach with a bottle I managed to smash on a wall. The other snuck up behind me and delivered the last of it. He had shiny boots,' he added, his gaze distant, 'I saw them as I fell.' He shook the memory off. 'Not just a regular ruffian.'

Genevieve spoke 'Do you know why, Dickie?'

Benedict turned to his sister, as if he had not heard. 'Orry, I'm hungry,' he held his hand up to stop her interrupting. 'Do you think you might make some of Mama's posset for me?'

'Of course, but you don't like—'

'I have a need for it.'

Honoria bent and kissed him lightly and melted away towards the kitchen.

'I have your money,' he said to Genevieve.

'*What* did you do, you silly boy?'

'I just won back your inheritance.'

'Then that belongs to my husband.'

Benedict jerked, causing his ribs to tear into his inner organs and a wave of pain to erupt. 'It does not. It belongs to you and no one else. You will put me in a terrible fix if you—' he coughed and moaned in pain once more.

Genevieve sat on the bed beside him and echoed his sister in grasping his hand. 'I promise not to let him know. But Dickie, did you really think money would solve my problem?'

He closed his eyes. 'I wanted to go and shake an apology from the brute. But you were right. Hurting Sumner would have made me feel better, but would have rebounded on you.'

'I wish I'd never let you guess — this is all my fault.'

'Then I thought of my Aunt Millicent. And yes, I did think money was the thing.'

'Your aunt, Lady Millicent?'

'She is married, but lives separated from her husband in a way that the world accepts. Because she is rich.'

'And the daughter of an earl. She is allowed to be eccentric.'

'I had to do *something*, Jenny. If it was Honoria or Serena, I know my father would have done something, whatever he says about the sanctity of marriage. Your father is not such a man. But you do have a *brother*, Jenny. That is what I have always been to you.' She hung her head, too moved to speak, not wishing him to see the hot tears that sprang so easily to her eyes since he had been lifted from the filthy back alley where he had been found. 'No point in winning it from Sumner — he doesn't have it anymore,' continued Benedict. 'So I cheated the cheats. It turns out that I have a talent for it, so says my uncle. Most of the money is at Carstairs'. The last lot—'

'They didn't get it. It was still wrapped around your waist when you were discovered by the watch.'

'Then there is close to 10,000 guineas all told. For you to get away, Jenny. Europe is safer these days. You could live anywhere. If you are afraid, I'll come with you to see you settled.'

She could only imagine the scandal — what it would do to him. 'Can you imagine me in Europe? I hardly knew how to bear London. I'm a country girl.'

She could tell that Benedict was a little hurt. 'There is a deal of countryside in Europe, so I hear.'

She was frowning. Something was taking shape in her head. 'I'm sorry, Dickie. You are such an idiot you know, to risk yourself like that.' She rifled his hair as she'd used to. 'Thank you for caring — and if I can pull it off, I might, just might, be able to solve this problem.' She smiled at him and he looked relieved.

'I thought you might not take the money. Indeed, how to make you take it is all I've been thinking of for weeks before Shiny Boots attacked me.'

'I will take it — on the condition that you reserve £500 to buy your coronet.'

'Second lieutenant in the Hussars! But I cannot—'

'I'm afraid you must, if you want me to take it.'

'But I have it by cheating — I cannot start my career with dirty money!'

'And yet you wish me to.'

'That's different. I was returning your money to you when it was as good as stolen from your fool of a husband.'

'Do not speak so, Benedict. I cannot hear that from you.'

'I am sorry, Jenny. But you must see that it is different to give the money to you than to spend it on myself.'

'Oh, this is one of those strange rules of gentlemen that I do not understand. How is this then, if I can achieve my own plan, I will accept all 10,000 guineas. Other than that I will take nothing. If my plan works, however, after receiving the money I will make a gift — or a loan if you prefer — to my *brother* to buy himself a coronet and go and make mischief for King and Country rather than getting into scrapes here.'

'If your plan does not work?'

'Then all the money you have won will be better in a charitable trust for impoverished gentlemen cheated at cards or some such thing, for I will not take a penny of it. Hiding in Europe is not for me. I will have to lie in the bed of my own making.'

By the vengeful look in Benedict's eye, Genevieve guessed that her young protector had mentally reverted to his first plan, of shaking Sumner till his teeth rattled. Somehow she knew that Benedict would not come second to her husband, whom she realised she had begun to see as much more omnipotent than was real. He shrunk in the fire of Benedict's eyes. But that confrontation must not occur. Her plan must work for his sake too. At the very least, a scandal that dear Lady Fenton would not appreciate could be avoided.

Honoria came back with the posset and both ladies looked on as he scrunched his nose in displeasure, but ate it, duty-bound. Despite herself, Genevieve laughed. Benedict threw his damask napkin at her.

Chapter 19

Confiding

Mr Wilbert Fenton's valet had been up betimes to visit 32, Ludgate Hill, the well-known address of Rundell and Bridge, Jewellers, carrying a very large sapphire cravat pin (won at play from the Prince Regent himself) and a fine emerald ring that had once belonged to his father, but which was completely out of fashion at present. Mr Fenton often thought he had been born in the wrong age. He rather liked the fashions of his father's times, when gentlemen were expected to dress in silken brocade and show their handsome legs in white stockings and high-heeled shoes with silver buckles. But every age has its horrors. The wigs, hot and sticky and requiring one's head to be shaved — and the sparsity of well-washed linen, would not have suited the modern man of 1814. But he would be an antidote now if he wore his father's ring, however handsome it appeared on his hand, so to have it made into a ring for his intended was something he could surprise her with. The money from the cravat pin would frank him and his household comfortably until the marriage took place.

When Pierre returned, he handed his master the sheaf of bills he had received at the jeweller's, and a note that had been left on the hall table by a footman who knew better than to disturb his master at *l'heure de la toilette*.

Benedict awake, said Lady Sumner's note without preamble, *He has remarked on two things about his attack. One, he wounded one of them in the stomach with a broken bottle, and second, the man who felled him with the cudgel, the cur who had sneaked up behind him, had the high-polished boots of a gentleman. Lady S.*

Interesting. Which of the heads that Benedict had shaved recently would have been foolhardy enough, or enraged enough, to act personally. It seemed a trifle outlandish when there were villains enough (and more) in London to employ in such things. Any ale house in the wrong part of town would supply them, he believed. Someone so enraged or so coldly vengeful that he wished to see the assault on his prey, or even to offer violence himself. Did he mean murder? At least he had not taken care to avoid it. A cudgel to the head hardly leaves the victim in a chatty mood. He had wanted harm more than money, which he may have believed Benedict carried with him still. Or hoped, at least. For the chance of hunting through Lord Carstairs' rooms was far too dangerous. There was an army of staff who attended the rooms of the various young gentlemen who lived there, it would be more difficult to penetrate than one of the stylish houses in Grosvenor Square. No, attacking Benedict was the only hope to recover any money, but the vicious use of the cudgels talked of revenge.

It amused him that the fate of Benedict should be the sting to his sleeping conscience. His father, had repaid the indiscretions of Wilbert's youth by leaving not only the entailed property to Ranalph, but every other property and penny as well. The will left him only his father's ring, with a coarse adjuration not to exceed the pawnshop's term before he retrieved it. Apart from that, Wilbert had a monthly pittance that his mother had left him (which may have allowed him to live in a country cottage, keeping goats or some such thing) and his sense of injustice had put his conscience to sleep for the next twenty-five years. He went to the devil, secretly grateful for his brother's allowance to him, but the old ill-usage at his father's judgment and his falling in, at an early age, with the Prince Regent and his friends, had allowed him to continue a ruinous path. He lived with the knowledge that Ranalph would have to say no sometime, and he had been secretly resigned. When his brother helped him out again and again, Wilbert chose to suppose that though he had a growing brood of children (of whom Wilbert was surprisingly fond) the estate must be richer than might be supposed. And of course there was the occasional big win as his skills increased. But he had lived this life long after the attraction of it had palled, long after his youthful rebellion had passed. But he was lazy and selfish and continued on his comfortable but self-disparaging way, his soul eaten away by a hidden guilt.

Until Benedict had been left for dead in a dark alley, caused, in part, by Wilbert's inability to act in any but his own selfish interests.

It did not seem right that through this he was embarking on a new life, with a woman who had been his friend for a lifetime and who he now acknowledged might be the woman of his dreams. That under the arrangement he offered her he might find, at last, the love that his brother had had in his marriage. Shouldn't he have to pay? But giving up casual affairs with married women or light-skirts, or the same card parties with his cronies, didn't seem to give up much. He'd thought too, that he might have to leave society as the patron of a gaming house, but that at least he could offer his countess the only real talent he had — a knowledge of gaming. But as it turned, he was forbidden even this slight sacrifice, for he was to be a kept man once more. Husband to a very rich woman. A pity he thought, raising an eyebrow, but he expected he could live with it.

But first he would find who was responsible for Benedict's injury, and God knew what he would then do. It might end up with a trip to Tyburn to be hanged. A just God might make him pay yet.

Serena was tending to her brother that night. Though servants and a nurse were on hand, the ladies: mother, sisters and friend, had decided between them that they would continue to tend him in shifts at night when he was at his most fretful and his fever was at its worst. Their familiar voices seemed to calm him, and as Papa was unable not to fall asleep in the chair, and Mr Allison, the lieutenant and Mr Scribster were nearly strangers, all offered aid from them was denied.

Benedict was having one of the nightmares that his fever caused and he turned and twisted in his sheets, trapping himself in the folds. Serena was trying to untie him when he grabbed her arm and said 'Jenny! He shall not strike you again!' Serena gasped, appalled, but she put her hand on his grasping hand and said mechanically, 'No. He shall not,' whilst a great many things clicked into place. Had this occurred on some business of Jenny's? She was not, then, in love — but guilty. Serena did not spend a second considering that it was Genevieve's fault

— she knew Benedict's protective instinct too well. But surely it could not be Sumner who had struck his wife? How could that be?

She mopped his brow and straightened his sheets by means of brute force and turned his pillow to assuage the fever. He calmed down, falling into a deeper sleep, whilst Serena thought and thought, twisting her hands together as she did so.

Mama came to relieve her at 4 am, and was so sleepy herself that her usually alert response to her children's emotions escaped her and Serena was permitted to depart before she had to answer questions that she had no answer to. As she slipped out into the hall she heard the click of a ball against another and through an open door saw Mr Allison playing billiards by the light of two candelabra. She moved towards the stairs, but her host had heard her and called her name. 'Miss Serena!'

She paused and turned to him, aware that her face might betray her. Veiling her emotions was not her most strong talent, as Mama often reminded her.

'I do not wish to delay you from your bed, but only tell me how the patient is.'

He was near her now and with a terrible understanding, she wanted to throw herself on his chest and divest herself of all her worries. But he was not yet her brother and of course, she could not.

'He is better, but still restless, I'm afraid.'

He held out his hand to her unconsciously and in the same manner she took it. 'You are more worried than that description suggests. You had better tell me before you worry yourself to death. I expect that once you have said it, you can put it from you.'

She smiled at him. 'I don't think it is my right to speak of it. I believe Benedict said something in his fever that he would not wish me to know.'

'Yet you worry. Is it to do with his attack? Are you still afraid for him?'

'No, it is just that I think Benedict might have been acting for someone and his behaviour recently might be explained if I could just put the pieces together. And perhaps it is related to his attack.'

'Come with me into the green salon, sit just a little, you are too overborne to sleep right now. Tell me what you feel able to.'

What on earth, thought Serena, made Honoria afraid of this kind and charming man. Her hand trembled in his and he dropped it at once, but they moved together easily to the room.

Serena frowned. 'You do not know my brother Benedict well. But apart from his annoyingly teasing disposition and his recent fascination with Mr Brummel's manners, he is the bravest person I know. Whenever an animal or a person is in danger, he throws himself into the fray to save them. He cannot help it. And I think he learned something about a friend in danger and of course, he has just thrown himself into it. With no heed at all for his own safety. But I cannot quite understand — or indeed believe — what he said to me tonight. I might be all out in my understanding,' she looked into his eyes anxiously. 'Indeed, I think I *must* be.'

'I fancy your uncle knows something of it.'

'Oh, yes, yes. Uncle Wilbert! I must visit him tomorrow.'

'Might you let me speak on your behalf? I believe you must get your rest and your uncle might speak more freely to a gentleman. Even me, if I am able to say I ask on your behalf.'

'And you, Mr Allison? Will you find out what he says and then keep it from me merely because I am a lady? I would rather talk myself.' Her eyes sparkled and he was glad to see it, it drove the worry from them.

'I promise you that I will tell you exactly what I find out, Miss Fenton, if you will let me serve you thus.'

'I think you might.' She looked at him with her head tilted, considering. 'And will you tell me his exact words?'

'Absolutely not.' She gasped. 'Your uncle has a choice turn of phrase at times, not at all suitable for young ladies. But I will tell you his meaning.'

She laughed and rose, holding her hand out once more. 'Thank you. You will make the most wonderful brother, I think.'

He flushed and a moment later she did too. 'Please forgive me and forget my stupid tongue. I just mean that you are behaving as my brother might- oh, I'm going to bed now. So sorry.' She dropped his hand and ran from the room.

Lady Cynthia left Benedict's room to fetch her work from the salon, only to see Serena dash from it, and to see, through the open door, such a stricken look on Mr Allison's face that she decided to retreat. She moved back to Benedict's room, closing the door softly. Her son slept peacefully. But it was quite clear that she needed to pay more attention to her daughters. She had been uneasily aware for some time that this visit was going slightly astray, even forgetting the attack on Benedict. Some odd moments between the young people, some behaviours that she had seen unconsciously, and yet been too preoccupied to pursue, now gave her pause. She usually prided herself on understanding her children, on seeing what they might not wish to betray. Everything from Edward taking the blame for the cricket ball that had destroyed the library window to protect his younger brother, to thirteen-year-old Honoria's *tendre* or infatuation for the handsome new curate (thankfully only a visiting clergyman) — a mother knew all. She was on the alert now. She would watch and wait.

CHAPTER 20

Lady Cynthia Departs

Lady Cynthia's plans for keeping a regard on her girls was overturned when she arose from her few hours' sleep the next day. She nibbled a breakfast roll because she must, as an example to her daughters and Genevieve, all of whom seemed to have lost their appetites to the uncertain hours of nursing Benedict. She was adjuring them to do likewise, when a letter in the very precise hand of Nurse, of Fenton Manor, was handed to her.

'What next is the emergency?' said Sir Ranalph cheerfully. 'Does she think Angelica a servant of Satan because she hid her tatting?' He stopped because a line had crossed his wife's lovely forehead.

'Measles!' said her ladyship, 'They all have them!'

'Oh!' cried Genevieve.

'Good-oh,' said her husband, 'Get 'em over with.' But he grasped her hand comfortingly, for everyone from the Yorkshire set remembered the death of Genevieve's baby sister ten years ago, of the same disease.

Honoria held Genevieve's hand below the table. Scribster and Allison exchanged a look.

'They are in good hands, surely, Ma'am?' said Mr Allison.

'Oh the best,' said her ladyship, 'but I must go. When little Cedric is particularly ill he wants his mama, I am certain.' She rose and said what was necessary to her host, going quickly from the room, followed by her husband.

Once in their bedchamber she said, 'Benedict is better now, the fever almost broke. I am right to leave, my love, am I not?'

He grasped her hands and sat her down. 'Benedict is as strong as a horse. I must own I was worried, but now he speaks quite sensibly at times. He has received no lasting injury I am sure.'

She smiled and summoned her maid, making busy with her packing and issuing orders at the same time.

Everyone else must remain here until Benedict was quite well. Sir Ranalph must remain to make the girls' stay respectable. He must order a chaise directly, she would make the journey in as few stages as possible.

'Should not one or other of the girls accompany you, my dear?'

'Oh, no, no. I think not.'

'I don't think that anyone is thinking of a match at this moment, my lady.'

'No, very likely not. But I do not need them and Benedict does.'

'Benedict has quite enough nurses, I believe. Never has a poor boy been so beset by women.'

His daughters chose this time to make their appearance.

'Oh no, Mama. Are you going alone?'

'Nonsense — a maid will accompany me and a coachman too.'

'May not I come Mama?' said Serena in a rather desperate voice. 'Please.'

'No, no.' Lady Cynthia regarded her closely, noticing the red rimmed eyes of exhaustion — or maybe something else. Would it be better to take her? All of this was so strange. But her girls could take no hurt with their father present. Well, nearly no hurt. Her head swum with the glances that she had seen and had not had the energy to consider. Glances between the young people and behind their backs. She could make no sense of it now, she ached to get to Cedric and the others, but some instinct told her that a stew was boiling on the pot and it would be best not to stir it till it thickened. When her head failed her, a mother always relied on her heart.

She shooed the girls away and left instructions with her husband that troubled his integrity greatly. Men never understood when a little manipulation was necessary.

When she had kissed her secretive daughters goodbye, was dressed warmly (for it was a wet summer day) and tucked into the carriage seat, she took a small silver notebook and pencil from her reticule and strove to make sense of everything she had seen that did not fit into the original plan for the visit to Mr Allison.

A. Stiff and formal with H. Or overly attentive. Or as distant from her in a room as he could be. Easy with all of us. Fought with Serena? (her dreadful tongue at fault?)

H. &S not so often together as their wont. (a spat? — so unlike them) H. stiffly encouraging to A. (her shyness, her awareness of his intentions? R right. We should not have told her) Very friendly with the L. (a tendre? *I hope not — no money and very little sense)*

S. Friendly with the L. But obviously despises his intellect. Friendly with A. — but last night? Until recently — maybe the last three days, she was the making of the party.

G. Deeply affected by Benedict's attack. I hardly like to think why. But her regard pity? Guilt? Not romantic. I believe. But G. hard to read.

The L. Fond of both girls? Rather longer looks at H.

The Lieutenant was a fly in the ointment. How big a fly was yet to be decided. In all respects, Honoria should have been in love with Mr Allison who had shown himself to be truly kind as well as rich and handsome. And seeing Honoria care for her sick brother, seeing her character matching her beauty, should have sealed the deal before this. But in hoping Honoria would be more relaxed with Mr Allison, she realised that she had ignored this suave man of the world's stupid behaviour around her daughter. She became quite cross with him. It was beyond believable that he had reverted to a teenager, only able to behave clumsily before his beloved. But what had changed his mind, and *if* it had changed, why had he invited them all to stay in this absurd fashion?

Honour! She thought suddenly. Whenever a man behaves absurdly — like paying his gambling debts to a Duke who would hardly know the difference, rather than a tailor's bill which might very well bankrupt the poor tradesman — it was a tenet of the male honour code, so far from a woman's comprehension.

But what changed his mind? Her head ached and she had to stop and sleep before the fears for her little ones took over her whirling head. She would drive herself mad otherwise.

In all her cogitation, however, it never occurred to her that she had left one of the party completely out of her equations...

The gentleman about whom she had forgotten spent an unhappy morning trying to get Honoria on her own. It irked him to be part of this absurd imbroglio, rather than a spectator. He narrowly missed taking Honoria for a ride after her mother's departure, spiked by the dashing Lieutenant. 'Can I take you ladies out for your necessary breath of air? I have ordered the tilbury.' He knew, of course, that Serena was determined to sit with her brother this morning. She had said so earlier at breakfast, when she had, with great attention, avoided his friend's eye. Scribster had little to say to that now, he found his interest in his friend's problem decreased, but he was dashed if he was going to spend all morning awaiting Honoria in the hallway, or lurk around her bedroom in the hopes of a conversation. Apart from anything, if he became in any way obvious in his intentions, she would shy away. He was well aware that his sole charm for her was to be able to speak freely to one of no importance, and he hadn't fully worked out the winning lecture that would convince her to marry an ugly, unpleasant fellow with a moderate income. So when Allison put on his driving coat, he asked if he could accompany him on his errand.

His friend hesitated and then said, 'Best not Gus, I have a commission for a lady.'

How fetching lemons, or yet another cordial to try on Benedict was in any way secret escaped Scribster, but he merely nodded at his friend's offer to drop him at the club. He was sure he *would* lurk if left in Grosvenor Square alone. People in love, as he had often observed, but never understood till now, were unalterably stupid.

Honoria was his friend, the first true female friend he had had since his sister. Her beauty had shaken him when he had first seen her, but the beauty of many young women had shaken him and he maintained his *sang froid* — he merely switched his attention elsewhere. But corrupting Honoria's martyrdom had been so enjoyable that he had dropped his defences. They had crumbled when she was in his arms. If he were a better man he would wish her to have her desire — Prescott. A good man — but not someone who could be trusted to look after a dog long term, never mind a wife. He could see the fictional dog in his mind's eye — a little Jack Russell, white with a black eye and a wagging tail, approaching his empty food bowl. The brave Lieutenant would probably succumb to an excess of sensibility and cry at the sad fate of his poor doggie companion. But crying wouldn't feed him.

Most of Prescott's grandeur was provided 'on account' and his wife's must be the same. So he excused himself from wanting Honoria to make Darnley Prescott a better man. But he could find no such excuse to stop her picking his friend. He, too, was a good man, and when she got to know him (when Rowley finally abandoned his distant manner) she would be enchanted by him. She would be a great lady, she would have every elegance and amusement a female could desire and her own affectionate nature would ensure she would love him soon. Serena, the fly in the ointment, would come out next season and take the town by storm. She would marry well and Allison would forget her. So — encourage Honoria to wed Rowley, that is what a good man would do. Unfortunately, he had long recognised himself to be a very, very bad man.

Serena's face was usually an open book to Honoria, and however she tried to hide her feelings, there was too much intimacy between them for her sister not to guess at her pain. 'Serena, what is the matter?' asked Honoria as she fetched her shawl for the carriage ride with Lieutenant Prescott. 'My dear, please tell me.'

Serena was not sure of the exact nature of her troubles. But one portion she could pass to her sister. 'Benedict said something in his fever last night. But it concerns another, and I fear I must not divulge it. Oh, but Orry, I wish that I had gotten it wrong.'

'Does it concern the attack?'

'I fear so. But I cannot be sure. I have set Mr Allison to find out more from my uncle.'

'Mr. Allison?'

Serena blushed, 'Well, we have kept him from the sickroom, so he may as well be put to use, don't you think?' She saw Honoria still look concerned. 'You are still afraid of him? I can't see why. He found me last night after Benedict had spoken and I just — well more or less ordered him to talk to Uncle Wilbert.'

Honoria laughed. 'Oh, Serena — how like you! I am not quite easy with Mr Allison yet, but I am not afraid of him. He has been so kind to us all.'

'Yes,' said Serena bleakly.

'Is there anything else, dear?'

'Oh,' said Serena lightly. 'A great deal more. I wish Benedict looked more like himself and that we were home with the children.'

'You are not worried about the measles?'

'No, no. They are all so bouncing with health. Even little Angelica is as stout as an ox, but I suppose it has all gotten to me a little. And even we don't see enough of each other while we play at shifts looking after Dickie. I miss you.' She smiled, 'You'd better hurry if you don't want to keep the lieutenant waiting.'

The girls hugged, a little more fiercely than seemed necessary on being parted for the length of a drive. Then, with mutual sadness at the separation in their spirits, they parted quickly.

Lieutenant Prescott had driven his cousin's tilbury around the park once before Honoria could be brought to answer his questions with more than a syllable. Her shyness and decorum quite enchanted him — the wives and daughters who had attended the soirees in Lisbon were often loud and overly confident for females. He preferred this shy country beauty. The admiration he had often seen in her eyes also added to his consequence. Few ladies flattered him thus when he was with his equally handsome but massively richer cousin. Today, however, she did not turn her fluttering eyelashes in his direction. She was dressed in a yellow muslin and shawl, her bonnet a simple straw with long fawn ribbons, framing her dark curls and accenting the dark doe eyes. She looked like summer personified.

'You outshine the flowers today, Miss Fenton!'

She blushed. 'I — thank you.' But beyond the blush, her eyes returned to the path ahead, between the horse's ears. And to whatever the lieutenant said next, she simply nodded distractedly.

Allison's admittance to his master's *heure de la toilette* caused little more than an eye-rolling from Pierre.

'Entrez, m'sieur, I beg of you. How disappointing that you are alone. *C'est tout ouvert ici,* I assure you. *No-zeeeng* of importance is happening—'

Mr Allison glanced down at the tiny person with the high colour and the heaving chest and dismissed him with a glance. Wilbert Fenton, with a footman in white gloves at his feet applying brute force to putting on his master's boots, said, 'Allison. I thought that you would have been at your own toilette still.'

'In the season, you would perhaps be right, sir. But this is summer and I always keep country hours in the summer.'

Mr Fenton shuddered. 'Well, do you bring me news of Benedict?' He was drawling, but Allison caught the note of concern beneath and liked him the better for it.

'He continues to improve, sir. But I have come to you on another matter today — I am an emissary of your niece Serena.'

'Serena, eh? Thought you had eyes on Honoria.' Allison blanched. Looking at the small valet and the footman, 'My servants are blind and deaf. Think of the company I keep and you'll know why. To be other is to risk their heads.'

Mr Allison toyed with the fantasy that the Price Regent had a secret guillotine for gossiping servants, but he got the point.

'And what does Miss Serena think I can tell her?'

'Could we speak privately, sir?'

Fenton nodded the footman out and lifted an eyebrow at Pierre who had stiffened in place like a statue. With slow deliberation, the little man laid his burden of cravats on a chair, then left, not deigning to glance at Allison as he passed.

'If you stop calling me Sir, I'll talk to you. Call me Fenton.'

'Miss Serena harbours a suspicion, due to something her brother said in a fever, that the attack on Benedict was because of some business of Lady Sumner's.'

Fenton seemed to lose a little of his urbanity for a moment. 'It was, I believe. But *I* was the instrument of his undoing.'

'The money? It has something to do with the money that was tied around Benedict's waist?'

'His winnings.'

'Pretty steep winnings for a novice gambler.'

'Well, there are some games that don't involve gambling at all…'

'I don't believe it. Benedict? Where could he have learned—?' Allison stopped and Wilbert Fenton nodded.

'Yes, well, the world may not believe that I have much honour, but I trust you know I never used my — um, skills, in any but one type of situation.'

Alison grinned. 'When you were playing with a card swiveller.'

'And Benedict—'

Allison sat on the edge of an occasional table, one leg thrown over the inlaid top. 'Sumner was cheated; I suppose that made things difficult for Lady S. But I still don't see—'

'There were further factors. I am not at liberty to tell you what. But they were considered by Benedict to be unacceptable.'

'He's not enamoured—'

Fenton shook his head. 'I don't believe so, though Lady Sumner is quite a woman, I find. Benedict just throws his heart over the fence at times.'

'So he beat—?'

'The men who cheated Sumner.' His voice became tight. 'I gave him the names.'

There seemed to be nothing to be said about this, so Allison stayed still. 'What next?' he asked, eventually, automatically handing Fenton a starched neckcloth and watching, with sympathetic interest, while he dropped his chin in a ritualistic fashion to achieve the perfect folds.

'I am going to find out which one of the three set the brute on Benedict, then struck the final blow himself.' Mr Fenton was drawling once more, but Allison wasn't fooled. His anger was barely suppressed.

'Any help I can give you in that endeavour, just a note to me will suffice. And my friend Scribster, too, I can speak for him, I believe. We have both become very fond of your brother's family, Fenton.'

The flinty eyes of his senior regarded him in the glass. So much for the pudgy, lazy dandy Allison had always known. He would not like to look down the barrel to those eyes. It seemed as though Fenton might fob him off, but at last he said, 'I might take you up on that, Allison. Look for my note.

Chapter 21

Genevieve Saves Herself

Genevieve, Lady Sumner, had left Mr Allison's house before Lady Cynthia had even had time to pack, determined on her unpleasant course. The person she was going to see was someone that she had sought to avoid, but with Benedict waking up, she felt that she had better make this attempt to save herself before he had a chance to throw himself into another dreadful scrape, or worse — only for her.

She had ordered a closed carriage to the address, not a mile hence, and her bonnet was heavily veiled, perhaps against the summer insects, an onlooker might choose to believe. Ever mindful of the horses, she ordered the coachman to pull round to the stables in a nearby mews — she would either walk around later or send for him. She mounted the steps of the smart townhouse with trepidation, and the door flew open before she had time to ring the bell. A well trained footman had opened the door at the sight and sound of a respectable carriage, even though it was a little early for morning visitors.

Genevieve lifted her veil as enough of an introduction, and the footman bowed and said, 'I shall see if her ladyship is yet risen.'

She thought of following his blue liveried back up the stairs, to have the element of surprise, but thought again. Dignity was everything in this situation. Presently, the bewigged footman came down the stair and gestured her above. She squared her shoulders and followed.

She was ushered into a private sitting room, which she knew to be an anteroom to the bedchamber of her husband's aunt, Lady Harrington. This lady sat, dressed in a mauve wrap and lace cap, and looked at her a trifle more coldly than on her last meeting, but held up her cheek to be kissed, which Genevieve bent and did, briefly.

She drew back and stood ten feet away, looking down at the old lady's dark, glittering eyes.

'Sit!' said that lady, pettishly, 'you will give me the headache to be standing there so.' Genevieve did not move, and her ladyship's eyes narrowed. 'I suppose you are here to apologise to me for breaking our bargain. I hear that you spent time in Yorkshire whilst your husband remained in town.'

'I made no bargain with you.' As usual, Genevieve's tongue surprised her. It would have been more tactful to be quiet at this stage. 'But if you wish to talk of the bargain you proposed and perhaps made with my husband, then yes, I have broken it. And I make no apology.' "Be quiet, Genevieve," she thought, sourly. But Lady Harrington's kind of manipulation was an anathema to her honest spirit. 'Indeed, I intend to break it permanently.'

'I suppose you know what this will mean for you — beggary and shame. You will never be able to show your face in town again.' Genevieve gave a crack of laughter. 'Ah! That will not trouble you, but

I fancy Frederick will feel very differently. And I fancy he can make you do my will, and his.' The old lady gave the crack of laughter this time, though it was humourless. Genevieve was surprised to see how cold her eyes could be. Manipulating her family to dance to her tune was perhaps her last power, now that her famed beauty had gone, and Genevieve saw how she clung to it.

She pulled at the lace at her neck, 'You should be proud of how he makes me do his will.' The marks were faded now, but still colourful.

She saw Lady Harrington's eyes widen, but she soon had herself in check. 'Believe that I will speak to Frederick on this head, as on others. He will do as I bid him and desist, believe me.' But she plucked at the skirts of the wrap, unable to quite meet Genevieve's eyes.

'I do not think so. I wish to live on Sumner's stud farm. And for Frederick never to visit.'

'Here it is!' cried the old lady with fire in her eyes. 'You come here to show me your wounds in the hope that I will agree to a separation. But my husband's name must be carried on! You have made a bad bargain in Frederick. There, I admit it. But you shall have no money from me to live apart from your husband. He will likely have to sell the place anyway—'

'You know he cannot, however ruined it becomes. It is entailed.'

The old lady rose. 'I will not permit it. It is against God and—'

'I will not stay with him.'

'And what will you do? Go home to your father? Trust me, I know enough of Henry Horton to know that he will not aid you in making this scandal. He, too, will cast you off.'

'I will go to the stud farm and you will help me.'

'I will not frank your imperious behaviour my Lady Sumner,' said the old lady, dismissing her.

'I do not need your money.'

'Have you hidden money from your husband?' asked Lady Harrington, shocked.

Genevieve looked at her blankly. 'I have an investor, let us say. And trust me, I will make money for him. I am a very good judge of a horse.'

'No doubt,' said Lady Harrington, contemptuously, unable to approve of any but the most worldly of pursuits, 'but there is still your duty to your husband.'

'If it were just me, ma'am,' said Genevieve, touching her stomach, 'however dreadful, I suppose I would agree with you. But I won't let him knock this baby out of me. Or trust him to be a gentle father.'

Lady Harrington stumbled forward and grasped the reluctant Genevieve in her arms, 'A baby! Oh, my dear, my greatest wish. We must hope for a boy.'

'However it is, my lady, there will never be another.'

But her ladyship was all smiles. 'Please my dear, sit, sit,' she said in quite a different tone, and Genevieve did.

In the next hour of closeted confidences, Genevieve told Lady Harrington the bald facts. And they agreed that it was to be given out that Lady Sumner had retired quietly to the country estate to be confined, as she was not keeping well. Her husband would leave town to visit occasionally (though in reality he would be elsewhere) and she would remain to bring up her child. Not an unusual arrangement. Frederick would be allowed to visit his child when his aunt was present, and at no other time. This deal Lady Harrington would broker with her nephew.

No doubt it would cost her dear. Enough to keep Frederick in town in his usual high-spending manner.

If it were not a boy, well, said her ladyship, they could revisit the arrangement. If it were not a boy, thought Genevieve, it would be time to see the sights of Europe and find some secluded spot using some of the money Benedict had won. But this, of course, she failed to confide in the old dragon. In some ways, Genevieve liked the old woman, a female wielding power in a man's world, but she did not mistake — she would be thrown under the horses to further the old lady's ambition.

As Genevieve left, she reflected that she was still betting. It was the like a toss of a coin, a boy and problem solved. A girl and there were still phantoms to run from. Like marriage, she thought, a little cynically. But either way, she would see her child safe from Frederick.

She left the house with thoughts of how soon she could leave and if she should buy some horseflesh in town before she set off. The carriage was waiting for her, but before she mounted, she saw a smart high perch phaeton pass, ridden to an inch. Lord Carstairs was a passenger, but Genevieve was struck by the young man driving and stirred by a thought. She needed just such a gentleman to drive the horses she would choose and eventually breed. Taking the word of a lady when buying a horse was not an option for most gentlemen. Someone to show her horses to advantage would be the trick. Then his friends would clamour to own them. She wondered if Benedict could find out who this nonpareil was? She laughed. No doubt he'd think himself up to the task, but though Benedict could ride, his driving skills were not at all showy.

But as Lady Sumner was standing stock-still and unveiled in the street as the phaeton bowled away, she did not see the gentleman who was looking at her from across the road. And followed her carriage through the busy London streets.

Lady Cynthia had fallen into a troubled sleep and awoke with a start at the first stop. 'Oh, my goodness!' she cried. She jumped recklessly from the coach without waiting for the steps to be let down.

'My lady!' said the astonished coachman.

'Never mind. I must find some writing paper directly.' A portly man in a slightly grubby apron, who had come to offer her some warm punch and some cake in the comfort of her carriage, was pleased to lead her to a bedchamber. Her ladyship would have been pleased to see, if she had leisure for it, that it was a deal cleaner than the apron would have suggested. But she sat at a table and took a quill in hand and wrote a speedy note to her beloved.

My Love, (ran this tribute to brevity) *On no account* (underlined three times) *must Honoria be alone with either* (underlined twice) *Mr Allison or Lieutenant Prescott. I rely on you,*

Your own,

C

The landlord had only just finished enumerating the other comforts he could offer his guest (a heartier lunch, some wine or a fire to be lit) but no, her ladyship turned and said, 'Someone must ride back to London with this note directly. To the house of Mr Allison in Grosvenor Square.' The landlord's face had fallen, for on this busy road he could ill-afford to lose a staff member for the hours that it would take to ride to London and back. But Mr Allison's name cleared his brow. The leader of fashion was well known on this and every other post road in the country, keeping horses in the landlord's own stables. Whatever he lost in inconvenience, the large-handed gentleman could be depended upon to reimburse handsomely. So he bowed and said, 'Certainly, my lady!'

'Directly!' her ladyship warned him.

'Instantly, your ladyship.'

'Send some tea and my maid.'

Lady Cynthia's sleeping brain had solved at least some of the mysteries that had troubled her, and now she felt the pull of London rather more urgently than that of Yorkshire. Her children needed her, perhaps all of them at once. The younger children were sick, but her eldest daughter may be about to do something that would change all their lives forever and risk the happiness of her family in so many ways. Never had her mother's heart and duty been so torn. If it was not already too late, she must trust now to her husband, she thought, and laughed bitterly. She trusted her husband to die for her and her children, but in this case...

Chapter 22

Sir Ranalph Fails His Wife

'Oh, damnation!'

By the time Sir Ranalph received the missive at four of the afternoon, he knew that he had already failed his wife, for Honoria had left for her daily airing — with the lieutenant. He saw the swiftness of his wife's penmanship and the lurid under-linings (made with a rather spluttering pen) and judged her urgency. She depended on him in a matter he felt ill-equipped to deal with.

How on earth he was to change the relaxed atmosphere of intimacy they'd established here was more than he could say. And how could he stand guard on his girls all day, or forbid the gentlemen who obligingly tooled them around by carriage, or gave them an arm for a short walk in the park, all for their healthy exercise, away from the confines of the sickroom? He could hardly begin to play the stern father now, especially when they had all built such an easy rapport.

And why? What on earth did his Cynthia fear? But in the matter of his children, he had learned not to ask, but obey. His wife had a prescience that he never doubted.

He was seated in Allison's library, where he generally perused back copies of *The Sporting Magazine, (*or *Monthly Calendar of the transactions of the Turf, the Chase and every other diversion interesting to the Man of Pleasure, Enterprise and Spirit)*. He was reading a stirring blow by blow account of a cockfight which had taken place two and a half years ago, when Prescott came in.

'Might I have a word, sir?'

Sir Ranalph was no fool. If the lieutenant was asking for a word, rather than simply starting to talk, things may be worse than he'd thought. With a large wad of panic in his throat, he coughed and said, 'Not quite feeling the thing, my boy—' he stood up and cast the magazine to one side. He saw Prescott's surprise and softened his swift departure with a friendly hand on his shoulder as he passed, 'You'll excuse me, I know,' and he hurried from the room like a craven coward.

What to do? Things might be worse than he'd feared. If the lieutenant were to ask for Honoria (though how his wife had guessed at such a thing, and at a distance of forty miles, was beyond him) then Cynthia clearly did not wish it. This much he understood. But why Allison himself? Rowley Allison had shown himself to be everything he could have hoped for in a new member of the family — generous, considerate and amusing, nothing at all like his top-lofty reputation. And Cynthia herself had seemed delighted! How he was supposed to stop the lieutenant buttonholing him later this evening he had no idea.

He supposed that the lieutenant did not know that his cousin had indicated his interest in Honoria. He'd get Scribster to drop a hint in his ear. Scribster was strange fellow, with a face that suggested a miserable disposition, but he'd come to see beyond that and admire his off-hand humour. He was sure he could trust him — after all Allison, who suffered no fools, had him for a friend.

Benedict was sitting up, Serena was applying herself to her duties as nurse, which was trying brother and sister both, since Benedict refused to discuss the reasons for his visit to London with her and she had taken the huff. This treatment included bringing him ratafia instead of wine, hauling at his pillows in a dutiful but less than gentle manner, and talking to him in a martyred monotone which made Benedict cross.

'For dash sake, Serena, you treat your horses better than me. Put that plate of cakes nearer to me, I'm devilish hungry.'

'I do not think you should be eating cake, you have had three already.'

'The doctor said I should keep up my strength. Give 'em here.'

Serena moved them rather further away and said in a pious voice, 'I'm sure that the doctor meant that you should be having posset and, and— gruel and such stuff as that to keep up your strength. The cakes will very likely upset your stomach.'

'Yes, and next you'll be saying I should have nothing but a plate of bread and milk—'

'An excellent idea!' said the pious Serena.

'—but I am not two years old! For goodness sake, Serena, what is making you such a cat this morning?'

Serena looked a little ashamed, and a little confused. 'You frighten us all with the result of your schoolboy antics—'

'I don't remember being cudgelled to near death when I was at Harrow.'

'—and then you refuse to talk to anyone about it except Genevieve Horton.'

'Lady Sumner to you. Jenny's a deal older than you, Serena. Don't take it amiss that I confide a little—'

'Well, don't treat me like a baby!'

Benedict narrowed his eyes. 'There's more to this than what I am, or am not, telling you,' he said, sagely, 'What happened when I was asleep — someone upset you?' he paused then guessed, 'Allison?'

'Certainly not. He has been the most wonderful host—'

'Did you go to Astley's? You wrote me that you were coming to London for the express purpose of—'

'Yes Benedict. That and the balls and assemblies, not to say the morning calls, have kept us very busy.'

'Good!' approved her brother, 'glad you've seen a bit of the town, you might not get another chance—'

Serena threw a small satin pillow at him. 'Do you think we've been out carousing while you were at death's door, you horrible boy?'

'Hey! Mind the invalid, wildcat!' he leaned over and grabbed at the cake plate, wincing as his ribs moved, and ate with relish. 'You might have known I'd be alright, it was mostly my head he hurt.'

But Serena had processed his throwaway remark. 'What did you mean that I might not get a second chance? Do you mean to see London before I'm committed to my season? Honoria said Mama ran her out to social functions three and four times a day! I suppose there will not be much time to visit the sights. I should get one of the gentlemen to drive me up the mall to Buckingham House on my daily airings. How far is Newgate Prison? It is a bit grisly, but I own I have an urge to see the place where the Gentlemen Highwayman was held.'

'Poor Serena — did you not meet a gentleman of the road on your way to London and have him shoot you and take all your trinkets? How unfortunate for you. No need to worry, you'll be intimately acquainted with Newgate someday, I've no doubt.' Serena exclaimed, but she knew that whatever funning thing he had to say, Benedict was keeping something from her. And she resented it. More secrets. Orry, Genevieve, and even Benedict. It was too awful. If he were fully well, she might have chewed him up with questions until he broke, but— it was all too frustrating. Her own mood, usually so sunny, was chafing at her and she could not allow herself to think why.

She longed to be at home. And yet she didn't. She did not even know herself.

While Serena sat with Benedict, Mr Allison, Mr Scribster and Genevieve all seemed to have errands that sent them from the house, Honoria went to her room to salve an aching head whilst some new worry niggled at the back of her mind, not quite reaching her conscious thought. She would no doubt have to sit with Benedict this night, though he was beginning to 'wish his sisters at Jericho' as he said when conscious, encouraging them to leave his care to the servants. She could barely sleep and she felt hot and ill-tempered, not able to explain herself in any way. Benedict's improvement meant that the whole reason for this visit was coming ever nearer. Sometimes she doubted that Mr Allison would offer for her, but surely he would have warned her parents by now. On the other hand, even if he did not, she would still bear the burden of knowing that she had not helped at all — she had neither sought his attention or been encouraging on the one occasion when he really did speak. Even knowing what it would mean for poor Serena, she had shied away from him.

Serena occasionally spoke of next year's season and what a time they would have together. She did not know how to answer, so it was as well that they had the distractions of Benedict's care. It was her duty to — but to do what? The secret messages of encouragement that ladies from her grandmother's day had sent to gentlemen with the wave of a fan were not available to her. How did one encourage a gentleman these days? Though younger, she was quite sure Serena would know.

There was a knock on her door. Perhaps Serena, or even better, Mr Scribster. She could not tell him everything, but maybe he would see the things she could not and explain them to her — at least he would make her laugh.

She cast the shawl from her and sat up, swinging her legs to the floor. 'Come in,' she called.

It was her father who entered, and he smiled at her. 'I noticed at breakfast that you were not quite the thing, Orry. I think you should have dinner in your room this evening.'

'No, really, Papa. I am quite well. I will come down at the appointed hour.'

Her father adopted a stern voice that she seldom heard from him. 'You will please me by keeping to your room, Honoria. I do not wish to have another of my children laid by the heels through illness.'

'Of course Papa, if you wish it! I will try to rest—'

'There's a good girl,' said her father, returned to his good humour. 'Mind you don't get up for any reason. I myself might be at your uncle's this evening, but you must rest here till I see you at breakfast.' He pinched her chin, hugged her, then headed for the door, obviously pleased with himself. He stopped, and turned towards her once more. 'Did you enjoy your carriage ride this morning?'

'Wh—? Yes, it was very pleasant.'

His eyebrows rose, 'Pleasant?'

'Yes.' He apparently wanted a little more. 'The weather was clement.'

'Good, good. Clement, eh? Good.' He nodded and left.

"What was that about?" she thought, but she could not be sorry. An evening free of the exhaustion of secrets and pretence was liberating. She sank into the bed and when a young maid brought her dinner at seven, she was still fast asleep. She even missed Serena coming in — who, seeing her sister sleeping, adjusted her coverlet and kissed her cheek before she crept away.

Sir Ranalph had done his best for that night at least, but locking Honoria in her room till her mother returned to take care of whatever situation this was would hardly be possible. Anyway, by dining at Wilbert's (though his brother did not yet know) he could avoid whatever Prescott sought him for. It occurred to him that he might just want his opinion on a horse or some such thing, but he feared not. Niftily done, he was thinking, but he underestimated his stalker. Prescott was at the bottom of the stairs, with an anxious but hopeful smile on his face, saying, 'Sir — have you a moment?'

Behind him, Mr Scribster, taking his hat off in the hall, stopped with a frozen expression on his face.

Sir Ranalph panicked, 'Um, just heading out with Mr Scribster on a rather important matter.' The shoulder slap in the passing was a trifle repetitive, but it was the best he could do. Scribster, no laggard he, had put his hat back on over his shiny thick hair and had already nodded the footman to open the door once more and the two left, Sir Ranalph giving a gesture of gratitude with his chin to the inscrutable Mr Scribster.

The gentlemen headed down the townhouse steps together.

'Thanks for that, Scribster,' said the big bluff baronet as the two descended into the square, 'You must be wondering what on earth—'

'Not at all, sir,' lied Scribster manfully, 'None of my business.'

'Well, as it happens, my boy, it might be.' Scribster's face was as immobile as usual, and Sir Ranalph was suddenly finding it difficult to ask him for what had seemed a simple favour. It must be done however, so he put his arm around the man and led him to a coffee house where they could chat. 'Mr Allison's cousin wants to speak to me, you see. And as he'd just been driving Honoria, he might be about to make a request of me.' Scribster's face remained frozen — drat the man, would he not help at all? 'It occurs to me, therefore, that he is unaware of, well, of the purpose of his cousin's invitation to my family.' He raised his eyebrows to encourage some nod of understanding from Scribster, but his face... 'Drat it, sir, your friend must have confided in you. I know that nothing is settled yet due to the dashed business with Benedict, but...' Sir Ranalph sighed. He felt as winded by this conversation as if he had just climbed a mountain. 'Might you just mention it to Lieutenant Prescott? Put him in the picture before he...? Well. I suppose he might still—' Sir Ranalph was still floundering, 'It might save some embarrassment.'

Scribster, at last, broke his silence. 'My friend does not like his affairs talked of, you see. I don't really know if I am at liberty to mention to his cousin something he has not mentioned himself.' Sir Ranalph's face fell. 'But I can hint, perhaps.' He sipped his coffee, 'But presumably, Miss Fenton has given Prescott leave to talk to you?' His voice was bland, colourless. 'And perhaps my friend should be made aware of—'

'I beg of you, no sir.' said Sir Ranalph quickly. 'I do not know what my daughter is aware of and what not. Until I discover how it is, I do not wish anything said.' Scribster nodded. Sir Ranalph sat back, exhausted. 'My wife would know what to do. All this kind of this thing is her ladyship's purview. She understands the girls.' The baronet sighed even more deeply. Come to think of it, he was too narrowly defining his wife's purview, she understood her sons too. Even his brother understood Benedict better than he.

'Shall we go, Scribster?' he asked at last. Scribster, who he normally thought of as having a watching disposition, seemed to strive to come away from some dream.

'Certainly, sir,' his tall, strange companion said. Sir Ranalph eyed him. Scribster had always been the taciturn, detached member of their party, unaffected by much. Though the baronet had intuited his strength and on a few occasions his humour, he had never before seen the raw look in the urbane gentleman's eyes. But suddenly he was reminded of twelve-year-old Benedict after his favourite dog had died. It was but a minute, and the old cold stare was back.

If the baronet didn't have his own problems at present, he would have attempted to make the reticent young man confide in him. But he did. How on earth was he to keep his Honoria away from two perfectly pleasant young men who now stood in the relation of good friends? Well, tonight was dealt with. It was like Sir Ranalph to take this as a sunny thought and head for his club to take several cups of cheer before he confronted his brother.

Later that afternoon, Allison went to see how his young invalid was doing and found Benedict trying to get up, having swung his legs out of the bed and attempting to stand, his face as grey with pain as a ghost. Lady Sumner had a hand on his shoulder to keep him down and two footmen stood by, looking at a loss, Benedict ordering them to help him rise and Lady Sumner countermanding his orders. 'Do not dare!' she said to one of the hapless duo as he stepped forward according to Benedict's summons. The man froze. Her hair had escaped its confines once more and she looked like a raging virago.

'Dickie, if you don't sit still, I promise you it will be the worse for you. Your ribs are broken, you annoying young pup, you could be puncturing a lung or some such thing!' Still less than ever did Allison now think that the pair were lovers. His own elder sister addressed him in just such terms. Benedict still rose however until she said, 'I will not take your gift!' and whatever this meant, the boy sat down.

'Can I suggest a compromise, my lady?' said Allison entering the fray and nodding the footmen to the door.

'Not if it means he shall get up and ruin his rest,' said Lady Sumner pugnaciously.

'Lady Sumner — might I call you Jenny?' said Allison, bending his handsome head and smiling, 'Let Benedict agree to rest this afternoon—'

'If I rest any more I shall very likely—' objected Benedict.

'Be quiet, Benedict.' Benedict grinned and shut his mouth. Allison turned back to her ladyship, who was wearing a stubborn look and had her hands on her hips in the manner of a woman standing her ground. 'Later we will corset him in bandages so that he cannot move and we'll let some footmen carry him into dinner. How's that?'

'I do not need to be carried,' protested Benedict, 'There is nothing but bruises on my legs!'

'Be quiet!' one drawling and one angry voice said at once.

'Oh, very well,' Benedict agreed, swinging his legs back into the bed and wincing despite himself.

Genevieve did not look like she was quite finished, but Blake quietly entered and approached his master.

'Sir, Lord Sumner is in the hall and wishes to see her ladyship.'

Benedict's legs swung forward with alacrity and Genevieve descended from Virago to suppliant, her eyes big with panic. She began to say something.

Taking all this in at a glance, Allison answered, 'Lady Sumner is visiting with a party of friends, at present, Blake. Please inform his lordship that he is welcome to visit tomorrow morning, when no doubt her ladyship will be here.'

His master's word was a matter of faith for Blake, so naturally he did not so much as glance at the (absent) Lady Sumner as he left on his mission. The trio stood close, Benedict's hand had found Jenny's and Allison had allowed himself the intimacy of a reassuring hand on her shoulder. They froze as one until they heard the final closure of the front door.

'Jenny—' began Benedict.

But Lady Sumner had recovered herself. 'Back into bed, Dickie, or I swear I shall not be responsible for what I do.'

Benedict did as he was told, and Allison and she left the room. In the corridor, Allison spoke. 'Lady Sumner ...if there is something—.'

'It's Jenny. And heaven save me from any more knights-errant, Mr Allison. I admit that my husband's visit was — a surprise. I cannot disguise that it was an unpleasant one, for we are, um, — estranged — at the moment as you must have guessed.' He nodded gravely. 'We are too much like friends now for me to try to hide this from you. But I have already taken care of ... I need no help. It is just that for a moment, I—' She turned and squeezed his hand, looking up into his eyes frankly. 'You have given me just the delay I need to deal with him, fear not. And thank you.'

Watching her walk away, Mr Allison could not quite shake his worry, however. It was more than sullen reluctance or righteous anger he had seen in Genevieve Sumner's eyes when her husband was mentioned. It was fear. He knew Sumner as an overblown blowhard with occasional charm and no integrity. He was famous for his indulgence in any number of vices, but many men about town were — even the married ones. What singled Foxy Sumner out was the shady way he conducted his affairs. He didn't provide for his discarded mistresses as he should, was often late paying his gambling debts, had a loose tongue with the secrets of his friends and (the ultimate sin in gentlemanly circles) could not tell a thoroughbred from a donkey. Allison had seen enough of his wife to know that her strength of character could surely prevail against such a man, that though she might have found she had made a bad bargain in her husband, she would have lived with it and made do, as many married couples did. But she was afraid. Nothing in Sumner's weak arsenal of bumptiousness could cow such a woman. There was only one thing that could. Allison's blood ran cold.

He already liked Dickie Fenton, but now he began to understand him, too. He was trying somehow to act on Jenny's behalf. But did he think restoring her fortunes could be the easy answer? This showed the young gallant's naivety: money did not shield a wife from her husband's will. By all the laws of the land, the money would revert to him.

Though dinner that evening was enlivened by Benedict's presence, it was a duller-than-usual affair. His cousin the lieutenant seemed anxious and on edge; Scribster sat looking at some world as far away as his Scottish castle; Lady Sumner retired early; and Serena, who had hardly looked at him all evening, claimed her need to retire early too.

'A devilish set of dull dogs!' declared Benedict, 'Get a card deck, for goodness sake.'

The card table was set up near the fire, the brandy on a side table. After a couple of desultory hands, with Allison and Benedict bearing most of the conversational effort, Benedict bent forward, wincing only a little.

'I think, gentlemen, that we should raise the stakes.' Scribster raised an eyebrow. 'But if we do, I need all of you, on your honour, to forget what occurs here this evening.

'Benedict...' warned Allison.

But the young man, a little tipsy, had dancing eyes. 'Don't you trust them?'

Allison sat back and shrugged.

For the next few hands, Benedict won so consistently that it was perfectly obvious something was amiss. The others came to attention. With more brandy and eventual hilarity, they watched, trying to catch their young companion fuzzing the cards.

'You young scoundrel, Fenton. Don't try to join my club or I'll have you blackballed.' said Mr. Scribster with a laugh.

'I wouldn't—' objected Benedict seriously.

'It's a jest,' offered Allison helpfully.

'Does he jest?' asked Benedict.

'Often mistaken for rudeness,' said Scribster, dryly, 'you impudent young swindler. Deal on.'

'By all that's marvellous,' said Prescott, joyfully. 'Could you catch others at it? I'm sure there's a captain of the dragoons in Lisbon who's fleecing the new recruits—'

Over the next hour, until Allison decreed that the young ivory turner should be banished to bed, Benedict laughingly displayed his scandalous talent to his companions. He objected that it was but one of the clock and not time — but Allison directed, and there was no need to summon the footmen, for the lieutenant and Scribster lifted him in his chair and bore him raucously from the room, with Allison laughingly adjuring them not to wake the whole house.

Honoria stirred in her bed, awoken by she knew not what. Snuggled beside her, holding on for dear life, was Serena, her sleeping cheeks stained with tears. Honoria hugged her back, not able to understand why her own tears fell on Serena's hair, but comforted anyway by the nearness of her beloved sister.

CHAPTER 23

A Proposal

At the first stop on her way home, Lady Cynthia, in her distraction, had sent her letter to her husband and at the second, she herself received a missive. It was from Fenton Hall and delivered by her own groom. At the inn where she had elected to spend the night, Jenkins had caused her to be disturbed as she was dressing for bed before finishing the journey on the morrow. There were many inns on the post road from London to Harrogate, but fewer who catered for Quality. Therefore, when Jenkins had been tasked with finding her ladyship on the road, he had only had to visit three other establishments before finding her.

It was from Mrs Hall, her ladyship's excellent housekeeper. After the prerequisite politesse, Mrs Hall's robust voice sounded out to Lady Fenton from the paper.

'... I was most distressed to hear, my lady, that Mrs Bunter took it upon herself to write to you regarding the children contracting the

measles. Whilst usually a sensible woman, any form of illness in the children (as we know, my lady) seems to throw Bunter into what Mr Macleod calls her histrionic mode. That's as may be, but if it means she is more dramatic than an actress on the stage I fear he is right. Thankfully, with such a healthy family, these little fidgets of Mrs Bunter's are few, but in this case I was nearly brought to anger. What right has she to give you more distress, worriting about Mr Benedict as you must be, when it is Quite Unnecessary.

The boys are indeed covered in spots, but if making a noise and destroying their bedrooms, not to mention eating like 'ravaging hoards' (as Mr Macleod puts it) is anything to reckon by, I do not think there is any cause for alarm. Indeed, the spots were less today than yesterday, so they are on the mend. As for little Miss Angelica, she has thrown out only two spots and shows no inclination to throw out more, and after sleeping much for a few days, was looking bright-eyed this morning.

I know you, my lady, and I know that you will set out for home. So I am sending Jenkins to find you on the road (on Sir Ranalph's swiftest horse) to let you know that if you are still needed in London, you have no need to listen to Mrs Bunter's hysterics, which I know comes from a soft heart and an excess of sensibility. All the children (as even the physician says) will very likely be out of bed within a few days...

It was wonderful news, of course. She was perfectly sure that her phlegmatic butler Macleod and the sensible Mrs Hall were to be relied upon. Tomorrow, at break of dawn, she told Jenkins to tell the coachman and the inn landlord she would return to London, in time (she hoped) to save her girls.

It was like Sir Ranalph that now Benedict was on the mend and he needed a place to hide, good will was restored between the brothers.

Of the financial side they did not speak. Some line had been crossed there — and he could see that it had done his brother good.

Now the baronet shared his notion — brilliantly arrived at after the fifth glass of wine — that he should instruct his daughters, since their brother did not need so much attention, to accompany each other at all times, solving the chaperone problem.

When Countess Overton, the third member of their cosy supper party at Wilbert's house, laughed aloud, he said defensively, 'What amuses you, my lady?'

Her ladyship smiled. 'Do you think two young sisters will fail to accommodate the liaisons of lovers? Intrigue in love is a woman's natural nature.'

'Not my girls,' said Sir Ranalph with a studied dignity.

'Ranalph Fenton — did *you* not conspire with my sister to meet me behind the orangery at Mrs Frederick's ball?'

He looked sheepish. 'Well, my dear Aurora, you were ... are ... quite a beauty, how could I do other?'

'Stop flirting with my fiancée,' drawled Wilbert.

'She kissed me first,' said Sir Ranalph, in reminiscent tones.

'Did you?' his brother asked, mock shocked, at his pretty countess.

'Behind the very same orangery. It was my first kiss. What heady days they were.'

'So you see—' began Sir Ranalph jovially.

'But it was *I* who danced with you first,' said Wilbert smugly. 'Ranalph didn't have the address to penetrate the hordes of admirers that surrounded you.'

'Perhaps. And perhaps I helped you a little.'

'You preferred my brother to me all along. I was heartbroken,' sighed Sir Ranalph.

The countess was wearing a pale muslin gown encrusted with crystals at her bosom and they sparkled in the candlelight nearly as brightly as her eyes. Ranalph caught a merry look between the two others and he made a discovery. Whatever this engagement was, it was not just convenience. His brother looked younger and happier than he had seen him. The countess turned to the baronet.

'Your broken heart didn't last the season, as I remember.'

'No,' said Sir Ranalph, 'I met my lady, and that was that.'

'And your papa banished Wilbert to Fenton Manor for playing too much Faro, and I was auctioned off to my count.' Wilbert grasped her hand. 'But I made the best of it! We were content, in our way.'

'But I do believe,' said the baronet, sipping his sixth glass of claret, 'that my girls will be quite safe together. I shall speak to them before breakfast and let them know my decision.' The last he said rather pompously. When the other two laughed, he grinned however. 'Oh, goodness. I wish Cynthia had not had to go home.'

The hall clock chimed three as Sir Ranalph returned to Grosvenor Square. His course was set. He'd see the girls before breakfast, issue his instructions and relax — having done his fatherly duty. He thought of Aurora Overton's amusement — but was reassured by the fact that his girls were very special. Honoria was never disobedient and Serena, well, Serena meant well.

But he did not move the next morning as one of Mr Allison's attentive servants entered his room and pulled the curtains open. And by the time he'd arrived at the breakfast table, Honoria had already been alone with two gentlemen. And Serena — though there was no need to worry about Serena — one other.

The girls got ready early, strangely silent with each other, but dismissing the maid to assist each other to dress in their old way. Neither mentioned the tear-stained cheeks, merely using the jug and ewer to splash faces and eradicate the evidence. Honoria wondered at them, usually so chatty — now so full of things that they could not voice a word, except for inanities.

Serena was still piling her curls on her head, and a little maid was helping her thread ribbon through her topknot when Honoria said, 'My dear, I shall go down, now. I may look in on Benedict before breakfast.'

'Oh, very well,' sighed Serena, 'I shall see you downstairs, Orry.'

But Honoria knocked on Mr Scribster's door, just as he was opening it to leave.

'Miss Fenton,' he said, 'good morning.'

'Shall we have a walk before breakfast? I should so like to talk to you.'

'This isn't Bassington, Miss Fenton. I fear how our *tête-à-tête* might be seen in London, country ways are not quite permitted.' He had closed the door as he spoke and wandered past her to the stairs.

'Nonsense! No one could think that you and I...'

Scribster turned and raised a cold eyebrow, 'Beauty and the Beast, eh? No doubt — but nevertheless...' His head gave a stiff little nod, which she might take as a bow if she wished. She did not.

'*You too* reverting to the formalities?' she laughed a little harshly, for his dismissive manner was rather too much to bear. 'I thought that you had no truck with such things.'

'Did you?' His large dark eyes looked into hers, and a lock of hair fell over his already hooded eyes, 'Someone must!'

She blushed, thinking he was blaming her for her shocking behaviour in throwing herself into his arms. At the time, it was the most natural thing in the world, but now he had thought of it and—.

'I understand you, I suppose,' she said, angry but humiliated. And swept herself away from him to the stairs.

'No!' he said brokenly, so that she could not hear him, 'Honoria!' he said more loudly. She did not turn.

She looked into Benedict's room and the stench of brandy still hung over him as she bent over his unconscious form. No doubt she could guess how last night's dinner went. Serena had told her of Benedict's entry back into the world, and she sighed. He had surely overdone it. But the other gentlemen might have known. She left him to sleep and went to the breakfast room which was fast filling with the many essentials that Mr Allison thought necessary to the comfort of his guests. A choice of coffee, tea and chocolate, and along with the usual rolls and a selection of fruit preserves from Bassington, there were eggs and a choice of meats, as well as some small silver bowls of other strange and tempting compotes made by his French chef. Only one other man was present. Lieutenant Prescott looked so delighted to see her that she stepped back even as he moved forward. Some niggling thing about yesterday's drive oppressed her. If he were to ask her to drive today, she would deny herself somehow.

He moved another step and since she was backed against an elegant chair she could not well avoid him as he took her hand. She looked at the hand that held hers in amazement. Gentlemen did not do this, unless in a dance, or to hand a lady into a carriage.

'I have not yet been able to talk to your father,' he said urgently. 'But I shall do so as soon as I can this morning.'

'Talk to my father?'

'I was so happy when you gave me leave. I know I have no right to speak until then—'

Honoria looked at his passionate eyes and suddenly knew what had niggled at her all yesterday. Whilst her thoughts were otherwise, in some warm comfortable dream of her friend's room, or on worry for Benedict, she eventually heard something of what an earnest Lieutenant Prescott had said. 'You give me leave, then, Miss Fenton?' And she had nodded absently, whilst a silver snake of suspicion entered the back of her head, giving her the vague feeling of doing the wrong thing. He must have talked of marriage! This couldn't have happened. Was she engaged to yet another man — this time remembering his face at least, but completely blanking his words.

Honoria withdrew her hand jerkily and said, 'I must go, Lieutenant, indeed I must!'

She met her father in the hall, pulled up short and composed herself. 'Papa!'

'Have you just been to breakfast?'

'Not yet — I am just going to fetch Serena.'

'Good girl. And you may tell her from me that it is my wish that you two remain together at all times today. We have been a little lax in the conventions, my girl, given our situation with Benedict, but with your mama gone there will be no more carriage rides without each other, no—' he looked at her closely, for Honoria's face had fallen. 'Are you well, my dear?'

'Oh yes, Papa,' she said miserably. Could he know of her visit to Mr Scribster's room? But no — surely he would have berated her before now. 'I will fetch Serena...' she said and turned swiftly.

She heard her father enter the breakfast room and mutter an expletive. 'Damn, forgot something...' and shut it again.

She looked and saw her father turn swiftly and encounter Scribster coming out of the salon that had become Benedict's chamber. They appeared to have whispered words and her father's voice said, 'He's alone now!' and Mr Scribster made his relaxed way into the breakfast room.

She ran to the top of the stairs, still wondering at what she'd seen and made her morning by bumping into Mr. Allison on the stairs. 'Miss Fenton, do you not breakfast?' said he with a light touch on her shoulders to steady her.

'So sorry! Yes, I am just going to fetch my sister, sir.'

'Might we talk privately today, Miss Fenton?'

Honoria's eyes opened wide. 'I ... my father ... perhaps you should ... excuse me sir ...' she grasped what dignity she could and curtsied, leaving him stranded. Not for the first time.

She ran to her room, where Serena had just finished her toilette, the little maid curtsying as she left the room.

'Whatever is the matter, Orry?'

'Oh, Serena, I've done it again!' and she threw herself on the bed in a passion.

By the time she had explained herself to Serena, her sister had thrown herself on the bed next to her and she stopped crying and began to join her in laughing.

'Oh, Orry! If that isn't just like you — if your head is otherwise, you cannot hear a thing that is said,' Serena mopped her eyes with a wisp of lace that served as a handkerchief. 'Oh how ridiculous — wait till Dickie hears...'

That made Honoria sit up. 'You would not!'

Serena laughed, 'Now how can you be so unkind, my dear sister? The poor boy deserves to be cheered up after his great trials. It will be just the thing to set him up again!' she looked at Honoria with a wicked light in her eye. 'One suitor whose face you failed to remember and another a handsome nodcock who you agreed to marry without hearing.' This seemed to set her off again and she slid off the silken coverlet all the way to the floor, still laughing.

'He is not a nodcock! Lieutenant Prescott is handsome and noble and—'

'You cannot be in love with him! Why, if his horse were to throw a splint and limp he'd very likely think it was a dressage step.'

Honoria's eyes flashed. 'Believe it or not, Serena, knowledge of horse flesh is not the only quality necessary for a future spouse.'

Serena considered this. 'Not the only quality, but surely indispensable all the same. But you cannot wish to — his only conversation is of balls he's attended in Lisbon, or — I mean he must have bored you so much today that you just nodded off and missed the part where he proposed. You don't love him do you?'

Honoria, wringing her hands, said, 'What does it matter what I think? I cannot think of marriage when Dickie is laid up ... I, I...'

'You cannot prefer him to—' Serena stopped herself. There had been some of the sisterly joy together when Orry confessed herself in yet another scrape. She didn't wish to enter the other place of unsaid things that seemed to be keeping them apart. So she jumped to her feet and said, 'Just *wait* till Benedict hears!' and began to run from the room with Honoria at her heels, saying 'Serena, stop!' but Serena ran towards Benedict's room.

Genevieve called, 'Honoria!'

'Jenny?' Honoria was surprised at her friend's appearance. She wore a grey muslin gown that she recognised as her best before she had become her ladyship. It was simple and slim, made high at the neck with only the smallest embellishment of her grandmama's necklace, a handsome tear-shaped ruby on a chain. Her hair was piled on her head in a relaxed style, a simple ribbon threaded through. A few curls had been allowed to escape by an expert hand instead of its usual escaped bird's nest. Neat and tidy. Her eyes were a little strained but resolved. She looked so much more like herself than in the unbecoming fashions of Lady Sumner that Honoria hugged her. She would never be pretty, but Honoria did not value beauty much and she admired her enormously.

'Have you breakfasted?'

'Not yet.'

'Bear me company, my dear. I have to slay a dragon today and I fear I am in need of sustenance.'

'Of course,' said Honoria automatically, the pair descending the steps. 'Serena is with Benedict, I have to take her with us; Papa's orders.'

Genevieve raised her brows. 'I suppose we have all become a little too informal since we have been here. No doubt your father is worried now that your mama is not here. If I stay I will fill her place as chaperone. I should have been thinking of you girls, but I'm afraid I have been preoccupied by my own concerns.'

'It seems ridiculous that you be our chaperone. You are hardly older than me by three years.'

'I am a married lady,' she said with an edge to her voice. 'Besides, I am older. So very, very, much older than you, my dear.'

By this time, they had entered Benedict's room. They found him fully dressed, standing on his feet. His face was grey with pain. Serena was beside him, adjusting his handsome muslin cravat.

'There! That's the best I can do.'

'Where is Papa?' demanded Honoria.

'Oh, he had to go out, I believe. He told me not to get up.'

Serena sighed.

Genevieve joined her. 'So why—?'

'I don't forget you will have a visitor today, my lady. I don't intend that you will meet him alone.'

The girls looked at her. 'My husband is arriving,' she announced. 'And I do not need your help, Benedict.' Benedict's eyes flashed at her and she sighed once more. 'You are the most stubborn young idiot, Dickie... Let us just to breakfast.'

Chapter 24
Lady Cynthia Returns

Even when he'd had a house party for sixty at Bassington, his house had never seemed so full of people, Rowley Allison reflected, as he headed towards the dining room. Maybe it was because every person he encountered at *this* house party was full of emotional charge. In his normal life he was fond of a number of people, of course. But his great wealth had made him a little lacking in trust of friends — sooner or later they wanted something more from him than friendship. His sister he loved, but she lived her happy life far from the city or from Bassington with her impoverished baronet and her brood of children. Maybe the similarities to the Fentons (though Sir Ranalph was not quite impoverished, just neat in the funds) was part of what drew him to them. A happy family, as he had seen, even in this most strained of situations. One in which he would be privileged to be included. He also loved his tiresome and expensive mother, but he did not miss her when she travelled and he was quite sure that part of the drive to marry was to legitimately banish her to the Dower House whilst she was in England. Her demands infuriated him, even if he could afford them.

He was also fond, or indeed more than that, of Gus Scribster, who had saved his life more than once in battle — and the fact that he had returned the favour did not negate the fact. Gus and he rubbed along very well. Although he joked about having him for a pensioner, and that was probably the common notion of their relationship, they both knew that it was their bond that kept them together. That and Scribster's lack of love for the draughty Scottish castle that he had inherited. He knew, too, his friend's complete disinterest in his money. Though the new hat and the haircut worried him. Was Scribster embarking on a life of fashion? The very notion made him laugh.

But the Fentons had become important to him in a great many ways. The sisters confused and made his head spin in a manner that he strove not to examine too closely, but that he knew to have a ridiculous aspect. The parents were such as he would have wished for himself. Lady Cynthia beautiful and astute, as kind as Honoria with a great deal of Serena's spirit, obviously adored by her good natured husband. Benedict's merry spirit, full of courage and brio, had affected him as some of his junior officers had in the Hussars. He liked the boy for himself and was worried and wondering about the trouble that he was still in. Even Lady Sumner claimed a part in his concern. He had guessed at her predicament and unusually for him felt a call to action, one contrary to his knowledge that it was improper to meddle in 'what God has joined together'.

He walked into the breakfast room to find his friend and his cousin silent and intent on their coffee, the mood flat. It improved when the ladies arrived, bringing with them a drained looking Benedict. There was a lot of quite bright conversation but none of it seemed real — there were undercurrents even from his usually sanguine friend and cousin — and it mercifully stopped when Blake entered.

'Lord Sumner has arrived, your ladyship, and desires to see you.'

'Oh, for goodness sake,' ejaculated Lady Sumner, much in the old tones of their relationship, 'why must he pick today of all days to rise before ten of the clock?'

'I have shown his lordship into the library, Mr Allison,' uttered Blake as though he had not heard her.

Allison nodded, and the butler left.

'I'll go to meet him,' said Benedict, his eyes ablaze. 'You won't see him alone.'

Lieutenant Prescott, all at sea, said, 'I beg your pardon?' in a disapproving tone.

'I'll go and greet him,' drawled Allison with a restraining hand on Benedict's shoulder. He caught Serena's eyes — she gave him a grateful look and he smiled down at her.

But as he stood, there was a commotion in the hall.

Honoria jumped up. 'Mama! I'm sure it is!'

'How can it be?' said Serena.

But in another second, she was found to be correct. Lady Fenton arrived, still in her violet redingote, only having stopped to remove her bonnet, taking her gloves off and smiling.

Mr Allison was suave, 'Your ladyship,' he said, bowing over her hand. 'Welcome. Your son is fast recovering as you can see.'

Her ladyship threw a glance in her son's direction, a slight frown breaking her sunny looks. 'Up too early, you mean. No one need apologise. He always was a most stubborn boy.' Her son grinned.

'Mama!' said Honoria, finding herself desirous of throwing herself into her mother's arms.

'Yes, my dear. The children are well, do not fear — so I thought I should return. Where is Papa?'

'He went out earlier.'

'Probably to his club,' she said comfortably. 'Samuel, could you send a message to him to say I have returned?' she smiled at the footman who bowed and disappeared to ask Blake which of the London clubs Sir Ranalph frequented.

'Sit down, Jenny,' said her ladyship.

'My husband has just arrived,' explained Genevieve, 'You must forgive me, Lady Fenton.'

'At this hour? How disobliging of him. Well, he must wait. You clearly have not finished breakfast.' She removed her redingote which was silently whisked away by another footman. As she sat, Honoria brought her some chocolate and some sweet rolls. 'This is so welcome,' she said brightly, 'I have been travelling since daybreak, I must look a fright.'

But she did not, thought Honoria. Her mother's violet muslin was hardly crushed and her dark hair was not yet covered with one of the lace caps that normally covered her dark curls. But it was her comforting presence and the little tweak of mischief in her eyes today that somehow infused Honoria with confidence. Now that Mama was back, all would be well. She looked at Serena and saw a similar confidence in her eyes.

Genevieve was still tense. 'Inform Lord Sumner that his wife is at breakfast and she will be with him in due course.'

'Perhaps I—' began Mr Allison, but he was interrupted in his turn by Blake entering once more with a missive for his master. 'I'm afraid I've been called away,' he said, after giving this short note a glance. 'And Mr Scribster too.' His friend looked up and seemed anxious to leave.

'Might I be of service, cousin?' asked the lieutenant.

'Not at the moment, Darnley. Enjoy your breakfast.'

Lady Fenton sipped her chocolate contentedly. 'I hope that you will both be present a little before dinner this evening? In the green salon at seven?'

Allison, halted on his swift departure, merely bowed.

Lord Frederick Sumner was known as an easy man among his cohorts – except, of course, when in his cups. He was a known devil then, apt to take a man up on any perceived insult, unable to take a quiet word inducing him to calm himself a little, and generally someone better avoided at that time. Unless of course you were disposed to sell him a flashy mare for two hundred pounds more than it was worth, or beat him at cards. But he had not yet partaken of alcohol today, and he had been disposed to show himself a jolly good fellow in Allison's house. It wouldn't do to set the great Mr Allison against him. Town was becoming rather warm for him at the moment at any rate, on account of dunning tradesmen willing to insult a peer of the realm with dratted demands for money. So to make trouble in his own set was something he wished to avoid. He would call Genevieve to heel by apologising and letting her know what he really thought of her behaviour when they were alone. He had no particular desire to see her beyond the strictures of his aunt, always ready to give him some financial relief in return for obedience in the matter of conceiving a child.

So Lord Frederick's demeanour was relaxed and he even took up an edition of Ovid that was sitting on a small table near a chair and began to read, ready to show his best face to his host and his wife. After twenty minutes of this dull work, reading Latin about a man who was named after a dashed carriage, Lord Frederick's mood darkened. It was insulting to keep a man kicking his heels in your house this long. He was not used to such treatment. Just as he was about to throw the book at a wall, the butler came in to offer to escort him to his wife.

He was smiling charmingly as he entered the room, lest his host was present, but when he saw his wife standing upright by the fire, wearing one of the plain gowns he had forbidden her (as not befitting the status of his wife) and quite alone, his demeanour changed. 'Madame wife—' he began in a dark voice, but he was interrupted by the door to an adjoining room opening.

'Sit down Frederick!' said the familiar tones of his aunt.

Walking to the stables, Scribster asked disinterestedly. 'Care to tell me where we're going?'

'To save Benedict Fenton's hide, I believe.'

'Oh, well then,' said his companion, satisfied.

Mama had been jolly over breakfast and had sent her daughters to keep Benedict in his room until Lord Sumner left the house. It proved impossible to tell his parent, especially before the lieutenant, why he might be needed. He agreed to go with his sisters, but was determined to escape when away from his mother's eye. Honoria restrained him.

'I do not know what you are about, Dickie, but I assure you that from what I saw of Jenny today, she has her affairs in order. What right do you have to interrupt her? You must have faith.'

The usually silent footman, Samuel, who was aiding in the removal of Benedict's coat, said passionlessly. 'I believe Lady Harrington is also with Lady Sumner, miss.'

'There!' said Serena. 'I do not know why you should—' she saw a look pass between her brother and sister. 'Another of these horrid secrets in this house. You will tell me immediately, Orry, or I swear I shall never speak to you again.'

Honoria looked uncomfortable. 'I hardly know … I am not sure …'

Serena turned to Benedict. 'Dickie, I shall sit on your ribs if you do not…'

Honoria sighed, flopping onto the chair nearest the bed. 'Do not ask him. Do you not know that some manly code of honour keeps him silent?' Her tone did not suggest that this was a compliment. 'I have just had a feeling. I would probably have told you before, Serena, but we have not spoken so often of late.'

'I know,' said Serena in a small voice.

'You two haven't *spoken*?' said Benedict with unnecessary emphasis. 'Never known you two to be quiet. To think I slept through it!'

'Well, looking after you did not help — but it is more than that…' Honoria added honestly.

'What is it then?' said Benedict. But Honoria's eyes dropped.

'I'm not really sure. Anyway, this is not the time.'

'No,' agreed Serena hastily. 'Not the time. Tell me what you know of Genevieve.'

HONORIA AND THE FAMILY OBLIGATION

'I think, from some things she has said to me, that there is something wrong with her marriage.'

'Well, we could all guess that they are not particularly close. But that is hardly unusual in the polite world, surely?' said Serena airily. 'Of course, it is not what one would want, but I for one have resolved to make a sensible marriage if I can. One shouldn't marry to disoblige the family.' Honoria became pale at this, but Serena continued, unaware. 'If only my suitor has an interest in horses and Papa considers him sound, I shall say yes. I expect we shall rub along very well.'

'Serena — when did you become so unromantic?'

'Oh, I think love and all that is less important than people think. Why, many young girls fall in love with men who are quite unsuitable, I have heard. Rakes, or some such thing. Or men who are already in love with ... with ... other young ladies. You won't catch me falling into a decline over some dream of romance. Better to wed some sensible choice.'

'Maybe so, but sounds dashed dull to me. Too dull for you, at any event, Serena,' said Benedict, who had gratefully taken to lying on the bed once more.

'Orry, you were explaining about Genevieve.'

'I think that whatever it is with Genevieve and Lord Sumner, it is something very hard to live with. I have been most concerned about her. I think she is maybe even a little afraid...'

Serena looked at Benedict, whose face had become grave. 'And that is why you got involved. But surely there is nothing you could do — but you DID do something, and you got attacked by someone because of it — and that is why Jenny felt so guilty.' She ended with satisfaction. Then she sat on the bed, ignoring his wince as she brushed past a bruise. 'Surely it wasn't Sumner who did this to you?'

'No, no,' said Honoria. 'Remember the Watchman said it was a ruffian.'

'Or caused it to be done?' guessed Serena insistently.

'You're well off there, Mistress Poke-nose,' yawned Benedict, 'Sumner was at Ottershaw all this time and I don't suppose he had any notion or interest in *my* whereabouts. Why should he?'

'Because you poked your nose into *his* business.'

'*If* I had,' Benedict said with a grin, 'I'd have taken a precious care that he didn't find out.'

Serena collapsed. 'More secrets. I do not know what this family will become with all these unsaid things—'

'Well, Mama is here now,' Benedict yawned, 'so I don't suppose much will be left unsaid for any time longer. If we must all bare our souls what have *you* been keeping to yourself, miss?'

Serena blushed. 'Nothing at all,' she answered quickly. Then her voice changed to a teasing tone, 'but Honoria, on the other hand... You won't believe what a scrape she's got herself into now—'

Honoria protested, but it was not long before the other two had her laughing once more at her predicament.

'For someone so sensitive to other people's problems, Orry,' concluded Benedict, wiping his eyes, 'you walk through your own life with hardly any awareness at all — God preserve us from this fix.'

'He already has,' said Serena. 'He has brought Mama back to London.'

Chapter 25

Mama Untangles the Knots

'Gentlemen, welcome!' said Mr Wilbert Fenton as Mr Allison and Mr Scribster entered his drawing room. The revered dandy was sitting in the midst of this delicately appointed apartment on a chair whose legs were so ethereal as to make his safety from toppling a concern. He did not rise, and the gentlemen saw that his foot rested on a handsome silk footstool.

'Mr Fenton, are you injured?'

'I'm afraid I am, my boy,' drawled their host. 'Please sit. Though not for long, I fear, if you are as good as your word.'

Allison held his eyes. Mr Fenton's moved to his friend. 'Mr. Scribster. Not a known gossip.' He winced a little, and took a sip of wine from a glass placed near him.

'I am terribly afraid, gentlemen, that footpads still roam the city.'

'Indeed, sir. And have you been a victim?' said Mr Scribster.

'Hardly at all, gentlemen. But I did become injured in a dreadful attack on another gentleman. A Mr George Rennie, do you know him? I er, went to his aid but unfortunately there were two of them. Someone came up behind me, but I had my duelling pistol with me—'

'Fortunate!' drawled Allison.

'It was. And he ran off. A rough fellow, rather like my nephew's attacker. He has a hole in his shoulder. I think he will not be hard to find. Once I inform the Runners, of course.'

'Where did this occur?'

'In the little wood behind the Owl and Feather Inn.'

'A famous place for duels, so I hear.'

'In the past, perhaps. It is illegal these days, of course. But I did indeed think that Mr Rennie may have been meeting an adversary. Perhaps his rather tricky style of play had upset someone.'

'Like Benedict's.' It was Scribster, at his most laconic.

Wilbert Fenton turned rather cold eyes upon him. 'Not at all like Benedict. Mr Rennie is another sort of man.' Scribster's half grin was all the response he got. 'I think perhaps that someone challenged Mr Rennie to a meeting. Once there, perhaps that person thought better of it. Thought that only gentlemen should duel and that Mr Rennie fell short of being a gentleman. Perhaps that man had a cudgel with him and treated Mr Rennie as poor Benedict was treated.'

'I have always remarked,' mused Allison, 'on the remarkable shine on Mr Rennie's boots.'

'Yes he is quite vain about it I believe,' smiled Fenton. 'Well, I intervened, of course, and was rewarded by the other — *hidden* — gentleman's cudgel.'

'Where is Mr Rennie now?'

'There, gentlemen, is the problem. Mr Rennie is still, as far as I know, in the wood behind the Inn. My valet was able to help me to the carriage as I could still walk. But Mr Rennie is in rather worse shape, and my valet — being a little fellow as you know — could not move him.'

'Have you called a physician?'

'I had arranged for one to be aboard a yacht that is waiting for him in the Thames. I think Mr Rennie is in need of a recuperative sea cruise.'

'My God man, what state is he in?'

Wilbert Fenton's cold eyes turned on Allison this time. 'He is alive. Which is rather more than he planned for my nephew to be. I believe his vengeance was not yet finished.'

'A sea cruise seems just the thing,' said Scribster. 'Providing he returns.'

'Yes, though he will be given a message to delay his return until his duelling has been forgotten – perhaps a year. He may otherwise be arrested,' smiled the stout dandy in his usual tone, 'Perhaps you could help him on his way, gentlemen? I have a coach ready to be put to. It would take barely two hours to ensure he gets to the boat. I could have enlisted my footmen, but—'

'No need to explain. Just order the carriage.'

Mr Fenton obliged by ringing a little silver bell at his elbow. 'Sit, gentlemen. Tell me how my nephew and my two beauties go along...'

If the girls thought that their mother would demand confidences immediately, they were mistaken. Lady Cynthia was tired and needed to repose from her fatiguing journey. She asked that her daughters take a long carriage ride to Wimbledon to visit a second cousin and to take Genevieve too. They were to request a recipe of her grand-mama's against the fever, in case Benedict's should return. They protested Benedict's good health, but Mama was adamant. And a groom should drive, because the gentlemen were out — all except the lieutenant whom they should not disturb. He was looking, Mama said, a little strained. Probably from listening to too much feminine chatter, she added.

It was of no use arguing. Mama was plotting something and she wanted them away.

Meanwhile, the lieutenant was in a moral quandary. Scribster had heavily hinted that his cousin was interested in the eldest Fenton girl, while he had been sure from regarding him that his interest was in Serena. He had thought himself astute in such matters. Indeed, Lord Duncan had often remarked that the only reason he kept a noddy like him around was because of his remarkable social acuity. Prescott caught romance, slights, resentments and hopes among the Duncans' staff and its satellites nearly as keenly as a woman. Since Lady Duncan was still in London, he'd said, he'd have to make do with Noddy Prescott. The lieutenant was too good-natured to take offence. After all, most of the Duncans' staff had nicknames.

Had he known of Allison's interest, he would never have looked at Honoria as he now did, that would have been quite out of the question. But now he was in love, wasn't he? And he had her permission to speak to her papa. He examined himself on this point. Honoria had said yes, but hardly with the sparkling eyes and the heaving bosom that might be supposed to partner this moment. She had rather looked distracted. Of course, she was a very gentle, very shy creature, which was part of what he had always liked about her.

If Honoria wished to marry him, which admittedly was a bit of a leap on the present evidence, he must act — even if it disobliged his cousin. Things had gone too far. No, she could not wish to marry Rowley, despite his wealth. Her infatuation with himself had been most marked. He had seen it a time or two before among the Lisbon ladies, but he had never before reciprocated. His dalliances were all with women, not girls — whom he feared would desire a marriage he was not yet ready for. If Honoria wanted him, though, she would be his perfect bride. He would gain a position in London and no doubt Rowley would help him find a tidy little house. But of course Rowley might not be so disposed to aid him now...

Thus went the lieutenant's head. Knowing there was little chance of seeing the baronet before tonight, and still not quite sure how far his affection and respect for his cousin might change his notion of correct action, Darnley Prescott went out for a ride.

On the hour's drive out to Wimbledon, Genevieve was able to tell her most pressing news to the girls. She had already confessed her pregnancy to Benedict and told him about her deal with Lady Harrington. With bad grace, Frederick had accepted their terms. Immediate payment of his debts, a larger allowance (though her ladyship had made it clear she would not fund his gambling) and for this he would forgo seeing his wife.

'Such a lonely life Jenny.'

'No such thing. I shall have my child and my horses. And visits from my true friends. What more could I want?'

When Benedict hung his head, she'd said gently, 'You know, I was never one for the idea of marriage. It was just the thought of living with my sister that I could not imagine. So I married Frederick. And after him,' she said with a shudder, 'I would wish for no other.'

He raised his head again and said, 'So it was all for nothing. You don't need the money.'

'I shall never forget what you have done, Benedict, and I will take some money for stock. It will be like an investment. And if I were to have a girl...' her eyes filled. 'Then the stud farm will not be far enough away from him, for her ladyship will not protect me then. She wants an heir too much.'

'What will you do?'

'I shall then use the money you have offered and go to Europe. Somewhere in Spain where they train the most beautiful beasts. I have a widowed cousin who can accompany me. She is a trifle tedious, but a kind soul.' She held his cheek in her hand since he continued to look a little haunted. 'You have been the best brother to me Dickie. Your courage helped me find my own. But then you always did throw your heart over the jumps.'

'Go away, Jenny,' laughed Benedict, a little embarrassed. 'I need to sleep a little. These damned ribs.'

She did, and on the way to Wimbledon she poured her heart out to her two friends. They were delighted with her genuine joy in her increasing. Still they did not quite know the reasons for the estrangement, but they knew Jenny was too sensible to make a drama out of a mere argument. No, if she were to live apart from Sumner, she had her reasons, which Serena was able to guess after Benedict's fevered ramblings. Neither did she tell them of Benedict's exact role in the affair, but they entered into her plans for the stud farm (Serena) and house (Honoria and Serena both) with glee, so that by the time they came home, all friendly and sisterly relations had been resumed. This, thought Honoria, was Mama's gift. It was she who had sent them off together with no option but to talk — and see what peace now reigned.

The sisters, after the footman told them the whereabouts of their mama, ran to her chamber. But after they had blurted out Jenny's tale, they were once more halted in their readiness to confide. Mama instructed them to wear the dresses she had caused to be laid out for them, to take special care with their hair, and to wear the ornaments that Mama had bought when they were out. Tonight was a special occasion, she said. It was to be hoped that their papa returned in time for everything, for he had not been found at his club.

'A special occasion, Mama?'

'Of course, to celebrate Benedict's restoration to health. And I have a little announcement of my own.' She looked sternly at the girls. 'Go on! You have scarce an hour to get ready.'

'Yes Mama,' they chanted. Even Serena did not quarrel with that voice.

At that moment, Mr Allison and Mr Scribster were riding back through London. 'I've meant to ask you, Gus. The hat and the hair and your mood. Is there anything you'd like to tell me?'

'Yes,' said Gus Scribster with his usual honesty. 'But I find I cannot, quite yet.'

Allison let it go. It was unusual for his friend not to be blunt. But his head was given to his own problems, problems that got greater the more they neared home. He thought that her ladyship was going to forward his proposal in some way. And that was what he wanted, wasn't it? To be at last free of this ridiculous situation. For it all to be concluded.

As her ladyship had instructed, everyone had gathered in the green salon before dinner, excepting her husband. Her ladyship was sanguine. She had dealt with many a family emergency on her own while her husband was otherwise engaged. The ladies arrived all at once, with Lady Cynthia at the helm, and she gestured away the attendant footmen with a smile.

The gentlemen had been there for some minutes, the cousins looking like schoolboys about to discover their fates, Mr Scribster in the shadows as usual and only Benedict looking relaxed.

He smiled at Genevieve, wearing a yellow evening gown that did not become her, and she came to sit beside him. 'Dreadful colour, isn't it?' she whispered to him.

'On you, hideous,' he agreed sotto voice. 'One of the kittens might wear it.'

Everyone was looking at the picture the girls were making this evening, and even Lady Cynthia regarded it fondly as well she might, for she had painted it.

Honoria's gown was white, and with her hair piled high on her head and silver ribbons trailing to one side, which matched the broader silver ribbon under her bosom, the simple drapery made her look like a Greek goddess.

'Aphrodite!' breathed Prescott involuntarily.

Serena was dressed in the heavenly blue dress that became her so well, the same as she had worn last year at Harrogate. Its overdress sparkled in the candlelight and blue ribbons through her topknot, with its tumbling curls so much like her sister.

'Angels!' said Genevieve admiringly, without the least hint of envy. 'Sit, girls.'

The sisters did, together, feeling both conscious and excited, for their mother had imbued this meeting with mystery and anticipation.

Lady Cynthia took her place at the head of the rough circle of persons, standing in the glow of a candelabra — looking quite beautiful herself, in a red gown cut low at the bosom and with a wisp of lace on her dark curls that passed for a cap.

'I have gathered you all here this evening,' she began, the young people hanging on her every word, 'to—'

The door opened a little too forcefully and Sir Ranalph, whose day's occupation could be hazarded by anyone standing within ten feet of him, came in. 'My dearest!' he exclaimed. 'You're here! I am still in my dirt. Let me kiss you and I shall change quickly, have no fear.'

Her ladyship allowed the first, with only a slight tightening of her nostrils as her beloved approached, but she said, 'No, no, Ranalph. Stay as you are. We shall go to dinner soon, but first I wish to say something.'

Her husband, taking the hint, backed away and knocked into a chair at her side. Finding it behind him, he fell into it heavily and smiled sheepishly.

'Oh dear,' sighed his wife, regarding him. She straightened. 'I intend to be quite frank. We are all friends enough for that now, don't you think?' She smiled and her audience smiled back — well most of them.

She could not quite see Mr Scribster's face, but then he mattered in this scenario no more than Benedict or Genevieve.

'When I travelled to see my younger children, I found that my head was full of thoughts of this house instead. I allowed myself to ponder, because it distracted me from fearful thoughts of my little ones' malady. I had known that while we were all very amiable with each other, indeed remarkably so for such a short acquaintance, there was still a strange undercurrent, indeed a number of strange undercurrents, which were hard to put a finger on. At least,' she added proudly, 'they were hard because my attention was elsewhere. If I had not had Benedict to worry about, I should perhaps have fathomed it sooner. Because my mother's brain saw and lodged every inconsistency of behaviour and held it for later perusal,' she touched her temple as she spoke, 'and in the many hours of my journey I had the time for just that. On my way home, I received a missive that the children were nearly well and I resolved to come back here. Where all was *not* well, I feared.'

Hardly anyone breathed, she had their full attention. 'What were these behaviours? Too many to enumerate, but I finally I awoke with the key: blue slippers and torn French muslin.' She stopped and relished the gasps from her daughters. 'First, Mr Allison, there is the matter of the blue slippers. Do *you* wish to speak, or shall I explain for you?'

'He shaid that,' murmured Sir Ranalph in his chair, 'Why'd you shay that Allison? Always thought it was odd despite the faradiddle Serena told us.'

Serena made a noise of objection, her eyes a little panicked.

'I think Serena's faradiddle, as you call it sir, was not far from the truth, though perhaps not all of it. She did meet Mr Allison at that Assembly, in the dark of a garden, but what she did not know was that it meant rather more to Mr Allison than to her.' Serena turned full in her chair to Mr Allison, but he could not look away from her mother. 'He saw Honoria at the Carlisles' Ball and thought it was Serena. That is always occurring, but of course we didn't think of it in this case because the girls were separated. And then he approached you, sir,' she added to her husband.

'Of course! Blue slippers! That explains it—' he appeared to rest with this titbit and applied himself to a decanter handily nearby. 'Genius, my wife,' he confided to the brandy.

'I always wondered why he chose me after I stumbled through that stupid dance,' murmured Honoria, 'but Mama, should we be talking of this — I'm sure Mr Allison—'

'I would not embarrass him for the world. Serena had no idea that Mr Allison favoured her. How could she? He offered for you. And even though they laughed and rode together, she thought of him like a friend, I think. Until quite recently—'

'Of course!' said Genevieve, remembering much that she herself had seen.

Allison, who had been a statue, now turned to Serena , 'Is it true, Miss Serena are you ... have you—?'

Serena was shaking. 'Of course not! I — Honoria.'

Honoria held her hand. 'I *never* wanted to marry Mr Allison — you know that.'

'I'll bet you've never heard many women say that, have you Allison?' said Benedict genially, beginning to enjoy himself. 'Every girl falling over themselves to get to you when I was in town... Ouch!' he looked at Genevieve.

'But you changed your mind. You said—' objected Serena, her heart almost in her throat.

'Yes — she *said,*' uttered Lady Cynthia recalling them all to attend to her once more, 'and that is where the other part of the key comes in: the torn muslin.' She smiled. 'This is where I was very clever, my love,' she said to her husband — who snored. She sighed and turned to the others. 'Honoria came into the breakfast room one day with a slight tear in her muslin. I noticed it because it was the new French one we had just had made up. And I thought it was probably the rose bushes by the pillars, since they frequently catch on my shawl.'

'Mama!' protested Benedict against the beginning of feminine divergence into the arcane world of ladies' fashions.

His mama frowned him down. 'It meant that Honoria, caught on a rosebush, had heard a conversation that Papa and I had about a very large unexpected outlay—'

'I expect it was my Uncle Wilbert, he's shockingly expensive, you know,' her son informed Genevieve.

'Be quiet!' hissed Serena and Allison, both on their last nerves.

'—and how it might mean a few luxuries might have to be cut back. Including Benedict's coronetcy and your London season, Serena. And we may have added some savings for the children, too, I cannot quite remember—'

'How could you, Orry?' gasped Serena at the same time as Benedict said, 'Early Christian martyr, my sister.'

'And-' Lady Cynthia said, with less bravado, 'we discussed how the proposed marriage would change all that.'

'Well, Mama, I would never have thought it of you and Papa to be so vulgar as to—' began Benedict piously, his rollicking mood well on its way. Genevieve did her duty, 'Ouch!' he said again.

'You've sacrificed yourself for your family! If that isn't just like you, Orry.' said Serena crossly, 'And I thought—'

Mr Allison was suddenly in front of her. 'What did you think, Serena? I believe I have to know.'

She stood up, trembling, to face him. 'I didn't think anything for a long time. Only that Orry was a fool to avoid you, for to me you were so much fun. By the time I realised that I—' her eyes that had looked at him so candidly, dropped.

He could not stop himself taking her in his arms then, and she really couldn't breathe until he pulled away and lowered himself to her lips.

'I believe, Mr Allison,' said Lady Cynthia, in a gratified voice, 'that you had better apply to her father before you steal his daughter from him.' Allison turned, breathless and a little embarrassed. They both looked at the baronet, who snored again. 'Perhaps not,' she said. She smiled at Mr Allison once more. 'I take it, sir, that the wedding plans in my head have not all been in vain?'

'If you do not think her too young?' he said, tucking Serena's hand through his arm nevertheless. 'Should she not have her first season?'

'I expect Serena will enjoy her season as much as an engaged young lady as she will a single one.'

'Or a married one?' ventured Allison.

'I think you go too fast, sir,' she said reprovingly, 'but she will enjoy herself next season, providing you let her ride your horses.'

'But never drive my chestnuts!' laughed he down at his fiancé.

'We'll see,' said Serena, pertly. But her cheeks were flushed and she was trying to control the joy in her voice.

'A little hint, Allison,' said Benedict. 'Serena's a lot different from the other one. Don't tell her what not to do or she'll go out and do it.'

'I think that is rich coming from you,' said his sister, 'committing who knows what stupidities and *cheating* at cards!'

Honoria had moved to her mother's side and hugged her, both smiling at Serena's glowing face.

'And now, my kindest and gentlest daughter,' said Lady Cynthia, 'I could see what was happening to you, too. I just put it away in my head somewhere and did not make up the puzzle. Lieutenant Prescott-' Honoria stiffened.

Sir Ranalph woke up with a start. 'Eh? Who? That blasted man has been hounding me. I think-' he said to his wife in the loudest of drunken whispers, 'that he wants Honoria for himself. Confounded cheek. Follows me everywhere.' He frowned. 'Why has Allison got his hands round Serena? Thought it was 'tother he wanted.'

'Not now, my dear. Now he wants Serena,' explained his wife.

'He can't go around changing from one to other ... it's—' said Sir Ranalph, attempting to stand.

'It's quite alright my love,' said Lady Cynthia, 'I'll explain it all later,' and pushed him gently back.

Sir Ranalph took his seat, but glared at Mr Allison first and then at Lieutenant Prescott, who was looking intently between Lady Cynthia and Honoria.

'I saw the way you looked at Lieutenant Prescott, Honoria, and I have never seen you look at any other in quite that way. Not all throughout your season. And he too — well I believe that he has been wishing to ask your father—' she smiled. 'Maybe I should have left the evening as it is, but my dear, my good and self-sacrificing child — I want you to have what *you* want now, too.'

'Miss Fenton!' Lieutenant Prescott said, starting forward.

'No!' said Honoria, 'You are quite wrong Mama!' she cried, distressed.

'Tally-ho, child,' slurred her father, 'hold out for Allison!'

'Mr Allison's engaged to Serena, Papa,' said Benedict helpfully.

'Oh. Forgot.' Sir Ranalph slumped again.

His wife was not attending. Her self-satisfaction was seriously dented. 'I was *mistaken* — you did *not* favour the lieutenant?'

'You have *all* of it wrong! I am *not* your good and kind daughter. I am often angry and selfish and not at all good.' Another figure was standing now, emerging from the shadow, looking at the beauty in the white dress, even the hot tears on her cheeks failing to blight her charms. She was speaking her mind at last, and he was so proud of her. 'When I thought I would have to marry Mr Allison I thought I would die!'

'Have at you, again Allison! Not only didn't want you — would rather *die!* Can you ever rise in your own esteem again?' jeered Benedict,

'Difficult,' agreed Allison.

'But meanwhile I wanted to kick someone, *anyone* instead. Even you, Mama!' Honoria continued, ignoring the interruptions. As her mama's eyes opened wide she added, 'Only for a while, Mama.'

'Your sister really, *really* didn't want to marry me,' Mr Allison said to his love who grinned back impishly.

'Just as well you picked the less fastidious sister,' Serena smiled — but she was shocked too. She looked at the trembling Honoria and thought how much her sister had kept within herself.

'You were not *all* wrong, Mama. I did favour Lieutenant Prescott.' She held up her hand to stop Prescott coming forward. 'I was quite infatuated for a time. He was very like Mr Allison, but much more sensitive and mannerly to me.'

'I know, Benedict, I know,' intoned Allison resignedly before Benedict had a chance.

She turned to Lieutenant Prescott. 'I am so sorry, sir. I did not hear you when you asked if you could speak to my papa — I'm afraid my attention was other where.'

Prescott gulped.

'Does that mean the young dog will stop hounding me?' asked Sir Ranalph of his wife. 'Had to frequent three different establishments today. Every time a door opened, I thought it was he who had found me. Jumped like a rabbit. Didn't trust myself to be able to refuse him, and was unsure of what you wished for, my love.'

Prescott opened his mouth and closed it again, he stepped back, looking shattered.

'Didn't even notice you propose, Prescott. That's one at *you*.'

'Benedict. That is quite sufficient!' said Lady Cynthia in a tone that brooked no protest.

'Yes, Mama.'

'I'm sorry Lieutenant—' her ladyship said to Prescott, who nodded, still in shock. She turned to Honoria and said gently, 'I'm sorry I caused you all this worry and embarrassment, my dear. I believe that one day soon, a gentleman will come who will just be as kind and good as you — one who will be deserving of you.'

Honoria turned to her passionately. 'But I do not want such a man!'

Genevieve sat up. She had just bethought herself of a day at Bassington when she had looked down from her window and saw a strange pairing on an early walk.

'What *do* you want, Honoria?' she asked softly.

'I don't know! I want to be a good daughter, of course I do. To the best mama and papa in the world. And I want to be a good sister. Well, not to Benedict, obviously—'

'Hah!' said Allison in her brother's direction.

'—but to Serena and to the children of course. And I always will want that. But there must be somewhere where I don't have to be always good. Where I can be awful and mean-spirited and angry. I need a husband who is a friend who can allow me—' she stopped abruptly, her own words sinking in and there was in her aspect something that held the others silent. 'Oh!' she cried.

A voice sounded out suddenly. 'Is it me, Honoria?' and Mr Scribster moved forward.

There was a collective gasp. No one, except Genevieve, and that only for the last few seconds, could have guessed. Lady Cynthia could hardly look. This could not be possible.

'Can it be so?' said Honoria, wonderingly looking up at him, 'I didn't think I liked you till I came to your room—'

'Honoria!' said her mama, shocked.

'Only to cry, your ladyship,' offered Scribster, glancing her way a second, laughing at Honoria's finally uncensored mouth.

'And you were disgusted with me the next day—' protested Honoria..

'No. I thought you'd agreed to marry Prescott.'

'But how *could* I marry such a nodcock?'

'And another, Prescott!' whispered Benedict, beneath his mother's hearing, 'My saintly sister is firing them off tonight.'

'And I, Honoria? Could you marry me?' Scribster stood still, his hooded eyes letting out slivers of cruel, dark light.

'Ah!' said Allison to Serena '—the haircut!'

'The hat!' she replied.

Scribster was moving towards Honoria, slow and sinuous as a cat, and she left her mother to meet him. Her ladyship's hand clung a little to her arm, 'Honoria! Take care what you are about.'

'You are very ugly, you know—' her good daughter said.

'And you are very beautiful,' he said, touching her face, 'but I expect I could get used to it.'

'—But your face is the dearest face of all.'

He laughed like the crack of a fire and he dropped his forehead to hers. 'It is not your face I love you for, Honoria, it is your wicked heart.'

'Oh, no!' said Lady Cynthia, sitting at last, watching as her daughter was enveloped in the long arms of Mr Scribster. 'Now I suppose you shall run her off to Scotland!'

'Another family member has just bought Stane Castle, Lady Fenton – one who will appreciate it as I could not. I'd already purchased a manor house five miles from Bassington. It's why I've stayed there so long — overseeing the works.'

'What's Scribster doing with Honoria?' Sir Ranalph had rallied once more.

'They are getting married.'

'Really? Well, he can't be considered the best looking chap in the world,' he whispered at the drunken level.

'Oh, I don't know,' said Serena pertly, 'It would only take a relative to leave him twenty thousand a year to have him accounted desperately handsome.'

'You, my love,' said Mr Allison, smiling down at her, 'are going to be a handful.'

Sir Ranalph, regarding Scribster critically said, 'Ugly fellow. Pock marks. Not his fault, of course. But what he wants to have such a long face for is beyond me. Clever, though.'

'I expect she'll get used to it,' smiled her ladyship, meeting Mr Scribster's appreciative eye for a moment before he gave his whole attention once more to her eldest daughter. The way that certain people were looking at each other had to be stopped immediately lest another breach in etiquette, worse than the last minutes, occurred. 'Now, I think, we should all go in for dinner.'

'Has he any means?' whispered Sir Ranalph, the noise bouncing off the walls.

Lady Cynthia finally looked a little embarrassedly at Scribster.

'A man of Scottish descent will seldom admit to being wealthy. But I am well enough to support a wife.' He reassured her once more. He looked down at Honoria. 'Even one who has expensive tastes in gowns.' She smiled back at him with a smile that made her mother's heart stop beating. Her daughter gave herself in that moment and with his rarely seen answering smile, her ladyship was able to see that they had no barriers from each other. It was beyond either his bad looks or her beauty. They were one.

With a break in the convention of precedence, Benedict squired Genevieve to dinner first, only stopping to shake the bridegrooms' hands, then kiss his sisters heartily.

Sir Ranalph mustered his dignity to attempt to rise, something that kind Lieutenant Prescott came forward to help with. 'Ah!' said Sir Ranalph, jerking away as he stood. 'Cynthia, it's that fellow again. Fellow who's been hounding me.'

The lieutenant said, smiling politely at her ladyship, 'I shall dine at my club, I think,' and he bowed.

'Quite right!' said Sir Ranalph. 'Take yourself off! Can't have her — Allison's going to offer for her — any day now.'

'Yes sir!' He gave a weary salute to his cousin, who nodded gravely, and left.

Sir Ranalph and his wife made their rather stately way after him.

'Poor Lieutenant Prescott!' said Honoria. 'He didn't want to marry *me* you know.'

'Your father quite thinks he did,' said Allison, walking with a laughing Serena on his arm, behind them.

'Yes. But he wanted to marry the *good* Honoria. The one that would have fulfilled the family obligation,' she turned and smiled at them all, 'whereas *I* am very, very wicked.'

'You have insulted a great many people tonight, Orry. Including my affianced husband,' said Serena to that.

'I expect I shall be very ashamed of myself tomorrow,' sighed Honoria contentedly.

'What a family I am marrying into,' said Mr Allison. 'Benedict the card shark, your shady Uncle Wilbert—'

'Card shark? Shady? Oh, and dear Papa as a drunkard this evening,' laughed Serena. 'Do you really, truly, want to marry me?'

'No,' decided Mr Allison. 'I shall marry Honoria and have her smile falsely at me every morning so that she can fulfil the Family Obligation.'

That agreed, all four of the young people joined their family for dinner.

Chapter 26

Epilogue

Later that evening, Honoria and Serena lay in bed curled up and facing each other, finally confiding.

'What about your life of adventure?' giggled Honoria. 'You planned on marrying a sea captain or a highwayman.'

'Rowley is my own Highwayman, I told you that. He is also a bruising rider and he told me we will travel now that Napoleon is on Elba and Europe is safe. Don't be concerned, we shall have many adventures.'

'I almost pity him, being responsible for your scrapes.' Serena merely grinned. 'When did you know you loved him? And *why* could you not have told me?'

'It was such an advantageous match for you – how could I deprive you of it? And Mr Allison – Rowley — is so wonderful, I was sure you *would* be happy. How could you *not* be? And I didn't know how I felt for such a long time. I knew he was the most marvellous man of my acquaintance, but I also knew my acquaintance was not large. I only thought he would be the most wonderful brother. And then I realised that I could not bear him to be my brother. I wanted him so much. It was so *selfish—*'

'Ha! Who would have thought it? It is *you* who are the good, self-sacrificing sister! I was running and avoiding Mr Allison even when I had resolved to do my duty. *You* would give up your true love for the family.'

'Bunkum! I did no such thing. I had no notion that he thought of me as other than a silly child. I gave up nothing.'

Honoria rolled onto her back and gazed at the ceiling. 'It all seems ridiculously easy to see now. The way he was when he saw us together at Fenton, the Mystery of the Blue Slippers – what fools we all were not to guess.'

Serena propped her chin on hand to better see her sister's joyful face. 'We are so lucky!' she agreed. Then her naughtiness reasserted itself. 'What is *not* so easy is to see how you fell for Mr *Scribster*. When I think of what I thought of him when he arrived at Fenton Manor!'

'That is a rather contorted sentence, but I know what you mean — I too. But *he* saw my unhappiness when others did not. Somehow he read my face. And it was so comforting to be able to talk to someone without disguise. His own disregard for politeness made me so angry, especially since I was feeling so oppressed by my need to be polite and dutiful, and it made it possible to be very rude to him. He was a man of no redeeming virtues, I thought, so what did it matter—'

'Rowley said tonight that Scribster had saved his life in battle. That he was a bold and brave soldier.'

'Oh, do not tell me so! I rely upon his being shameless so that I can abuse him at will. You can have no idea how dreadful it was when each new virtue of Mr Allison became apparent. It gave me no excuse to escape.'

'Why did you want to? Of course, I am extremely glad you did – but what made you take such a disgust to Rowley?'

'Not disgust. I could not explain it – even to myself. But I think I may be vainer than we have supposed,' she confided. 'There simply seemed to be no reason why he should be attracted to me — I turned into an imbecile in his presence. I did not wish to marry a man who would prize my eyes or my figure over my imbecility. Imagine being pursued by a man who wanted you only because you might have handsome children together. It was like that all the time in London. I was not comfortable and so I uttered nonsensities or didn't speak at all. And yet many men still paid court to me. It gave me a very poor opinion of them.'

'Oh, my sister, you think much too much. I should have been flirtatious and flattered probably, no matter what their motives.'

'As though *you* suffer fools!' scoffed Honoria. She rolled back to face her sister. 'No, I wanted a marriage like Mama and Papa. Mr Allison seemed to have none but questionable reasons for choosing me. Of course, we did none of us realise that it was *your* personality that he really admired. Mine I don't think he ever saw.'

'But Mr Scribster saw it.'

'The worst of it, I fear. But it amused him. And soon I grew so close to him and I never really saw it happen.'

'You went to his room! That seems more like my sort of a scrape than yours—'

'How shocking to think of it! But it seemed imperative to tell him how vengeful and violent I felt when I thought of Benedict's attackers. Mama would have given me a Biblical lecture on "Vengeance is mine" which of course I know. I just needed to *say* it!'

'How dreadful!' said Serena comfortably.

'Poor Mr Scribster, I fairly threw myself into his arms.'

'Orry! He certainly seems to bring out a different side of you.'

'He does. When Mama let us walk on the terrace after dinner, he told me that that was when he realised he wanted me for himself. He calls us Beauty and the Beast! How absurd. I do think he is just a little handsome now that he has cut his hair.'

'A vast improvement. And I trust you'll take care of his clothes soon. Perhaps Uncle Wilbert could help.' They both giggled at the picture this created of Mr Scribster in one of Mr Wilbert Fenton's more florid outfits. 'Rowley said he has resisted his invitations to visit his tailor, but holds out hope now that you are around.' Honoria blushed. 'Rowley said,' and now her sister was laughing at her oft-to-be-repeated phrase, 'that Mr Scribster's buying the Manor House nearby was a –'

'Oh, Serena, we shall only be five miles apart!'

'I know, my dearest Orry. But do you know why?'

'He did not like his castle I suppose.'

'He did not. But after the battleground, when the two were so much together, Rowley found it difficult for some time to be parted from Scribster. I remarked that they were strange friends and Rowley explained to me that such awful things had happened to him that it was only his friend who kept him sane. Indeed, he begged him to buy the Manor house.'

There was a silence. 'Pray do not tell me any more virtues of my Mr Scribster. Soon you will make it quite impossible for me to do less than admire him greatly. Which would be fatal.' They both laughed. 'Oh, Serena. Winter in London to choose our bride clothes! Going to balls and parties together where I do not have to be afraid being courted and admired. It was very uncomfortable, I assure you. We shall have such fun.'

'But how will Mama and Papa afford it?'

'Settlements!'

'Thank goodness for that! I intend to be a most expensive fiancée.'

'Serena!'

Her sister's eyes glistened.

'Well, it is wonderful to be in love. But so much more wonderful to be in love with a *very* rich man. I understand your manor will have only ten bedrooms. Never mind, my dear, the spare children can reside at Bassington.'

Lady Cynthia, awake in the next room while her husband snored, heard the shrieks of outrage and laughter coming from Honoria's room and glowed with maternal pride and happiness.

Mr Scribster and Mr Allison, playing billiards and drinking brandy below, heard it too, and held each other's eyes. It was almost too much to see the other's happiness, redoubling their own. They broke off looking and went back to the game. Both rather flushed.

It had been an exceptional day, thought Benedict, regarding them from a table in the corner where he turned over cards idly, making some disappear into his jacket. He would soon be in Wellington's army – though in this year of 1814 there wouldn't be too many of the good scraps left – but he'd be in a scarlet coat, with hope of adventure, as he'd always wanted. Genevieve would be gone to a better life in a couple of days, his Uncle Wilbert was engaged to the lovely Countess Overton and Serena set to make the richest, most fashionable man in England the naughtiest wife he could wish for. Yes, Scribster was a strange partner for Orry, but Benedict had seen him look at her. He was not such another as Sumner. Sumner was a charming veneer hiding a black heart. Gus Scribster was the opposite.

He silently toasted the family Fenton. Out of the suds with barely a scratch!

About Author

Alicia Cameron lives between her homes in rural Scotland and rural France. She reads avidly, laughs a lot, and is newly addicted, unfortunately, to Korean Dramas ... for which she refuses treatment. Here is a link to get **Angelique and the Pursuit of Destiny** for FREE! https://BookHip.com/XSNQVM It puts you on the list to receive Alicia Cameron's book news and offers, occasionally.

All Alicia books are available on Amazon and as audiobooks on Audible. Some are available in several languages, German and Spanish especially.

You can find out more here :

The website   https://aliciacameron.co.uk
Facebook   https://www.facebook.com/aliciacameron.100
Twitter   https://twitter.com/aliciaclarissa2
Bookbub   https://www.bookbub.com/authors/alicia-cameron

Also By

Regency Romance

Angelique and the Pursuit of Destiny: getbook.at/Angelique
Angelique was named by her French grandmother, but now lives as Ann, ignored by her aristocratic relations. Can she find the courage to pursue her Destiny, reluctantly aided by her suave cousin Ferdinand?

Beth and the Mistaken Identity: getbook.at/Beth
Beth has been cast off as lady's maid to the pert young Sophy Ludgate, but is mistaken as a lady herself by a handsome marquis and his princess sister. Desperate to save the coach fare to London, she goes along with them, but they do not let her escape so easily.

Clarissa and the Poor Relations: getbook.at/Clarissa
Clarissa Thorne and her three friends have to leave their cosy School for Young Ladies after the death of Clarissa's mama. all must be sent off

as poor relations to their families. However, Clarissa suddenly inherits Ashcroft Manor, and persuades the ladies to make a bid for freedom. But can she escape their unpleasant families? The Earl of Grandiston might help.

Delphine and the Dangerous Arrangement: getbook.at/Delphine

Delphine Delacroix was brought up by her mother alone, a cold and unloving childhood. With her mother dead, she has become the richest young lady in England, and is taken under the wing of her three aunts, Not quite trusting them, Delphine enters a dangerous arrangement with the handsome Viscount Gascoigne - but will this lead to her downfall?

The Fentons Series (Regency)

Honoria and the Family Obligation, **The Fentons 1** https://getbook.at/Honoria

Honoria Fenton has been informed that the famous Mr Allison is to come to her home. His purpose? To woo her. She cannot recall what he looks like, since he made her nervous when they met in Town. Her sister Serena is amused, but when Allison arrives, it seems that a mistake might cost all three there happiness.

Felicity and the Damaged Reputation, **The Fentons 2**
https://getbook.at/Felicity

On her way to London to take a post as governess, Felicity Oldfield is intercepted by xx, who asks her to impersonate his cousin for an hour. When, in an unexpected turn of events, Felicity is able to enjoy a London Season, this encounter damages her reputation.

Euphemia and the Unexpected Enchantment, The Fentons 3
https://getbook.at/Euphemia

Euphemia, plain and near forty, is on her way to live with her dear friend Felicity and her husband when she is diverted to the home of Baron x, a bear of a man as huge and loud as Euphemia is small and quiet. Everything in her timid life begins to change.

Ianthe and the Fighting Foxes: The Fentons 4 https://getbook.at/Ianthe

The Fighting Foxes, Lord Edward, his half-brother Curtis and Lady Fox, his stepmother, are awaiting the arrival from France of a poor relation, Miss Ianthe Eames. But when Ianthe turns up, nothing could be further from their idea of a supplicant. Richly dressed and in high good humour, Ianthe takes the Foxes by storm.

The Sisters of Castle Fortune Series (Regency)

Georgette and the Unrequited Love: Sisters of Castle Fortune 1
https://getbook.at/Georgette

Georgette Fortune, one of ten sisters, lives as a spinster in Castle Fortune. She refused all offers during her London Seasons, since she fell in love, at first glance with the dashing Lord Onslow. He hardly knew she existed, however, but now he has arrived at the castle for a house party, and Georgette is fearful of exposing her feelings. She tries to avoid him, but Onslow treats her as a friend, making Georgette's pain worse, even as he makes her laugh.

Jocasta and the Cruelty of Kindness: Sisters of Castle Fortune 2
https://getbook.at/Jocasta

At a house party in Castle Fortune, Jocasta's beau had fallen for her sister, Portia. Now Jocasta is back in London and has to suffer the pity of the friends and family that care for her. Only Sir Damon Regis treats her without pity, and she is strangely drawn to him because of it.

Katerina and the Reclusive Earl: Sisters of Castle Fortune 3

Katerina Fortune has only one desire, to avoid going on her London Season altogether. On the journey, she hears of a recluse, who dislikes people as much as she. Katerina escapes her father and drives to offer a convenient marriage to the earl, who refuses. But an accident necessitates her stay at his home, and they discover they have more in common than either could have believed.

Leonora and the Lion's Venture: Sisters of Castle Fortune 4

At the Castle Fortune house party three years ago, fourteen year-old Leonora fell out of a tree and into the arms of the the shy Mr Linton Carswell. From that minute on she decided to wed him and secretly prepared herself to be a good wife. Leonora's goals are known as the Lion's Ventures to her sisters, but although the know she has a new venture, not even her twin Marguerite knows what it is precisely. But when the lovely twins arrive in London, they begin to realise her unlikely target. Foggy

Carswell, not a marrying man, begins to suspect too and hides from his pursuer. But Leonora, the most determined of her sisters, is set on him. But when she sets him free at last, the tables finally turn.

Edwardian Inspirational Romance
(typewriters, bicycles, and leg-of-mutton sleeves!)

Francine and the Art of Transformation: getbook.at/FrancineT
Francine is fired as a lady's maid, but she is a woman who has planned for every eventuality. Meeting Miss Philpott, a timid, unemployed governess, Francine transforms her into the Fascinating Mathilde and offers her another, self directed life. Together, they help countless other women get control over their lives.

Francine and the Winter's Gift: getbook.at/FrancineW
Francine and Mathilde continue to save young girls from dreadful marriages, while seeing to their own romances. In Francine, Sir Hugo Portas, government minister, meets a woman he could never have imagined. Will society's rules stop their union, or can Francine even accept the shackles of being in a relationship?

A chapter of Clarissa and the Poor Relations to tempt you...

Chapter 1

Clarissa Convinces

Looking down upon the curate's thinning hair from her vantage point of the library chair Miss Clarissa Thorne felt herself to have borne enough.

'Do please rise, Mr Peterkin. I would myself if you hadn't quite caught yourself in my skirts.' she said tartly. She was quite a young lady, about eighteen summers, but with a determined chin set in a face surrounded by mousy ringlets caught up carelessly in a rather tattered ribbon. She wore a plainly cut black muslin, as befitted her mourning state. She might have been passably pretty had she not had a quite unladylike air of certainty in her large grey eyes.

The Reverend Mr Peterkin rose at once and was about to deliver himself of a lecture as to the tones young ladies should adopt when speaking to members of the clergy, when he recollected that this would not forward his case.

'Indeed, Miss Thorne, it is only my sincere intention to throw myself at your feet, to act as your solace your comforter in this harsh world that caused me to...' But his companion had already pulled a decrepit bell chain and was holding out her hand to bid him farewell in an unmistakable fashion.

'I am obliged to you for your charitable sentiments, sir, but you have now received your answer and must take your leave.'

As Mr Peterkin grasped her hand automatically, he felt he was losing control of the situation. He gulped and said, 'But Miss Thorne, you cannot have considered your position, your parents both dead...you need a man to guide you...'

She withdrew her hand and looked past him at her superior servant.

'Ah, Sullivan, here is Mr Peterkin taking his leave of us, please show him out.' she said, with the utmost cheerfulness.

'Certainly, miss.' said the impassive Sullivan, holding the door as the curate left the room in some disorder. As they descended the stairs, Mr Peterkin stared with dislike at Sullivan's back. How Mrs Thorne's Academy for young Ladies had ever merited a servant who gave himself such superior airs as Sullivan was a mystery to most in the county, but not to the curate. When Viscount Ashcroft's daughter had married mere Mr Thorne, a writer and free thinker and a younger son to boot, the First footman of the Ashcroft estate had accompanied her to her new home bringing with him such an elegance of manner as to terrify the local gentry but to reassure the parents of the young ladies who were educated there.

'I beg your pardon, sir, for the circumstance of you finding yourself ushered into Miss's presence alone. Might you tell me which of the servants should have done such a thing?' Whenever Sullivan alluded to the other servants, he did so with the air of one still presiding over a multitude instead of the cook, parlour maid and groom that was all that the house boasted beyond term time.

Mr Peterkin was jamming on his hat hurriedly and had the grace to blush. 'Well, as to that …I let myself in through the garden door… as I wished to offer… religious comfort at this time mourning for Miss Thorne.'

'Indeed sir?' Sullivan's eyebrows raised a little at this and Mr Peterkin, knowing himself to be the butler's social superior wondered why he should feel a wish to explain himself. 'Perhaps you will allow me to announce you next time sir, and then you would find miss properly accompanied by one of the other ladies.'

'Well, yes. But if you wish to infer…It is not your place, Sullivan to… a clergyman's case is very… Good day.'

'And Good day to you my slimy weasel done up in a clerical collar,' said Sullivan after he closed the door behind him, 'and a good riddance to you. And if it's not my place to be guarding my young lady from the likes of you, I don't know whose it is.'

Clarissa meanwhile had thrown herself into an adjoining room wherein lay three ladies variously occupied in packing up the contents of the room.

'That's it.' She said imperiously, as she entered the room. Her eyes were flashing and her cheeks flushed and she looked quite arresting, despite her dull gown.

A lady of some forty-five years in an unbecoming round dress of mud coloured cambric looked up from her employment of sorting through piles of dusty books, and said, 'My dear Clarissa, whatever can have upset you?'

'I have just had to suffer the impertinence of an offer from Mr Peterkin, so now you will all *have* to listen to me.' Clarissa declared. She moved a work box from a red velveteen chair and sat down whilst with exclamations of astonishment her companions abandoned their tasks and joined her, two sitting on the sofa and the other at her on the footstool by her chair chafing her hands to soothe her evident agitation.

The ladies on the sofa could not have provided a greater contrast. True both were dressed in sober grey gowns, made up at the neck and free of any softening touches such as lace or the sad knots of ribbon with which the third lady had sought to relieve the severity of her attire. But then Miss Appleby, seated at Clarissa's feet, was of a romantical disposition and she still held a faint flame alight for the gentleman who might one day seek her hand. That this gentleman was very late in appearing, no one could doubt. The other two ladies would have scorned such hopes. Therein lay their only similarity.

Miss Oriana Petersham was without doubt a beauty of the first water and though she pulled back her golden hair severely and simply pinned in a loop at her neck she could not help the little ringlets that escaped to frame her heart-shaped face or the darker lashes that curled around her large green eyes, or the perfection of her pert nose and bow-shaped mouth. It did her no good either, to wear the sober unadorned gown, which served only to act as a foil to her magnificent figure and beautiful face. That face at the moment wore an expression of great concern, for too often had the beautiful Oriana Petersham been the object of unsolicited male attentions for her to be anything but unsympathetic to the Clarissa's ordeal.

Alongside her sat a lady probably fifteen years her senior at thirty-five, her figure as stolid as her companion's was lithe, her complexion as ruddy as Oriana's was delicate, her hair as dark and straight as was the other's pale and curled. Her brows were dangerously close to meeting over her determined brown eyes, but her face was so impassive that it was hard to know how she had taken Clarissa's outburst. Miss Augusta Micklethwaite's face did not betray her thoughts.

Miss Appleby, her grey and brown ringlets (owing a great deal to a hot iron) bouncing thinly about her face as she agitatedly chafed at Clarissa's hand, 'Oh, how can this be ... Mr.Peterkin, so romantic. To have harboured a *tendre* for you all this time...I should never have guessed...Indeed, I always thought that he disliked you, Clarissa, for do you not remember how he scolded you over that button that you put in the poor box...But that was quite some time ago now...' She broke off in agitation as Clarissa withdrew her hand.

'*Tendre?* You can scare be serious.' uttered Clarissa. Her anger gave way to a giggle at the memory of Mr Peterkin's obsequiousness

Miss Micklethwaite said in her plain northern voice, 'He has heard about the inheritance, of course. You are a fool Louisa.'

Miss Appleby was too used to Miss Micklethwaite's unfurbished mode of conversation to take offence at this statement. 'Oh he would not...I'm sure...But how could he?' she finished and her watery eyes were bright with agitation. What was once a frail beauty was now a scrawny, but wirier face and figure with a resilience borne of hardship in the service of various households as a drudge-governess until her last five years of bliss as a teacher at the Academy that her old school friend has established. Here she had been coddled, she thought, treated with real respect by dear Clarissa's mama, now sadly dead.

'I should imagine that it has something to do with Jane...' Oriana saw that Miss Appleby was still looking confused and explained. 'Our cook, Jane is second cousin to Lottie, the Parlour maid at the Vicarage.'

'Servants know everything.' exclaimed Miss Appleby.

'Mr Peterkin said that he was wishful to marry me to give comfort to a motherless waif.' said Clarissa, her voice tragic.

Oriana's eyes danced, 'He never did. And I always thought him a man of no address.'

'Well it is not funny. And when I asked him if he was in a position to support a wife...'

'Oh, Clarissa, you did not.' interjected Miss Appleby, in shocked accents.

'Well, I did. I said I did not scruple to ask him such a question since I had no parents to ask it for me,' said Clarissa pertly, but with her eyes dancing quite as much as Oriana's, 'and he stammered and said that he did not at the moment have the means, but that if I should prove to have a little competence from my mamma, he believed that I would need a man of his experience to manage it for me. He gave himself away completely. Depend upon it, he has offered for me because he has heard of my cousin's death and my inheriting Ashcroft manor.'

'I'm sure you must be correct,' said Oriana with sparkling eyes. 'What a ridiculous little man. He seeks to profit from an alliance with one to whom he has shown naught but impatience any time these last three years.'

'But surely he is correct, my dear Oriana. Clarissa *does* stand in need of guidance at this difficult time. A gentleman's strong shoulder, his decisive nature...'

'Bah.' ejaculated Miss Micklethwaite, impatiently, 'He cannot even decide between chicken or dressed crab for dinner. He can little pretend to have offered much in the way of support to Clarissa in these last months since her dear mamma has passed away. It is Mr Norbert who has behaved as a vicar should, even though we were all cast into the doldrums anytime his visit lasted above twenty minutes. If she needs guidance then no doubt her brother may offer it to her, even he's as stiff-rumped a young long-wind as you may meet in a twelvemonth.'

'Augusta.' said Miss Appleby, in a faint but pleading tone, 'you must not say such things of Mr Thorne. To be sure he is a man of high principals and strong views....'

'Dearest Appleby, it is no more than my mother used to say, for try as she might she could never warm to her stepson. Even my father felt that he had adopted his air of outraged virtue only as a reaction to his and my mother's more liberal views. He could never bear to be thought of as different or *eccentric* as they were. Father blamed Harrow.' As Clarissa spoke her large eyes took on an affectionate twinkle as she thought of her parents, dead within a year of each other, united in Heaven as they had been in life. She sighed and looked at each of her friends in turn. 'You are quite right, however. John does mean to visit me on Monday, as he informs me in his letter. He further informs me that he has taken the liberty to visit Ashcroft and finds it in a very sorry state. He also advises me that he has set his lawyers on to sell it, there being no objection now that the succession is broken and the entail is ended, he is sure that will be my wish. As for the rest, he invites me to go and stay with him, where he is sure, SURE, mind you, that I will be of help to Cornelia with the children.' For most of this speech, Clarissa had been wringing a lace handkerchief to death whilst pacing passionately about the room. 'I have been brought up to be of independent mind---can you *imagine* what my life would be in such a household? I should die.'

'I have often thought that your mother did not know what she did when she allowed you so much free rein in your thinking and behaviour. *Here* your education stood you in good stead, but out in the world people take a dim view of young ladies who set themselves up against men's opinions, or seek to take part in political debate. I spoke to her many times on this matter, but she did not expect to leave you unprotected so soon.' So said Miss Micklethwaite, whilst she wiped away what might have been a tear from her fierce eyes.

'Yes, but I have a plan. I shall not be here to listen to John's advice—for I shall be at Ashcroft. And all of you shall go with me.'

'But you cannot' squeaked Miss Appleby.

'Clarissa, you cannot have considered.' said Miss Petersham.

'Dear Appleby, only listen. Of course I cannot go with no respectable female to accompany me, but with three of you we shall do splendidly. John can hardly object to the respectability of that.'

'I should rather think he would object to us hanging onto your coattails.' said Miss Micklethwaite roundly.

'Yes, and he'd be right. Take Miss Appleby, by all means, but there is no need to take on all of us. I could not be your pensioner at any cost,' declared the beautiful Miss Petersham, the flush on her face causing her to look even lovelier than normal.

'Do you wish to go and live with your brother who will try to sell you in marriage to the highest bidder again?' demanded Clarissa.

'I shall be there only long enough to find a new situation.' declared Oriana. 'Besides, he cannot force me.'

'But he can make life as unbearable for you as John can for me. You know that getting another position is unlikely. Finding this situation suited you, but you are far too beautiful to be accepted as a governess in most houses.'

Oriana bent her head and bit her lip. Clarissa leant forward and grasped her tightly clasped hands in both of her own.

'Would you not rather be of use to me?' She said pleadingly. 'Look, when mamma died and we knew we had to close the school at the end of the year, all of us thought that we would need to part, to break up our cosy life here. Then, when my cousin died so unexpectedly, I thought I could use my inheritance to help us all.' She turned impulsively, 'Appleby, dearest, you do not really wish to go and live with your cousin Farnham and all those dreadful little children, do you? You know that you'll be treated as an unpaid servant in that house. I remember the exhausted state you were in when you returned from there last summer.' Miss Appleby made inarticulate noises in faint protest. 'I truly need a companion, one who I can talk to of my mamma and papa and who understands me as well as you do. You would not abandon me?'

Miss Appleby took the badly used handkerchief from Clarissa's grasp and sobbed into it. 'Oh, my dear Clarissa - so kind...if I could only be sure I would not be a burden to you...'

Clarissa turned her burning eyes and determined young face to her other friends, not so easily moved as Miss Appleby.

'You have not thought, my dear Clarissa, what living in a house such as Ashcroft would entail. If your brother is right and the estate has been neglected then perhaps it is right to sell. Then you and Miss Appleby could set up your own establishment in Bath.' Oriana's honeyed voice sought to calm down Clarissa's spirits.

'You are correct in thinking that I do know what running an estate entails - that is why I need *you* to show me, Oriana.'

Sir Ralph Petersham had involved his daughter in many male pursuits, riding roughshod over her mother's complaints. He had included her in all estate matters and she had proved so apt a pupil that he had left a deal of responsibility in her hands. When his son Fitzroy came home from Cambridge in the vacations, he was often adjured to 'Ask Oriana what's what.' When the young man had shied away from including Oriana in what he had felt to be his domain and had thus done something unwise, his father had trenchantly ordered, 'Leave it to your sister next time.' Sir Ralph had meant his beautiful daughter to be the wife of a great man, able to stand at his side as an equal, as his own wife had never done, and had he lived who knows what might not have happened.

As it was, a jealous brother had been the one to oversee Oriana's come-out in London and he had been pleased to accept, on her behalf, an offer from an Earl who was both wealthy and approaching sixty. Oriana's disgrace in calling off her wedding and her brother's consequent anger had induced her to seek her position at Mrs Thorne's Academy. Her brother, still questioned by the world about the fate of his beautiful sister, had never forgiven her.

'Mother always said that Ashcroft was a prosperous estate at the time of my uncle and my cousin has only owned it for five years. He was a sad rake and possibly a libertine but *surely* he could not have done so much harm in that time. Oriana, you could help me make it prosperous again. Don't you see, far from being a *tax* on me you can be a *real help* to me.'

Oriana's eyes sparkled then dulled again, 'If only I could, my dear. We do not know the people… they would have to come to *trust* us Clarissa, but with the help of a good agent…' She tried to look in Clarissa's eyes for signs of the charity that she would so deplore but saw only hope and determination. 'Oh, *could* we?' she said.

Clarissa leapt to her feet and danced Oriana to hers. 'My dear, so you'll come.' She and Oriana shrieked and danced about the room. Just as abruptly she stopped and turned to Miss Micklethwaite.

'Dearest Waity, you know that I shall need you to help me set the house in order.'

Miss Micklethwaite's frown became more terrible. 'You do not need me to feed as well.'

'For all my Greek and Latin, I have not learned any of the house-keeping things a lady should know, for how could dear mamma teach me what she did not know herself? And we need you to scare away the dragons, Waity. Just *think* what attentions I might receive from mushrooms like the curate if I have not you by me to lend respectability. As for Oriana, you know we dare not send her out without she comes home followed by some smitten gentleman.'

A gasp from Oriana at this made Miss Micklethwaite smile sourly.

'And I should *so* value your support my dear Augusta,' said Miss Appleby gently, 'for in the absence of any gentleman, I cannot but feel you are the next best thing. - Why, what can I have said to make you go into such transports of laughter, Clarissa, Oriana.'

But the young ladies were laughing so hard at the outrage on Waity's face that they had to grasp onto each other to keep upright. Miss Micklethwaite's forehead smoothed a trifle.

'I think, Louisa, that you and I will be needed to keep these two in check.' she said.

'Well, if you think so, Augusta, then of course we shall go.' said Miss Appleby in a confused voice.

'I do,' said Miss Micklethwaite, her grim voice repressing the unseemly levity of the young ladies, 'And what is more we had better go now to change for dinner. Perhaps I can find some knee breeches.'

'*Knee breeches*. Whatever can you mean?' said Miss Appleby to the retreating back of her friend. 'Girls?' she uttered vaguely. But it was no use the two young ladies had collapsed in an unseemly heap onto the sofa, in helpless gales of laughter.

Later that evening, Clarissa sat in bed hugging her knees. A life with her brother and his wife was a bad enough thought, but she was determined that no such fate must touch her friends. She had seen too well the life of the despised poor relations, women who drudge for their families for a little more status than a maid and less money - for rare indeed was the family who took on the responsibility of a portionless female with any acceptance of equality. They must be grateful for the benefits of their position, the benefits which might include insult, humiliation and exhaustion from the performance of a hundred thankless tasks each day: the complete inability to order a second of one's own life. Even if she could bear it, her dear, dear, friends must not.

Chapter 2
The Ladies Contrive

If they were to quit the Academy before the arrival of Mr Thorne, the ladies had a great deal to do. Miss Micklethwaite did venture the opinion that it would be better to await his arrival and inform him of her decision, but when Clarissa declared that it would be better if he were faced with a *fait accompli* she could not but see the force of it. A young man of overbearing manner who was ten years her senior, Mr Thorne would not take kindly to his wishes being overset. No doubt, thought Augusta, he also had some plans as to how to *manage* Clarissa's money for her: plans that might be to his advantage. Of this, she said nothing, merely marshalling the ladies in the packing.

They could now take all the books that they had been so unwilling to leave behind (even though *Basic Arithmetic for young Scholars* was unlikely to be of use in a country house), for Sullivan had declared his intention of travelling ahead with the trunks, whilst Mary could accompany the ladies on the hired postchaise. This was a relief, for who knows what state the house would be in and Sullivan could be depended upon to provide the basic comforts for their arrival.

He had something to say to Clarissa before he left. 'You have not been wont to worry much about your mode of dress here miss, quite understandable, I'm sure. But it will not do to arrive in Hertfordshire looking, well...' Sullivan paused, embarrassed.

'Shabby genteel. I know.' said Clarissa. 'But there is hardly time...I'll discuss it with the ladies. Thank you Sullivan'

'Very good, ma'am.'

Oriana had already done some thinking about this she confided when Clarissa brought up the subject. 'And I believe I have the very solution, if you will not take it amiss. Your mama's wardrobe and some chests of fabric that I found have given us some unexpected treasures. If you would not object to having her black silk evening gown altered for you, I should think that would be the very thing. Plus the two black muslin gowns that Mrs Trimble in town is making for you will be sufficient for daywear until we find someone in Hertfordshire.'

'Yes,' said Clarissa, blushing, 'But will they be grand enough for the lady of the manor? I wish to be taken seriously when I deal with the locals. I do not want feminine folderols, but only to at least look like a lady of quality rather than the silly schoolgirl that I fear I am.'

Oriana suppressed a sigh and grabbed at her hand. 'Only come with me and see what your mamma has been hiding...'

getBook.at/Clarissa

Printed in Great Britain
by Amazon